Who woul̶ ̶ ̶ ̶ ̶ ̶ ̶ ̶ ̶ ̶ ̶ ̶ ̶ ̶ ̶ ̶ ̶ ̶ ̶ ̶ ̶omer? Someone ̶ ̶ ̶ ̶ ̶ ̶ ̶ ̶ ̶ ir at the post office? Despite her Zen nature, Aunt Claire did have a knack for getting into confrontations with certain folks. This child of the sixties was also a real activist, holding meetings for causes like workers' rights and animal rights every week in the store. Suddenly, I heard a startled gasp from behind me. "What happened?"

Turning around, I found Aunt Claire's passive-aggressive right hand, Janice Dorian, a stricken look on her face. Despite being surrounded by natural ways to calm down, she was an uptight forty-something, with a perpetually pinched face. "What have you done to her?"

"Nothing!" There was no one I loved more than my beloved Aunt Claire. "She's gone, Janice. The police will be here any minute."

Janice pushed past me and bent over Aunt Claire's body. "Everything was fine until you came home. I've never seen her so agitated since you arrived."

This was true but had to do with my efforts to bring my mother and Aunt Claire back together. Or maybe, her agitation had something to do with her new business venture. Even then, she hid it very well. "Janice, you know that we loved each other very much." I pointed to the bottle of Mimulus. "I think she was murdered." I explained my theory.

She snatched up the bottle before I could stop her and snarled, "You did this!" She waved the bottle at me. "This is your fault!"

This title is also available as an eBook

Dedicated to My Detective Dachshunds:
Holmes, Fletcher, and Wallander.
Best Friends, Protectors, Muses.

# death
# drops

A Natural Remedies Mystery

## Chrystle Fiedler

## Gallery Books

New York   London   Toronto   Sydney   New Delhi

Gallery Books
A Division of Simon & Schuster, Inc.
1230 Avenue of the Americas
New York, NY 10020

First Gallery Books trade paperback edition February 2012

GALLERY BOOKS and colophon are registered trademarks of Simon & Schuster, Inc.

For information about special discounts for bulk purchases, please contact Simon & Schuster Special Sales at 1-866-506-1949 or business@simonandschuster.com.

The Simon & Schuster Speakers Bureau can bring authors to your live event. For more information or to book an event contact the Simon & Schuster Speakers Bureau at 1-866-248-3049 or visit our website at www.simonspeakers.com.

Designed by Jacquelynne Hudson

Manufactured in the United States of America

10  9  8  7  6  5  4  3  2  1

Library of Congress Cataloging-in-Publication Data

Fiedler, Chrystle.
Death drops / Chrystle Fiedler.—1st Gallery Books trade paperback ed.
    p. cm.—(Natural remedies mystery series)
1.  Naturopathy—Fiction.  I. Title.
PS3606.I327D43 2012
813'.6—dc23                                                    2011043575

ISBN 978-1-4516-4360-2
ISBN 978-1-4516-4362-6 (ebook)

# acknowledgments

My heartfelt thanks go to my agent Ann Collette, for her insight and support; the wonderful team at Gallery/Simon & Schuster, especially Mitchell Ivers, Megan McKeever, and Stephanie Evans; all the alternative health experts who have been my teachers, including herbalist Brigitte Mars, Suzy Cohen, RPh, Deborah Wiancek, ND, and Jacob Teitelbaum, MD; and my mother, Marion Fiedler, who started me on the alternative path. Thank you all!

# death drops

# chapter one

**Dear Dr. McQuade,**
**Help! I've been feeling anxious and stressed to the max ever since I started my new job. Is there anything natural I can take to help me chill out?**
    **Signed,**
    **Stressed Out**

**Dear Stressed Out,**
**Have no fear. One of the best natural remedies for stress is flower essences, which help to correct emotional imbalances. There are thirty-eight flower essences, developed by Dr. Edward Bach in 1934. Just put a few drops of Bach Rescue Remedy—a combination of rockrose for terror and panic, impatiens for irritation and impatience, clematis for inattentiveness, star-of-Bethlehem for shock, and cherry plum for irrational thoughts—under your tongue and you'll begin to chill big-time. You'll find it at your local health food store.**
    **Signed,**
    **Willow McQuade, ND**

Call me a nature nut. I love nature. I like to walk in nature, I use natural remedies, and I practice natural medicine as a naturopathic doctor in Los Angeles. So my "green exercise," walking in the forest, this Friday morning fit right into that theme.

It was part of the reason I'd traveled to Long Island, two hours east of New York City at the beginning of June, wanting to absorb by osmosis nature's finest in a preserve the Nature Conservancy called one of nature's last, best places. I'd come back to my hometown of Greenport, New York, an idyllic fishing village turned tourist mecca, to stay with my beloved aunt Claire, master herbalist and owner of Nature's Way Market and Café, for my annual summer visit and to rest and recuperate.

I desperately needed these two weeks away after a punishing spring that involved joining a new holistic medical practice in West Hollywood, traveling biweekly to consult at the Arizona Center for Integrative Medicine, writing a blog and numerous articles for *Nature's Remedy*—an online magazine—and handling a high-maintenance boyfriend, now my ex. More about him later.

Right now the forest, dappled in sunshine, was spread before me like a visual all-you-can-see feast. Splashes of color from blooming cosmos, hibiscus, and Rose of Sharon bushes saturated the landscape. Bluebirds cawed and flitted from tree to tree, while squirrels skittered down the path, looking for breakfast. The woodsy smell of foliage, flowers, and crusty earth was intoxicating. Through the canopy of trees I could just see a wink of clear, blue sky.

I'd driven to this nature preserve walk every day for the past week. Although it was just outside of town, I felt transported to Eden. I focused on being here now, feeling my legs move in rhythm with my breathing, one-two, one-two, concentrating on every butter-yellow-Croc-soled step, and making it a walking meditation.

Still, in spite of my best intentions, my thoughts kept returning to the conversation I'd had this morning with Aunt Claire, which had left me worried. I'd come downstairs from my bedroom on the third floor to discover her working feverishly on her computer. For years Aunt Claire was a real technophobe, but once she made the leap into the twenty-first century, she never looked back. She even used an iPhone.

She glanced up at me, smiled, and pushed a wisp of shoulder-length blond hair behind her ear. She was dressed in her usual casual style—a T-shirt, denim shorts, and hemp sandals—although the vegetarian message on her T-shirt, Love Animals, Don't Eat Them, was anything but.

"Honey, did I wake you?"

I'd been sleeping in Aunt Claire's guest room, across the hall from her bedroom, above Nature's Way Market and Café for the past week and a half. I hadn't heard her get up, probably because my white-noise machine was on. Although there weren't the traffic sounds I was used to hearing in L.A., just the sounds of crickets to keep me company, I couldn't break myself of the habit.

That morning I woke up at six thirty, hopped out of my cocoon of a bed, did my morning reading of inspirational authors such as Thich Nhat Hanh and Eckhart Tolle, and meditated for fifteen minutes. Feeling centered and at peace with the world, I dressed in shorts, a T-shirt, and my yellow rubber sandals and headed downstairs. On the way out, I found Aunt Claire working away in her office before the store and café opened at eight.

"I didn't hear a thing." I walked over to the desk, kissed her smooth cheek, and looked at the computer screen. "What are you working on?"

"The fountain of youth."

I blinked. "Say what?"

She chuckled. "I'm working with a company in New York on an age-defying herbal cream."

"So that's your secret." I appraised her. Nary a wrinkle; clear, vibrant skin; sparkling aquamarine eyes. Aunt Claire glowed with vibrant health. Her calendar age was sixty-seven, but she looked a good ten years younger.

She pushed Send and reached for a steaming cup of herbal tea. It smelled delicious, like licorice and fennel. She pointed to the pot of tea on the desk and an extra cup. "You could say that. I first started using this specific combination of herbs when I was researching my book."

Aunt Claire had written *The Complete Encyclopedia of Herbs* a few years ago and *The Complete Encyclopedia of Herbs for Beauty* last spring. She'd circled the world to complete her research, traveling from the Amazonian rain forests to the Himalayas. "The cream is full of herbs, antioxidants, and lots of other goodies."

"Sounds great. And people are really into that kind of thing. I'd use it."

She shook her head and smiled. "Sweetheart, you don't need it. Your skin is beautiful, just like the rest of you."

Giving her shoulder an affectionate squeeze, I circled the desk and caught sight of myself in the large, wooden-framed mirror on the wall. Not for the first time, I noticed how much I looked like my aunt Claire, instead of my own mother, a petite brunette. Although I was twenty-eight and Aunt Claire was sixty-seven, both of us were tall, thin, and blond, with angular features, good skin, model-like cheekbones, and excellent teeth. "The teeth of the tiger," my aunt always said, as neither of us spent any time in the dentist's chair.

Overall, we were presentable and personable. People liked us, a good thing, since I was a doctor and she was a business owner. I was glad the gene fairy had given me Aunt Claire's characteristics rather than my mother's. In fact, Aunt Claire felt more like my mother than my own mother did. She was a nurturing soul and accepted me the way I was. My mother always wanted me to be different, more like my sister, the "real" doctor, and less interested in "whoo-whoo" medicine, which is what she called my chosen profession.

I sat down and reached for the ceramic teapot, with its bold red-and-yellow floral design, and poured tea into the matching cup. The chair was comfy, as was the office, with overstuffed couches, bookshelves crammed with natural, new age, and vegetarian-themed books, and pictures on the wall of various herbs and yoga positions. Above the doorway was a sign with the word *Peace* in big, bold letters. On her desk in a place of honor was a picture of me receiving my degree in naturopathic medicine from the Southwest College of Natural Medicine and Health Sciences. Aunt Claire, my inspiration in all things natural, was the only family member to fly out for the ceremony.

My mother considered my pursuit of natural medicine foolish; why, she asked, hadn't I gone to a real medical school like my sister, who graduated from Harvard? I was tired of trying to convince her that naturopathic doctors are "real" doctors, too. Our training is rigorous, and I'd even stepped it up by learning from some of the best and brightest—namely, Ray Richmond-Safer, MD, a nationally renowned holistic physician (and bestselling author and talk show favorite) at the cutting-edge Arizona Center for the Advancement of Natural Medicine.

Unlike traditional doctors, naturopaths are taught to take into consideration a client's entire body, mind, and spirit before rendering a diagnosis. After such an assessment, if I believed a patient (many of whom were bicoastal entertainment types: actors, agents, and studio execs) could benefit from more conventional medicine, I referred him or her to integrative doctor friends—those who had *MD* after their names but were open to natural medicine approaches—in L.A. or New York. My aunt Claire couldn't be more proud and my mother, Daisy, more dismissive.

The fact that my mother would not support me in my chosen field was a constant source of friction between them. There had been many arguments and tears. Then, last September, when my mother was admitted to the hospital for heart problems, Aunt Claire wanted to help restore her health with natural remedies, but my sister rebuffed her. Now, even though my mother lived in Greenport and my sister lived in Southold, seven minutes away, the three women still weren't talking.

"Have you been working on this long?"

Aunt Claire picked up a bottle of vitamins and turned the label toward me. "Green Focus, the company that makes this line of vitamins, approached me about creating beauty products after my book topped the *New York Times* non-fiction list last fall. I've been working on it all winter. You know I've always wanted to have my own line."

I did. For as long as I could remember, Aunt Claire had been working on formulas to address different health conditions, first in her native Australia, then in London, then when she came to Greenport one summer to visit us and ended up training with master herbalist Nick Holmes, now her boyfriend of more than fifteen years (neither believed in marriage). I'd always been fascinated by stories about exotic Aunt Claire, a professional herbalist who'd traveled to distant lands like Japan, India, and China, so when she came to the East End, twenty years ago, I'd been a sponge ready to absorb everything about her.

She was fascinated by natural remedies and the way the body could use these cures to make itself well. Her curiosity was boundless, and she'd drawn me into her quest more than once. I'd been a guinea pig for her black tea compresses for sunburn, ginger-garlic soup for viruses, and special salve for poison ivy. She sold the ginger-garlic soup in the café, but the other remedies had never been packaged for her customers. Creating and distributing her own line was a dream come true. Sipping the tea, I savored the warm spices and kick of fennel and the happiness I felt for her.

"When will your anti-aging formula be on the market? Or should I say, in your market?" I smiled.

She beamed back at me. "I'm hoping Fresh Face, that's the name of the line, will be on the shelves by year's end. But for now, don't say anything about it. It's all very hush-hush. I've been instructed to keep it—what do you kids say? On the down low. They don't want anyone to scoop us."

The phone rang, startling her, which I found strange. Aunt Claire was usually as serene and immovable as a rock. She answered, "Claire Hagan here," listened, and then covered the receiver with her hand and cocked her head. "Honey, this is going to take a while. Would you mind?"

"Not at all. It's time for my morning walk anyway." I headed for the door. As I did, Aunt Claire reached into her drawer, grabbed a small vial, and untwisted the cap. As she listened to the person on the other end, she furrowed her brow and emptied a dropperful of the contents into her tea. It looked like a bottle of flower essences that help relieve emotional upset and bring you back into balance. Was Aunt Claire worried about something? Thanks to her practice of meditation, yoga, and Zen thinking, she was always the picture of calm. I shook off the thought. It must be the new formula. As she said, she'd never worked on something like this. She probably felt as if it was her big break. Still . . .

As I crossed a footbridge over a small stream, my review of our conversation was interrupted by my cell phone ringing. A few yards away, an elegant, long-necked white egret glanced at me, and then promptly flew off. The phone's caller ID said: Aunt Claire and showed a picture of her smiling.

Answering, I said, "Hello? Aunt Claire?" but the reception was terrible and I couldn't hear her.

Several seconds passed with no reply. I disconnected the call and was about to dial back when I received another call from the same number. I answered again, wondering what was going on, when I was again greeted with static. *Damn these cell phone towers,* I thought. Reception in some places was the absolute pits.

"Aunt Claire? I can't hear you."

Through the earpiece I heard garbled words, followed by a loud crash. Then the line went dead.

Not knowing what was wrong but already cursing myself for not staying at the store and waiting to find out what was upsetting her, I screeched her PT Cruiser to a halt in front of Nature's Way and jumped out. Even though I was in a mad panic, I still couldn't help but notice the care and attention Aunt Claire had paid to the three-story gingerbread Victorian exterior, with its bright yellow paint and red trim.

Squinting at the sign in the early morning sun, I realized again how much I loved this place. My aunt's store, my home away from home, and most delightful, home to natural remedies. I'd been introduced to many of those elixirs as a teenager, after my Aunt Claire returned to the States from the UK to be near my mom and opened the store. Brightly colored posters in the windows announced everything from "CoQ-10 on Sale!" to

"Yes, We Have Burt's Bees!" to "Scrumptious Organic Rasp-berries!"

Thousands of tiny white lights hung from the roof, and on top of the building stood a ship's weathervane, a nod to our village's nautical heritage. Three white metal tables and chairs had been placed on the porch for al fresco dining.

I sped up the path lined with perennial plants of every size, shape, and color that Aunt Claire had bought, nurtured and watered faithfully, bolted up the steps, and pushed at the fire-engine-red front door. It was locked. In a town as safe as this, I found it odd that she'd bothered to do so, unless she wanted to make sure no early bird customers drifted in. Reaching for my key, I slipped it into the lock, pushed the door open, and stepped inside. It was eerily quiet. I looked around and, not seeing her, called her name several times. "Aunt Claire? Are you okay?" I felt panic rise in my throat.

Getting no reply, I headed farther inside, past the bright and cheery café section, with more white metal tables and chairs; bookshelves bursting at the seams with volumes on everything from vegan eating to yoga to meditation; and the oversize cork-board displaying the daily specials along with funky artwork and postcards from customers around the world. The smell of patchouli filled the air, giving the space a warm, musky scent.

I walked past the kitchen and the wood-paneled, square checkout station, which was situated in the middle of the bright green-and-blue space, facilitating attention to custom-ers' needs. Featured at the checkout station were items that were likely to be bought spontaneously, such as lip balm, stress mints, bug repellent, and bars of organic milk chocolate, along with magazines like *Nature's Remedy*, *Yoga Journal*, and *Natural Health*. The sun coming through the skylights spilled over the entire area, bathing it in an ethereal glow. Pushing open the office door, I peered inside to where I'd left her only an hour before. Aunt Claire's teacup sat empty, as did her chair.

Turning around, I walked back into the store, past the display of eco-friendly cleaning products, to the produce aisle, which led to the stairs. Perhaps Aunt Claire had felt ill, headed upstairs to lie down, and fallen. I hoped not. The stairs were narrow and winding; one slip, and you could really hurt yourself. But I didn't get that far. As I rounded the corner, I spotted her.

She lay in the fetal position on the floor, the bottle of flower essences resting next to her left hand. Her tabby cats, Ginger and Ginkgo, a brother and sister she'd adopted from a local animal-welfare foundation, were circling her, mewing. Had she fainted?

Dropping to my knees, I put my head to her chest. Was she breathing? No. Oh, God. Her eyes were closed and her face was pink, as if she'd stayed in the sun too long.

I put my head to her chest again and hoped against hope that I was wrong. No, she wasn't breathing. I grabbed my iPhone, called 911, and then started to perform CPR. But it was no use. She didn't respond. I kept trying. Moments later the EMT's arrived and took over. After a few minutes of trying to resuscitate her, they told me that Claire was gone. The shock of her death reverberated through me. I wanted to throw up.

As I fought back nausea, my gaze landed on the bottle next to her left hand. I bent over her and inspected it. It was the flower essence Mimulus, which is taken for "Fear of worldly things, illness, pain, accidents, poverty, of dark, of being alone, of misfortune. The fears of everyday life. These people quietly and secretly bear their dread; they do not freely speak of it to others," according to its creator, the British doctor Edward Bach, who'd discovered and patented the power of certain flower essences in 1934.

I went to the desk and got a napkin in case someone's finger-prints besides Claire's were on the bottle and carefully picked it up by the top of the dropper. When I opened the top and smelled the liquid inside, it didn't smell like any flower essence I'd ever used with patients. Had someone put something into the bottle with the intent to kill?

My world tilted on its axis. Aunt Claire had been dealing with something big. Something so foreboding that she'd chosen this cure. And it had killed her.

# chapter two

Dear Dr. McQuade,
I've been feeling really low for over a month now. I can't point to a specific reason, although I have had several personal setbacks this year: I lost my job, my husband left me, and my goldfish died.
   Signed,
   Feeling Down

Dear Feeling Down,
For mild to moderate depression, you may want to try Saint John's wort. It's been proven in many studies to be effective. However, if you're feeling depressed and it's getting worse, it's time to see a professional. Remember, it takes a strong person to ask for help when she needs it. Feel better!
   Signed,
   Dr. Willow McQuade

I don't know how long I sat there and cried with the cats keeping me company, dissolved in a puddle of goo and using the recycled-paper towels from the display to mop up my tears. I think subliminally I hoped that if I cried hard enough, I could will her back to me. But Aunt Claire had definitely, as she would often say when others died, gone to the other side. She was probably looking down on me right now. In spite of everything, I found this somewhat comforting.

The EMS volunteers had come and assessed the situation after I'd carefully replaced the bottle in its original position. When I told them my suspicions, they called the police, who asked me to sit tight until they arrived. While the EMS techs went outside for a smoke, I stayed where I was, by her side, a lump in my throat and thoughts buzzing around in my head like bees. Why did she choose this essence? What was she afraid of? Why didn't she confide her fears to me? Had someone put something in this bottle to try and kill her?

But who would want to hurt Aunt Claire? A disgruntled customer? Someone she ticked off at the post office? Despite her Zen nature, Aunt Claire did have a knack for getting into confrontations with certain folks. This child of the sixties was also a real activist, holding meetings for causes like workers' rights and animal rights every week in the store.

Suddenly I heard a startled gasp from behind me. "What happened?"

Turning around, I found Aunt Claire's passive-aggressive right hand, Janice Dorian, a stricken look on her face. Despite being surrounded by natural ways to calm down, Janice was an uptight forty-something with a perpetually pinched-looking face. She wore the Nature's Way green apron, khakis, and a white T-shirt, hair stuffed into a crisp ponytail. "What have you done to her?"

"Nothing!" There was no one I loved more than my beloved Aunt Claire. Checking my temper, even though I wanted to deck her, I steadied my voice and said, "She's gone, Janice. The police will be here any minute."

Janice pushed past me and bent over Aunt Claire's body. "Everything was fine until you came home. I've never seen her so agitated since you arrived."

This was true but had to do with my efforts to bring my mother and Aunt Claire back together. Or maybe her agitation had something to do with her new business venture, Fresh Face. Even then she hid it very well. "Janice, you know that we loved each other very much." I pointed to the bottle of Mimulus. "I think she may have been murdered," I said, and shared my thoughts about the strange smell.

Janice snatched up the bottle before I could stop her and snarled, "You did this!" She waved the bottle at me. "This is your fault!"

"No, Janice," I said, feeling tears well up again. Dealing with Janice in this situation was like rubbing sand into a wound. "You're wrong. That is simply not true."

"I'll take that." I turned around to see that the cops had arrived, a few patrolmen and two men in street clothes who were most likely detectives. One of them, a tall, lanky guy with close-cropped brown hair, put gloves on and took the bottle from Janice. He dropped it into a plastic bag and gave her a withering look. "Nothing like contaminating the evidence."

"That's her fault," Janice huffed. "She's the one who told me about it."

The other detective, short and stocky with an athletic build, got right down to business. "I'm Detective Koren. This is Detective Coyle. You are?"

"I'm Willow McQuade," I said, and wiped away fresh tears with a Kleenex. "This is Janice Dorian."

"I can speak for myself," Janice huffed again.

"Fine," I said, weary of her attitude.

Detective Koren arched an eyebrow. "Problem?"

"She's the problem," Janice said, and pointed at me. "Everything was fine until she came here. Claire and I worked together as a team. She trusted me. We built this business to where it is today. Then she comes and ruins everything! I'll bet she killed her!"

The cops gave me a quizzical look.

A wave of dread washed over me. I took a deep breath to steady myself. "She was my aunt. I loved her. I did not kill her." I told them my theory about what might have happened this morning.

Detective Coyle narrowed his eyes at me. "What makes you an expert?"

"I'm a doctor. A naturopathic doctor."

"Oh." Coyle smirked. "So you're not a real doctor."

I stiffened. I'd heard this before, but it just wasn't true.

"Why don't you two take a seat," Koren said. "We need to take a closer look, and then we'll have some questions for you both."

Janice paced by the door and I watched from a table in the café with a knot in my stomach as Koren and Coyle examined Aunt Claire's body and the area around her. After that, Koren separately questioned us about our connections to Aunt Claire and to the store, our contact information, and our movements this morning while Coyle took notes.

When I mentioned finding Aunt Claire and the bottle, Coyle held up the plastic bag and squinted at the label. "Mimulus? What's this for? Some kind of quack cure?"

*Okay, Willow, don't take offense. You know that lots of people think natural medicine is quackery, but you know better. Your Aunt Claire knew better. Don't go to the dark side.* "It isn't a quack cure," I said briskly. "It's what is known as a flower essence, which is used for specific situations."

"What kind of situations?"

"When you have an emotional imbalance, you choose a flower essence to help put you back in balance. In this case it looks like she was afraid of something." I explained the properties of Mimulus to him.

Detective Koren, who was clearly the fashion-forward member of the team in an Armani knockoff, while his partner made do with JCPenney garb, grabbed the bag. " 'Fear of worldly things, illness, pain, accidents . . . misfortune'? That's quite a list. You on that list?"

"No, officer, we had the best of relationships."

Janice huffed her disapproval. "Then why did you fight?"

I shrugged like it was no big deal. "Like all people who love each other, we had our disagreements. Mostly about my mother. She and Aunt Claire are, I mean were, estranged. I was trying to bring them back together. Aunt Claire was, well, resistant. She didn't give up a grudge easily."

Koren held up his index finger. "Wait a minute, your aunt"—he glanced at Aunt Claire's body—"had a grudge against your mother? Was it mutual?"

I was already getting tired of his questions, but I answered, "When my mother was in the hospital last year with heart problems, my aunt Claire disagreed with what the doctors were doing for her. She wanted to add some natural remedies. My sister and my mother rebuffed her. They still hadn't made up."

Detective Koren handed the plastic bag back to Coyle and drilled me with a look. "They local? I'll need their addresses and phone numbers for follow-up." He flipped open a small notebook.

"Yes," I said, thinking about how much my mother and sister were going to dislike talking to a cop. "My mother lives in Greenport." I gave him her address and my sister's in Southold.

He scribbled down the information. "Do you live around here?"

"No," Janice said with a sniff. "She lives in L.A."

Was that a crime? Some locals thought so. They called us citidiots. Pushy city folks clogging up the streets, the grocery store, and the beaches. "That's right. I was here visiting Aunt Claire."

"And you're staying where?"

"I'm staying here, upstairs, and I'm not leaving until this is settled. Aunt Claire just had a clean bill of health from her doctor yesterday. Something is very wrong here. Like I told you, I think she was murdered."

He gave me a look I didn't like. "Why don't you let us worry about that?" he said as he flipped the pad closed and put it in his jacket pocket. "And staying put is a real good plan. Why don't you tell your mother and sister to stay put, too? Sounds like we all need to talk."

The coroner arrived a few minutes later and removed Aunt Claire's body.

The day wore on into evening, and the cops worked late into the night processing the scene as I cried myself to sleep upstairs, which worked better than the valerian I took for my occasional insomnia. Valerian root, like chamomile, lemon balm, and lady slipper is an herb known as a nervine, which soothes and calms the nervous system. But tonight my tears did the trick.

Saturday morning, I awoke to the rhythmic pat-pat-pat of rain on the bedroom window and the crackle of thunder in the distance. When I got up to close the window, droplets peppered the windowsill. Ginger and Ginkgo both stirred, stretched, hit the floor, and then followed me as I crossed the hall to make sure the windows were closed in Aunt Claire's room.

When I opened the door, her presence was so strong it felt like a punch to the chest. Even though I knew her spirit was gone, the room was all so *her,* everything from the art on the walls depicting Australia and London, two of her favorite places, to her beloved, worn cotton comforter, the books on the shelves, even the lavender smell of a large pillar candle. It had been her favorite scent.

I lit the lavender candle, which was also good for relieving stress, sat on the bed, and reached for the book on her nightstand, *The Power of Now,* a classic by Eckhart Tolle. Hers was well-worn and dog-eared; she'd obviously referred to it constantly. Perhaps even more so of late, since she clearly was troubled by something. Lying back on the bed, the grief like lead in my chest, I stared at the flickering candle and sifted through what could possibly have been troubling Aunt Claire.

A knock on the door disturbed my reverie. I blew out the candle and padded out of the room. When I opened the front door I found Merrily Scott, one of the café waitresses, dressed in the standard Nature's Way uniform—jeans, a white T-shirt, and a green apron with the logo on the front. On top of her head she had twisted her bright red hair into tufts with fluorescent blue, green, and orange rubber bands.

Merrily was hypercheerful and hyperenergized, probably from the energy drink she constantly was holding. Today, though, her usual good cheer had been replaced with sadness and tears.

"I'm so sorry about Claire," she said, her red eyes moist. "She was always so good to me."

"Thanks, Merrily," I said, verging on tears myself. "We're all going to miss her." I put my arm around her shoulders. "But why are you here? I told you to stay home." I'd told Janice as much yesterday before she left. "We aren't going to open today."

She wiped tears from her eyes. "I can't just sit home. I'll drive myself nuts. I have to keep busy. Even if we aren't open, I have things I can do, like ordering products, cleaning, stuff like that. Oh, and I have a message for you." She handed me a message scribbled on a piece of recycled notepaper and took a sip of her drink. "This is for you. It's from Mr. Matthews, Claire's lawyer. He wants to see you right away. This morning. Now." She chomped her gum a few times for good measure.

I looked at the note with his name, address, and phone number. Mr. Matthews had been Aunt Claire's lawyer for more than twenty years. I knew she'd been fond of him, and more important, trusted him. "Did he say why?"

"No. Just that he wanted to see you."

"Okay, thanks." I began to close the door, but she stopped it with her foot. "Like, he wants to see you right now."

"I know, Merrily, I just want to take a shower first."

She thought about this. "Well, okay. He just sounded like he was in a really big hurry to see you."

"Okay, Merrily, I'll be down in a minute."

Closing the door after Ginger and Ginkgo scampered down the stairs, I went into my room, stripped, and headed into the shower. As the warm water gushed down over my head and body, I wondered why Mr. Matthews wanted to see me so urgently. Was it something about the business? About Aunt Claire's will? Surely that could wait until after the funeral. I grabbed the organic green tea and fennel shampoo (not tested on animals, of course) and lathered up as I considered the possibilities.

An hour later, after grabbing a quick breakfast of fresh fruit and granola with plain low-fat yogurt, I grabbed an umbrella and headed out. After a brisk walk through the raindrops in the tangy, salty morning air, I arrived at Aunt Claire's lawyer's office. Located upstairs in a two-story white house (a dentist's office was on the first floor), it was smack in the middle of Main Street, one of two busy thoroughfares in town along with Front Street.

Greenport had a quaint charm that came from its mix of longtime businesses such as the nautical ship and shore emporium, the drugstore, the old-fashioned department store, and the post office side by side with new, upscale boutiques, seafood restaurants, tea and coffee shops, antiques dealers, ice cream stands, and art galleries. I loved it and always got a thrill when I walked or drove through town, with its multicolored awnings, bright facades, and wooden signs. Tourists loved it, too. From Memorial Day to Labor Day, throngs of visitors packed the sidewalks sampling fare, shopping, and enjoying the seaside environs. Forbes even named Greenport one of America's prettiest villages.

Today, though, it felt like a dark cloud hovered over the town. I was sure that everyone was shocked and afraid by what had happened. A murderer was among us. On a practical level, townsfolk were probably also concerned about the effect a murder would have on business. Would tourists be scared away?

I tried to shake off the cornucopia of fear I felt and knocked on Mr. Matthews's office door. Receiving no reply, I went inside anyway. He wanted to see me right away, didn't he? I stepped into the nondescript waiting area, which consisted of a threadbare couch, a few tired magazines, and a door that led to his office.

Sitting down, I checked my iPhone for messages. I'd received three e-mails from my assistant, Patty, in L.A. regarding various patients, and I replied with a request to please refer the cases to my boss and fellow alum, William Cohen, as she had done with other patients since I'd been away.

A few moments later, Patty e-mailed again, telling me that she would handle everything and not to worry. But I *was* worried. I couldn't stay away too long or my new practice would suffer. But since I was the executor of Aunt Claire's will, I would be responsible for the time-consuming task of settling her estate.

I pocketed the phone when Mr. Matthews appeared. Dressed in a tired-looking business suit, he was balding and had small, round spectacles perched on his nose. He popped a breath mint into his mouth as he crossed the room to me.

"Dr. McQuade, thank you for coming over," he said as he took my hand. "I'm so sorry about Claire. She will be missed."

"Thank you," I said, on the verge of crying again. Any mention of Claire made me feel like dissolving into tears, a reaction I was sure would continue for a long, long time, maybe forever.

Matthews popped another mint into his mouth. "Mint?"

Waving him off, I said, "No thanks." That brand was filled with artificial sweeteners I wanted no part of. I was off sugar, had been for the past five years, since I realized it depleted my energy reserves. If I needed a sweet fix, I used Truvia or Stevia, natural sugars with a glycemic index of zero, meaning they kept my blood sugar stable and didn't zap my energy.

He shook his head. "I've been popping these constantly. I've got this strange metallic taste in my mouth that I can't get rid of."

I got the feeling he was looking for some free natural medical advice. As much as I wanted to get to the point of today's meeting, I couldn't resist giving him some. "Have you tried a tongue scraper?"

He gave me a blank look. "A tongue scraper?"

"It's a U-shaped device that you use to scrape bacteria off your tongue. It might help. You might also want to try some chlorophyll tablets to help correct your pH balance, make it more alkaline, which is better for your health. If you come to the store, I'll give you some. Have you seen a dentist? It's possible something's wrong with a tooth as well."

He put his hand to his face. "I'm not in any pain, but I'm due for a checkup. I'll make an appointment and try what you suggested. Now, let's go into my office, shall we?" He motioned to the door.

Inside, sitting on the couch, was my mother, Daisy; my sister, Natasha; and Janice.

My petite mother, dressed in a sunny yellow suit, brunette hair in an updo, jumped up and stood on tiptoe to kiss me on both cheeks. "Darling!" she chirped in her Australian accent. A transplant, she'd lived in the States ever since marrying my dad thirty-five years ago. They'd met in London while he was in Boston University's student-exchange program and she was working as a magazine editor for British *Vogue*. "Are you okay? I called and called yesterday, but you didn't answer."

Wanting to be alone with my grief, I'd turned my cell phone off and had let the phone in the market go to voice mail. I also knew that my mother would be of no comfort to me, as she invariably said the wrong thing and made the situation worse.

Mother lived in her own universe, which after my father's death from cancer eight years ago, revolved around trips to New York—especially during Fashion Week—charity fashion shows in Greenport, lunch at the country club, and worldwide vacations on cruise ships. Ditto for my older sister, Natasha, thirty-two, who worked 24/7 to ensure her new practice in Southold thrived.

"I'm fine," I said, feeling tears welling up behind my eyes.

"You don't look fine. You look pale and drawn, doesn't she, Natasha?"

Natasha, with her fine-boned face, chic haircut, and designer suit, stayed on the couch. We, like my mother and Aunt Claire, had been estranged since clashing over Mother's treatment. I hadn't expected a warm, sisterly embrace, so her ice-princess attitude was not a surprise. Janice, Ms. Passive-Aggressive, gave me a nasty look and refolded her hands firmly on her lap.

Mr. Matthews rounded the desk and sat down. The space was decorated in generic blues and browns, with an oversize desk for Matthews, one guest chair, and two couches. The art on the wall was mostly by local artists, including one by my cousin, who'd achieved local fame for his seascapes.

The energy in the room felt stagnant. Perhaps Matthews didn't have many clients, or the ones he saw had issues. I always tuned in to the feeling of a place. While Aunt Claire's store felt light and vibrant, this office felt dark and oppressive. I decided that smudging the room, the practice of burning dried sage and allowing the vapors to clear the space of bad energy, would certainly help.

Mr. Matthews interrupted my musings by saying, "The reason I've asked you here is to make you aware that there are some surprises in Claire's will. I thought it was best to get them out of the way immediately."

"Surprises?" Natasha, a petite brunette like my mother, arched a carefully manicured eyebrow. "I'll bet this has to do with that ridiculous fight last September when you were in the hospital," she said, turning to my mother, who'd sat down next to her. "What did she do, change the will?"

In case this was true, I plopped down in the office chair. I wanted to be as far away from them as possible when the stuff hit the fan.

"She did," Mr. Matthews said, taking off his glasses and cleaning them before putting them back on. He blew out a sigh. "She came to me in October and said she wanted to make some changes."

"I don't believe this," my mother said. "She must have been feeling particularly vindictive."

"Don't talk about her that way," I said vehemently. "She was never vindictive. I'm sure she felt she had her reasons."

Mr. Matthews picked up a sheaf of papers and looked at me. "She wanted to give everything to you, Willow."

I gulped. "Everything?"

"I don't believe this," Natasha said, drilling me with a nasty look. "You always were her favorite."

I shot back, "You didn't help matters any when you barred her from Mom's hospital room. You completely took over and pushed us away. She was very hurt."

"I did it for Mother's own good," Natasha huffed. "She was causing a nuisance."

"She was trying to help," I replied. "You made her feel excluded, like she was in the way. She had a right to be there." I dug my fingers into the leather chair.

Natasha waved my comment away. "If I hadn't protected Mother, who knows what Aunt Claire would have recommended? Mother had a heart condition. She didn't need any of

Aunt Claire's quack remedies; she needed good, solid medical care."

"She was just trying to offer alternatives," I said, now really peeved. "That's what she believed in. But she never would have hurt Mother." My phone rang, and I looked at the caller ID. It was the store. I ignored it—I had enough to handle right now.

Mr. Matthews cleared his throat to get our attention. "In this, her last will and testament, she's left Nature's Way Market and Café to you, Willow, along with the rights to an anti-aging cream called Fresh Face she'd been developing for Green Focus Nutraceuticals."

I was surprised. I knew I had a special place in Aunt Claire's heart, but how did she think I could manage the business from L.A.? Had she expected me to move to Greenport? I considered the possibilities. It seemed as if I might have a choice to make, and soon.

"This is outrageous!" Janice stood up and pointed to herself. "Claire always indicated that I was to get the store and café. I've slaved for over ten years helping her build the business. And the formula—that could be worth millions! Fresh Face was her own exclusive blend. You're not going to get away with this! I'm going to contest the will." She shook her fist in my face. "You have some nerve! First you kill her, and now you're trying to take everything she had!"

"What?" My mother gasped.

"Now, wait a minute," I said, taking deep yoga breaths known as pranayama, trying to remain calm. "I did not kill her, but I do think that someone may have added something to the flower essence formula she was taking. I believe that's what killed her."

"Why would anyone want to kill her?" my mother asked. "Are you sure?"

I nodded. "Aunt Claire received a clean bill of health from Dr. Murphy two days ago. She was a very healthy woman, in great shape for sixty-seven. She didn't eat meat and always was careful to eat plenty of fresh fruits and vegetables and take vitamin supplements. She didn't smoke, she didn't drink. When I left her yesterday morning, she was taking these drops, this flower essence," I explained. "When I found her, the bottle was on the floor beside her."

"It also makes sense that you're a suspect, since you found her," Janice sneered. "That's what the police think."

"What?" I felt my stomach drop.

"The first person at the scene is always a suspect. My cousin Bobbie told me. She's married to Kenneth, Detective Koren." She pointed to Mom and Natasha. "The cops also want to talk to *you*, because of the fight you had with her."

My sister stared at me with narrowed eyes. "And who told them about that? As if I didn't know."

Mom put her hand to her chest and sucked in a breath. "Oh, my lord."

"Are you okay?" Natasha asked, putting a hand on Mom's shoulder.

She locked eyes with Natasha, a worried look on her face. "I feel a little strange. Are they going to arrest us?"

Natasha gritted her teeth. "Now look what you've done, Willow, and with her heart problems. You should be ashamed of yourself."

Shame was something I was accustomed to when it came to my mother and sister. They tried to use it to control and dominate and make themselves feel superior, but I didn't buy into it. I got up and went over to sit next to my mother. "I'm sorry. I didn't mean to tell the police—it just came out. Are you okay?" It was hard to tell if this was real or if she was just putting on a show. Imaginary chest pains were not beyond her, as she had pushed the heart attack button more than once since September to get what she wanted.

Mother sat between us looking stricken, her face a chalky white.

"I'm taking you to the ER right now," Natasha said briskly. "We aren't taking any chances. Not after last fall." She got up and began to hustle our mother to the door. "I hope you're happy," she said as she turned and shot me a nasty look.

Between my mother's real or imagined heart attack, the police's suspicions about me, and Aunt Claire's murder, I felt anything but.

# chapter three

Dear Dr. McQuade,
I have been spending my nights tossing and turning.
David Letterman and Craig Ferguson are becoming my
new best friends. What can I do to sleep through the
night?
    Signed,
    Counting Sheep

Dear Counting Sheep,
There are several things you can try. Known in herbal-
medicine lingo as a nervine, valerian root is very relaxing. You may also want to try melatonin. Take a
small dose, 1 to 3 milligrams, to see how it affects you.
Finally, why not try a relaxing meditation tape? It will
help you de-stress and drift off to sleep naturally.
    Signed,
    Dr. Willow McQuade

On the way to the hospital, which was a few blocks away on Manor Place, I checked my messages again. There was one from Merrily, wondering how things were going, and oh, by the way, she'd found a small stray dog under the front porch. What should she do? I quickly called her back and got the 411 on the situation. The dog, a friendly mutt that was probably a terrier mix, didn't have a collar or a license and seemed malnourished. He also had a large gash on his neck that looked infected. She'd fed him some organic dog food and he was now resting in Aunt Claire's office.

I suggested she call the animal shelter to see if anyone had lost a dog. She said she would but was worried that she wouldn't find the owner. The dog really needed to see a vet straightaway. I asked her to take a picture of the wound and e-mail it to me.

I got it a few moments later. The wound did look nasty, deep and infected. I decided the dog needed immediate care, so I told her to go ahead and take him to the vet. We could look for the owner later. If we didn't find him or her, I'd pay the bill. I'd been an animal lover since my childhood, when my father had rescued animals of all different types: birds, rabbits, bats, opossums, and mice. The local vet knew my family well.

That attended to, I turned my attention to the ER. When I arrived, my mother and sister had already gone into the patient area. I checked in with the receptionist and asked if I could join them. She pushed an intercom button, talked to the nurse on duty, and then waved me over to the door.

I stepped into a cold, white hallway and asked a nearby nurse where my mother was. She pointed to the right, so I headed down the hallway, looking into the stations that had all the latest monitoring equipment for emergencies. I spotted my mother and sister in the second one, engaged in deep conversation. My mother lay in the bed, already hooked up to an IV and heart monitor.

I interrupted them. "Are you okay, Mom?"

Natasha gave me a dismissive look. "No, she's not okay. They're running tests. They don't know for sure what's going on. But that scene in the lawyer's office didn't help. Good going."

I pushed past her and went to the head of the bed. "I was talking to my mother."

Mom put her hand to her chest, where it fluttered nervously. "My heart just feels like it's beating a little too fast."

Natasha took mother's wrist and looked at her watch, preparing to take her pulse. "She has an arrhythmia, Willow. If you'd been here last September, you'd know that."

Since both Aunt Claire and I had been barred from the hospital room, I'd been forced to get reports secondhand from the nurse, who hadn't been very forthcoming. I let Natasha's remark pass, not wanting to further upset my mother.

I leaned over to talk to her. "Is there anything I can do? Do you need anything?"

"I'm fine, honey," she said, patting my hand. "My nerves are just so jangled right now." She began to mist up, and Natasha handed her a tissue. "I can't believe Claire is gone, and this business with the will is unsettling. I don't know what Claire was thinking."

I felt close to tears myself but focused on her. "Maybe some Rescue Remedy would help you calm down," I suggested, and pulled a bottle of the flower essences from my pocketbook. I thought of Aunt Claire but pushed the memory out of my mind. Later.

"Willow. Outside," Natasha commanded.

We left Mother's station and walked down the hallway to the door that led to the reception area.

"Are you out of your mind? Giving her that stuff?" Natasha snapped.

"It's perfectly harmless and could help calm her. It wouldn't interfere with anything they need to do here. You can see she's a nervous wreck."

"This is so like you. You just don't get it, do you? This is a serious condition. We need to run tests. She may have to stay here overnight or for a few days. I'm not going to allow her to take any of your quack remedies. Especially not until we know what's really wrong with her."

Sucking in a breath, I said, "You're not going to allow her? Who do you think you are? Who put you in charge?"

"This," Natasha said as she reached into her pocketbook, pulled out her wallet, and flipped me her AMA card. "I'm a real doctor: you're not. I'll call you when we know something. Good-bye, Willow." She turned on her heel and headed back to Mother.

Natasha's words stung, but I knew that trying to talk to either my sister or my mother right now would just make things worse. So I sat in the parking lot of the hospital feeling upset and bereft. I'd held it together in the lawyer's office and in the hospital, but now that I was alone again my defenses were down. My grief engulfed me like a shroud, and I started to sob uncontrollably. People passed me going to the ER or to their cars, and I just kept on crying. I didn't care. My best friend was gone. I was alone.

After a while, I reached into the glove compartment, found some tissues, and wiped my face and blew my nose. I tried to compose myself by taking a few deep breaths. I felt exhausted and had decided to go back to the store and lie down (although it worried me that the murderer might return, and then what would I do?), when my phone rang. It was Nick and he sounded awful. He asked me to take care of the funeral arrangements. He just couldn't do it.

Yesterday morning, when I'd called him with the news of Aunt Claire's death, he'd hurried to the store. When he saw her, he dropped to his knees and began sobbing. After the police left, so did he, without a word about where he was going. I'd called him repeatedly, but he didn't answer. Finally, he called me back last night, sounding drunk, which was atypical for him but certainly understandable given the circumstances. The love of his life was gone. I'd checked with him again early this morning, waking him up, and he said he'd call later.

I told him I'd take care of the funeral.

I drove the two blocks from the hospital to the funeral home and pulled in front of the green-and-white clapboard building. The rain had stopped, but the stone walkway to the door was still wet as I walked up to it and rang the bell.

Ralph Chadway came to the door. The self-assured, fit, and handsome man in a tailored black suit and azure tie barely resembled the boy I knew in high school, who'd been tortured for being openly gay.

He saw my red face and eyes but didn't comment. Instead, he pulled me into a hug. "I'm sorry about your aunt. I know you were very close."

He led me into the lobby. To the left was a viewing room that was thankfully empty. I didn't feel up to seeing another dead body, not today. "Let's go in here to talk." He led me around the corner to a living-room-type area with lots of plush couches and boxes of tissues. All the shades were pulled down halfway, creating a gloomy atmosphere, like that of *Six Feet Under,* which I guessed was fitting.

Ralph sat down at his desk, which was pushed against a

wall, in front of a window, and motioned to the guest chair. He immediately grabbed a tissue and sneezed.

"Bless you," I said, sitting down and taking a closer look at him. His eyes and nose were red. "Are you not feeling well?"

He threw the tissue into the waste basket, already full of discarded ones. "Allergies. I'm in misery. I can't stop sneezing, my nose is runny, my eyes are itchy. I've tried everything. Nothing works."

"Have you tried natural remedies?"

He shook his head no.

Despite my grief, I knew that Aunt Claire would want me to help. "Natural remedies support your body's innate healing process, so you can feel better faster. I often suggest my patients take quercetin. It's a bioflavonoid found in the skin of red apples, red grapes, and red onions. You can take it with green tea, a natural antihistamine, and bromelain, which comes from the enzymes in pineapple stems and helps the quercetin be absorbed. Stinging nettle is also a good antihistamine. I have supplements for all these nutrients at the store."

He smiled. "That sounds good. You're actually giving me hope. Anything else I could try?"

"I'd start with those, but you can also take fish oils, which contain essential omega-three fatty acids, specifically EPA and DHA, to reduce inflammation. Zinc is another good immune booster. You take it in lozenges and supplements. Homeopathic remedies like histaminum and apis can work well for some people, too. You should also use a neti lota pot."

"A what?"

"A neti lota pot. It's from the practice of yoga. You use it to wash the allergens out of your nose with a solution of warm water, a quarter teaspoon of noniodized salt or sea salt, and a quarter teaspoon of baking soda. Use it once or twice a day as you need it."

"I feel like I should pay you for this visit," he said and smiled.

I waved his comment away. "That's not necessary."

"But you do have a practice, don't you?"

"I see clients in L.A. but haven't set up an office here. Right now my main priority is to keep Aunt Claire's business open." After that, I didn't know. My phone rang again, and I looked at the display: Merrily. I excused myself and answered.

"Hi, Merrily, what's happening? Could you find the owner?"

"No, I called the animal shelter and the police, but no one has reported a dog missing, so I brought him here. They haven't had any calls about him, either."

"Have they treated him?"

"Yes, they treated the wound and gave him a shot of antibiotics. I have cleanser and salve to keep it clean. The thing is, I can't have animals at my house—it's a rental. Can he stay with you at the store? I'm on my way back there now."

Ginger and Ginkgo might not like it, but the dog needed a place to stay. "That's fine," I said. "I'll be back in a little while."

"That's great, Willow," Merrily gushed. "I'm so happy that you'll be able to take care of him. I'll see you soon."

Ralph gave me a concerned look. "Anything wrong?"

"We've got a stray dog on our hands. Merrily just took him to the vet. It looks like he's going to be okay." I blew out a breath, feeling even more overwhelmed.

"You've got your hands full with everything that's happened, haven't you? How can I help?"

I focused on the task at hand. "I need to take care of Aunt Claire's funeral arrangements." I eyed the box of tissues, glad they were there in case I had another meltdown.

"No need, no need. She was in here last week and arranged everything."

My eyebrows shot up. Aunt Claire lived in the moment.

The idea that she would think ahead and take care of such things was a surprise, to say the least. And what prompted her to come here last week? Did she have a premonition that something bad was going to happen? Suddenly I couldn't breathe.

He riffled through a pile of papers, grabbed a blue folder, and continued. "It's very common. People do it so their loved ones don't have to deal with such matters in a time of grief. If you think about it, it's actually quite thoughtful."

"Yes, you're right, it is," I said, forcing myself to take a deep breath. "But did she say why she decided to come in?"

Ralph checked his notes. "Not really. She just said she wanted to get it over with."

"Get it over with? What do you think she meant by that?"

He closed the folder. "From what I could tell, the subject had been on her mind. Something she wanted to take care of. But if my experience is any guide, people, even if they know what they'd like done, often delay coming in to see me because it makes it real."

"Did she seem upset? Did she say anything about someone trying to harm her?"

"Harm her?" He frowned. "No, she certainly did not. She was very businesslike. She told me what she wanted done, that she wanted her body to be cremated. Just a memorial service at the church, no wake. She said she didn't want a viewing. She found it maudlin. I told her the wake wasn't for her but for her family and loved ones, but she was immovable."

"Sounds like Aunt Claire," I said, in shock.

He handed me a tissue. "She was a woman who knew what she wanted."

I couldn't help but wonder if what Aunt Claire "wanted," whatever it was, had put her at cross-purposes with her killer. If so, her stubbornness may have led to her being murdered.

# chapter four

Dear Dr. McQuade,
I have a terrible, annoying high-pitched sound in both of my ears. Someone told me that it's called tinnitus. My regular doctor sent me for a hearing test and he says my ears are fine. But the buzzing is driving me crazy. Can you help?
    Signed,
    Seeking Silence

Dear Seeking Silence,
Tinnitus can be very troublesome. It can be caused by overuse of nonsteroidal anti-inflammatories like aspirin, by wax in the ears, or even by allergies. For relief, you'll want to increase circulation and decrease inflammation. High doses of ginger, say 300 milligrams, can be helpful, as can the herb feverfew. A good homeopathic remedy is kali carbonicum. Another way to ease tinnitus is through craniosacral therapy. Developed by the osteopathic physician and surgeon John E. Upledger, the treatment uses light pressure (the weight of a nickel) to release restrictions in the craniosacral system, which comprises the membranes that surround the brain and spinal cord. You can find a practitioner at www.upledger.com.
    Signed,
    Willow McQuade, ND

We'd scheduled the memorial service for Monday. Ralph had kindly offered to contact the pastor and arrange all the details, and Merrily was more than willing to call Claire's friends. Like Nick, I just couldn't face it.

After my meeting with Ralph, I pulled into the parking lot behind Nature's Way and headed for the back door. Before I could open it, Merrily did. Her eyes were as red as mine. It was a tough day all around.

"How's the dog?"

"He's resting in the office. I put him on the couch. I hope that's okay."

"That's fine."

As I stepped in the doorway of Aunt Claire's office, the dog jumped off the couch and came over to me. He was a cute little shaggy thing, brown, black, and gray with a furiously wagging tail.

"Hi, sweetie. How're you doing?" I looked closely at the wound on his neck. It was red and ugly and looked painful. "What did they give you to care for the wound?"

"The vet said to clean the wound out every day with this." Merrily held up a bottle of blue liquid. "Dry it and apply this." She showed me a tube of ointment.

"Okay," I said. "I'll add an ointment Aunt Claire carries, too." Natural remedies can often be used effectively along with many prescription meds, although there are a few exceptions. Like the fact that you shouldn't take Saint John's wort if you are already on prescription antidepressants.

The shelf across from the checkout counter was chock-full of remedies for dogs, cats, and horses. I plucked off an ointment that contained calendula extract and *Hypericum* and a bottle of calendula 6x homeopathic pills.

I picked up the dog and put him on the couch. "Merrily, can you please hold him?"

Merrily sat down next to him and put her hand on his back while I applied the cream to the wound. "This will help speed healing." Next I popped a few calendula pills into his mouth which would dissolve instantly. "The homeopathic calendula will help heal the skin, too."

"Should I keep looking for his owner?"

I looked at the malnourished dog, with his sad eyes and gaping wound. The sore around his throat was where a collar would have been. Probably the gash was the result of an ill-fitting collar and/or the dog being tied up most of the time.

"I think he's a victim of neglect. So let's not worry about that. He can have a home here. Maybe he was brought to us for a reason."

Merrily brightened. "That's what I was thinking! But he'll need a name."

I looked at the dog. "How about Qigong?" Qigong, pronounced chee-gung, or Chinese Yoga is a five-thousand-year-old practice that combines breathing techniques, postures, and meditation to balance vital life energy. It is used in Traditional Chinese Medicine along with acupuncture, acupressure, and herbal medicine. The name would only help speed the dog's recovery.

Merrily clapped her hands. "I love it! Good doggie, good Qigong!" Qigong wagged his tail.

"I believe we have a winner," I said, and smiled at Merrily.

"I think so, too. But I'd better get back to what I was doing."

"Merrily, that can wait. Why don't you go home?"

"I can't go," she said, misting up. "Not yet. I've got a few more calls to make about the memorial service."

I pulled her into a hug. "Thank you so much, Merrily. You're a lifesaver."

"For Claire," she said. "Anything."

After she went back out to the store, Qigong curled up in a corner of the comfy couch and promptly went to sleep. It seemed like a good idea, so I grabbed a pillow from one of the chairs, lay down at the other end of the couch, and pulled a blanket over both of us.

When I woke up an hour later, Merrily had gone, leaving me a note on the desk that she'd see me in the morning. Alone again, I felt the darkness creep over me, and the tears came.

After the crying jag ended, I realized I was very much alone, and I suddenly felt afraid. Would Aunt Claire's murderer come back? Should I be staying here by myself? The other choices were to stay in a hotel, which I'm sure wouldn't allow dogs, or with my mother or sister, ditto. Nick lived in a tiny one-bedroom cottage in East Marion, so that was out, too. I had taken self-defense classes in college, so I knew I could protect myself. I decided to be brave and stay the night.

Next I realized I needed to check on my mother. I tried Natasha first, but when the call went to voice mail, I called the ER and was only told by the nurse on duty that my mother was to be admitted, but as a precaution, since she was stable. They were just waiting for the results of a few more tests. Nice of Natasha to let me know.

I was grinding my teeth together in aggravation over Natasha's selfish behavior when there was a knock on the door. Nick walked in looking completely devastated. I was surprised to see him after our last conversation.

Now, wordlessly, he came over to me and hugged me. If it was possible, I could feel that his heart had been broken. He seemed so frail, instead of his usual robust self, ready for any adventure. He had accompanied Aunt Claire around the world three times.

Nick's focus over the past decade, though, had been on meditation and yoga, which he taught in the studio on the second floor. His classes on Wednesday, Thursday, Friday, and Sunday mornings were always well attended. His style was gentle and inspirational, yet practical. He encouraged his students to master the postures but never to the point of straining. People left feeling relaxed and renewed. I'd taken his classes many times over the years.

Dressed in his usual garb of polo shirt, jeans, and brown Crocs, he, like Aunt Claire, looked a good ten years younger than his actual age of sixty-eight. Eating vegetarian, teaching yoga, practicing meditation, and thinking Zen thoughts will do that to you.

He spotted Qigong and his eyes lit up. "Who have we here?"

Qigong wagged his tail but stayed put.

"He's a rescue," I said, and told him what had happened.

"Good for you. Claire would have approved."

"I know."

He patted Qigong on the head and sat in the chair opposite Aunt Claire's desk. Up close, I could see that his piercing green eyes were red from crying. Being alone with his thoughts must have been hell.

"I'm surprised to see you out," I said.

"I wanted to bring this to you," he said, pulling a letter out of his pocket and handing it to me. "I thought you should see it right away."

"What is it?" I turned the letter over and saw that Aunt Claire had printed *For Willow* on the envelope.

"I don't know. She told me to give it to you if something happened to her."

"When did she write this?"

He shifted in his chair. "I'm not sure. Something had been troubling her lately, but she wouldn't talk about it. Believe me, I tried to find out."

I prepared myself as well as I could for whatever lay inside, opened the letter, and began reading:

> *My dearest Willow,*
>
> *If you are reading this letter, it is because I had to leave you much too soon. You know I don't have any fear about death, so I urge you not to worry about me or the state of my soul. God is good and I know that all will be well. My concern, dear niece, is for you and your happiness. I'm so proud of what you've been able to accomplish! It is my sweetest satisfaction that you are as passionate about natural remedies as I am. You know by now that I've willed Nature's Way Market and Café to you, but you probably have questions about why. Here is my answer: I want you to carry on my life's work here by helping the community you and I both love. Life is meant to be lived in balance, and I feel you can find that balance here, along with joy and love. Be well, my dear niece.*
>
> *I love you,*
> *Aunt Claire*

My eyes filled with tears, which overflowed and plopped on the sheet of paper. I grabbed a Kleenex from the box on top of the desk and handed the letter to Nick. He read it and nodded. "She wanted you here. I know she talked to you more than once about working together."

I nodded. "She did, but I was involved with Simon. Plus William had asked me to join his holistic medical practice in West Hollywood. California is on the cutting edge when it comes to holistic treatments, so it seemed like a good place to start my career." Naturopaths were also licensed to practice in California, while legislation was still pending for New York. I could see patients in New York, but my ND title had more acceptance on the West rather than the East Coast.

"But you missed home."

"Of course. But basically I was doing okay."

He gave me a skeptical look. "Okay is not wonderful. That's what she wanted for you, to live life fully, joyfully. Can you honestly say that's what you've been doing, living so far away, living in a city, in L.A.?"

"Well, no. It's difficult there. It's noisy, the beaches aren't the same, there's no space or seasons. I miss . . ."

He held up the letter. "You miss Greenport. She knew that, and in the event of her death, she wanted to help you find your way back here, Willow. Back to your home."

I grabbed another Kleenex and blew my nose. "But why did it have to be this way? Why didn't she tell me about her concerns?"

He thought for a moment. "I think she wanted to, but she also didn't want to step on your independence. You were doing very well, from all outside appearances."

"But she knew better."

He nodded. "And she wanted to help you."

I thought about how I'd been feeling lately, especially after my ex and I split. Out of balance, annoyed by city living. L.A. was less claustrophobic than, say, New York, but it was still a city. Everything from shopping for groceries to doing laundry to getting to work was a hassle. How many hours had I spent in traffic on the 405? In airports traveling back and forth between L.A. and Arizona? Yes, my neighborhood in Studio City, near CBS Studio Center, was nice, but it wasn't the country. It was, in fact, one street over from bustling Ventura Boulevard.

The Pacific Ocean was wonderful, but I was tired of going to the beach with a thousand other people. It wasn't the same as walking on the beach along the bay or the Sound and relishing the solitude. It wasn't the same as being home. In Greenport. I'd often yearned for a simpler life, but not this way. Not with Aunt Claire gone, and under such suspicious circumstances.

"Willow, Claire wanted you to be happy. Be happy."

I sniffed back tears. "How can I be happy if I feel guilty?"

"It's not your fault she's gone."

I didn't say anything.

"Willow?" He arched an eyebrow and leaned forward in his chair. "What are you thinking?"

"I think she was murdered and that Janice did it," I blurted out, telling him about the scene in the lawyer's office.

Nick made a face. "I'd be thinking the same thing, only I don't believe Janice would do anything to Claire. She seemed to revere her. I'd look at Gavin Milton. He's that bodybuilder who owns the health food store across the street and has been hassling Claire ever since he opened last year. He's been trying to drive her out of business by doing things like undercutting prices and spreading rumors that Nature's Way has roaches."

"Drive her out of business? But she's been here for twenty years!"

He shook his head. "He doesn't care. It made her very upset. She was worried about the Fresh Face formula, too. She was very nervous that she'd be scooped."

"Is it really that unique?"

He walked around the desk, opened a drawer, and pulled out a key. Walking back around the desk, he went over to a dark brown floorboard and pulled it up. It was the kind of hidey-hole Lane on *Gilmore Girls* used for her favorite music. Underneath was a strongbox. Nick used the key to open it and plucked out a

large sheaf of papers, which he handed to me. "This is the formula. You could say that it's the culmination of her life's work.
She'd traveled the world looking for the right combination of
ingredients. This time, finally, she was sure she had it. It made
her excited and nervous, very atypical for Claire."

"I'll say." I glanced through the papers and found a list
of ingredients she planned to use, including lavender, plantain, sunflower and borage oils, willow bark, and peppermint
extract. She'd listed at least a dozen more ingredients. "Is this
the only copy?"

"I'm not sure." Nick put the papers, the floorboard, and the
key back as he said, "But I think that's why she wrote this letter.
Maybe she had a feeling something bad was going to happen.
She wanted to provide you with guidance."

Maybe she wrote the letter for the same reason she'd gone
to the funeral home. Aunt Claire's "feelings" were the same
kind of intuitive nudges I received from my inner self. Meditation, which both she and I practiced faithfully each morning,
only made it stronger. Aunt Claire's radar was right on when
it came to people, situations, or places. Mine was pretty finely
tuned, too, which meant I might be able to use it to find some
answers . . . namely, who killed her.

Aunt Claire had been my surrogate mother, best friend,
inspiration, and moral compass. Suddenly I knew what I had to
do. I would stay in Greenport and carry on her vision and her
work with the community and find her killer. I owed her that
much, no matter the risk.


That night, sleep did not come easily. Thoughts about Aunt
Claire's letter, what Nick had said, and what I'd decided kept
me as awake as if I'd had ten cups of organic coffee. Was I

crazy? What did I know about running a health food store and café? Sure, I'd watched Aunt Claire handle things with ease for more than twenty years now, but that wasn't the same as doing it myself.

And what did I know about conducting a murder investigation? Was a personal stake enough? Plus, could I really just leave L.A.?

One thing I did know was that I liked the idea of providing naturopathic care to patients in New York. The more naturopaths there were in New York, the more likely New York would be to license them. We would gain further acceptance nationwide as an alternative to traditional care.

I tried to push past and future thoughts out of my mind. I'd never get to sleep this way. I heard a thump, then another. A few moments later Ginger and Ginkgo jumped on my bed and purred soothingly. I guess they'd been in Aunt Claire's room sleeping, probably because they felt closer to her there. I petted them as they arranged themselves, one around my head, the other by my feet. Their routine would definitely bring me warmth this winter. I'd need to get Qigong up here, too. But for tonight he'd stubbornly insisted on staying downstairs on the couch in the office.

To ease myself into sleep, I repeated one of my favorite mantras from Louise Hay, the grande dame of the positive-thinking movement. "All is well. Everything is working out for my highest good. . . . I am safe." Affirmations work by changing thoughts from negative to positive, which in turn changes the way one feels.

I was just drifting off to sleep when I heard a huge crash downstairs. Qigong started barking. Sitting bolt upright, I considered the possibilities. Had something fallen over in the store? Or in the office?

Or was it something more sinister, someone making trouble? The cats looked at me as if to say, "What are you going to do about it?" I glanced at the phone but decided against calling the cops until I knew more.

Pushing back the covers, I crawled out of bed and headed downstairs. Halfway down, I heard movement in Aunt Claire's office. Scurrying the rest of the way, I found Qigong waiting for me, barking loudly.

"Are you okay, buddy?"

He barked some more, wagged his tail, and headed for the office. As we rounded the corner into the produce, dry foods, and tea aisle, I saw someone running through the store, something tucked under his arm. It sure wasn't organic lettuce. Qigong, barking, took chase.

"Hey! You!" I yelled. "Get back here." This declaration fell on deaf ears as the person headed out the door, down the steps, and into the black night.

I grabbed a wooden yoga block and a purple strap, used for doing certain poses, as weapons and headed for the door to make sure the intruder was gone. Yes, according to every horror movie ever made, this was exactly what I shouldn't have been doing. But I did it anyway.

As I rounded the checkout counter, I discovered that the front window had been shattered with a brick, which now lay on the floor. That was the crash I'd heard just moments before.

I zoomed outside. The intruder had disappeared. But where was Qigong? I called for him, and he ran up to me, tail wagging, a piece of fabric in his teeth. Not only had he taken to his new name but he'd brought me a prize. I bent down, gave him a hug, and gently removed the fabric from his mouth.

"Good dog! I knew you came here for a reason."

Under the porch light I looked at the piece of orange fabric

Qigong had retrieved. It seemed unremarkable except for a label with the name of a popular organic clothing manufacturer. Maybe the organic clothing store in town sold this brand. I'd have to check it out.

In Aunt Claire's office, Qigong jumped back up on the couch. The office looked undisturbed except for where the piece of floorboard had been moved away. Below it was a black hole. I grabbed a flashlight, looked into the hole, and felt my stomach drop. The strongbox was gone, and with it the formula, Claire's life's work! Too late I realized I should have put the formula in a safe-deposit box at the bank. I had failed Aunt Claire.

Feeling sick, I went back into the store and surveyed the damage. Picking up the brick, I noticed that tied around it was a white sheet of paper, attached by a rubber band. I pulled it off and, holding it by the edges to avoid smudging any existing fingerprints, turned it over. It read: *Get OUT or ELSE!* I felt a chilly sensation wend its way down my spine as if caused by a ghost's cold finger. Creepy, and expensive, I thought as I looked at the big gap in the wall and broken shards of glass on the floor. Someone obviously wanted me gone. Was it the same person who had killed Aunt Claire? I shuddered at the thought as I reached for the phone to call the police.

# chapter five

Dear Dr. McQuade,
I have suffered from migraine headaches since I was a teenager. I've been to see a neurologist and taken prescription medications, but nothing really works. Or it works, but then I get a headache again. I'd rather not take some pill to get rid of my headache, anyway. Could you recommend a natural remedy?
    Signed,
    Still Suffering

Dear Still Suffering,
I give you credit for wanting to treat your headaches naturally. Natural remedies can be very effective at preventing migraines. You'll want to take vitamin B2 (riboflavin) and magnesium. Butterbur is also very effective, and you can't go wrong supplementing with a good-quality fish oil and co-enzyme Q10. Make it a habit to include these nutrients and watch your incidence of migraines decrease markedly.
    Signed,
    Dr. Willow McQuade

The bleat of a tugboat out in the harbor woke me Sunday morning. Hoping the sight and smells of the sea would help soothe the raw wound of Aunt Claire's death, I padded into her room and stepped out onto the small balcony. The view of the horseshoe-shaped harbor was spectacular twinkling in the early morning sun and populated by motor- and sailboats moored to the dockings in front of Mitchell Park. I sucked in a breath of fresh, salty-sweet air. This is what I missed living in L.A.

I thought about Aunt Claire and what she'd wanted for me, to stay here and carry on her business and serve the community. It seemed more right than ever, and today, in spite of the break-in, I decided to commit myself to my new role as the owner of the store and café. And to finding Aunt Claire's killer and the missing formula. The cops had secured the scene last night, and I expected the detectives this morning. I also needed to call a locksmith right away. I knew Janice had a key, but I wasn't sure who else did.

After doing a short seated meditation, showering, and dressing in my Be.Peaceful T-shirt, khaki capris, and hemp sneakers, I headed downstairs. Merrily was standing in the middle of the store, holding yet another energy drink and looking dumbfoundingly at the shards of broken glass.

She turned to me and said, "This is weird. And a mess. What happened?" She took a sip.

"I think someone is trying to send me a message." Message received. Not that I was going to follow its dictates and "Get OUT!" Qigong trotted out of the office. I patted him on the head and examined his wound, noting that it already looked much better.

Merrily squinched up her face, thinking. "Who would do that?"

"I'm not sure," I said, heading for the office. "But, Merrily, we've got a big problem. They took Aunt Claire's anti-aging formula." I went to the desk and began to search for a copy of the formula.

"Oh no!" Merrily's eyes opened wide. "We all knew she was working on something big and that it had to do with a new product, but we didn't know the details." She began to tear up. "Claire was so good. Why did all of this have to happen? This sucks."

That was putting it mildly. I didn't find anything pertaining to the formula on the desktop, so I opened the top drawer of the desk. Whoever had stolen the formula must have known that Aunt Claire was very close to getting it exactly right, to the point where it would be a bestseller and be worth millions. What I couldn't figure out was how they thought they would get away with pretending the formula was their idea.

Finding nothing, I closed the drawer. "Do you think Janice would do something like this? Throw the brick through the window and take the formula? Do you know if there's another copy somewhere?"

Merrily twirled her hair around her finger. She'd yet to put it up into various tiny ponytails with colored bands. "I don't know about a copy. As far as Janice goes, she was pretty upset on the phone yesterday when she called to say she wasn't coming in. I didn't tell you, but she was accusing you of having killed Claire. But I knew you couldn't do that. I saw how you two were together."

Shaking my head at Janice's audacity, I moved on to the rest of the desk drawers but found nothing.

Merrily headed out to the store, and I followed her, saying, "Janice seems to be under the impression that Aunt Claire owed her something for her work here at the store." Like the store, café, and formula, for example.

Merrily picked up a big shard of glass and carefully placed it in the oversized garbage can behind the checkout desk. "Janice felt like she gave her life to the store." She gave me a meaningful look. "Of course, that was her choice, and when she'd complain about it, that's what Claire told her. She didn't ask Janice to be on call twenty-four/seven; she just doesn't have a life outside of here."

"What kinds of things did she do?" I grabbed a shard, careful to avoid the sharp end.

"She handled all the staff, the ordering, the books. She was always on call in case Claire needed something. She was devoted to her." Merrily picked up another fragment and put it in the trash can.

"Then why change the will?"

"I don't know. Ouch!" Merrily put her finger to her mouth. "Crap. I cut my finger. Now I'm wounded just like Qigong." Qigong gave her a sympathetic look before padding back into the office.

Putting down the piece of glass I was holding, I grabbed a napkin from one of the tables and handed it to her. "Keep this on. Hold it tight." I headed for the counter and the first-aid kit I knew was there. I rounded the spot where the brick sat; that and the window area had been cordoned off with police tape. Trying to ignore the creeps the police tape gave me, I entered the square counterspace and went to the cash register, below which was the first-aid kit. Opening the bright red box, I found some hydrogen peroxide.

"Let's go in the bathroom. The blood will clean out the wound, but we need to clean it further with the hydrogen peroxide, then I'll take a look at it." I headed toward the tiny, white-tiled bathroom next to the back stairs, picking up some tea tree oil soap and lavender oil along the way.

"It's a good thing for me and Qigong that you're a doctor," Merrily said, holding her finger and smiling as she followed.

Why didn't my mother or Natasha feel that way? *Stop it, Willow,* I admonished. *Focus on the task at hand.* I poured the hydrogen peroxide on the wound, an inch long but not very deep. "You won't need stitches. But because it's a fingertip wound, it'll bleed more than, say, a wound on your elbow would."

I handed her the bar of soap. "From now on, use this tea tree oil soap so you don't destroy new cells that will help heal the wound."

She washed her finger, and then I applied lavender oil to further disinfect the wound.

I'd also grabbed an herbal salve containing comfrey, calendula, lavender, and vitamin E, and I applied it to the wound to help it heal. Finally, I covered the wound with gauze and taped it in place. "There, good as new!"

Back in the store, I scanned the homeopathic remedies and picked out Saint John's wort. "This is good for a wound where there are lots of nerve endings, like your finger. Take it four times a day until you feel better," I instructed, handing it to Merrily.

"Thanks, Dr. McQuade."

"Willow, please."

In the office, I grabbed the yellow pages and found a local glass company. As I dialed the number, I hoped I had enough money in the till to pay for it. I wouldn't be able to touch Aunt Claire's bank accounts until the will was probated. Hopefully, there wouldn't be any more incidents. Fingers crossed. As I made an appointment for the window to be replaced later in the day, the store's other service assistant, Julian, a tall, bookish guy headed for Cornell in the fall, arrived. He took one look at the mess and grabbed a broom while Merrily filled him in on what had happened.

Next on the list was a locksmith. Locating one in the yellow pages, I scheduled for him to be here within the hour.

That taken care of, I decided to check Aunt Claire's computer for an electronic copy of the formula. I fired up the computer and fruitlessly searched the desktop. My anxiety grew and I sucked in a breath. There was nothing left to do but deliver the bad news to Green Focus. Riffling through Aunt Claire's Rolodex, I found the name and home number for her contact at the company, a development executive named Randy McCarty. I had to inform them that their secret project was compromised and also make sure they had a copy of the herbal formula. Randy answered on the second ring. I explained who I was and what had happened and was greeted with stunned silence.

"Claire is dead? Oh my God." He sucked in a breath. "She was such a lovely person."

"Yes, she was," I said, my heart aching.

"And they took the formula?"

"Yes, and I need to know if that was the only copy." It just couldn't be, I told myself as I prepared for the worst.

"Dr. McQuade, we have a formula, but it doesn't include her recent changes. She was working on the final touches. I don't know what she planned to add next. We were told she had a secure location for the formula. I thought she kept it in a safe; not in the floor in a strongbox." He stammered, "I-I have to call the president of the company. I'll be in touch."

I hung up the phone feeling stunned. I had to find that formula. My gut told me that Janice must know something, but how would I get her to talk? I stewed about this in the office for a few minutes, until my stomach started grumbling for breakfast.

In the kitchen area I peered into the glass cases, looking for something that would hit the spot.

I noticed some sugar-free cranberry-apple bran muffins that looked yummy and went around to the back of the case to grab one.

"What do you think you're doing?"

Startled, I turned around, and who should be glaring at me but Janice, old Miss Pinch Face, dressed in a red-and-orange T-shirt with Peace on the front and black running shorts, sweat dotting her forehead. "You're not supposed to be back there. It's for the help only."

"I'm getting something to eat." This is my store and café after all, I wanted to say, but didn't want to rub it in. Instead I said, "Did you know the Fresh Face formula was stolen, Janice?"

"I don't know anything about that. I'm here to get my pay-check. I forgot it yesterday." She hustled past me and headed for the office. Merrily and I raised our eyebrows at each other.

On the counter I noticed several bottles of oil. "Is she planning on taking these as well?" I looked at the bottles more closely: lavender, plantain, and sunflower and borage oils, some of the ingredients for Fresh Face.

"Sometimes she takes products home to try them," Merrily said.

Or to try and replicate Aunt Claire's formula, I thought.

A few moments later Janice emerged from the office, with Qigong following her. That was strange, I thought. She was the first person who'd come into the store that he seemed overly interested in. Now, why was that?

Janice pointed at Qigong. "What is that doing in the store? We could be cited by the health department. He can't be here."

"His name is Qigong, and I decide whether he stays or goes," I said, standing firm. "He stays." Still, I thought I'd better get a baby gate for the office so he would stay put during the hours we were open. I'd have to take him out to pee and for a walk several times a day. It would give us both some exercise. He could also stay in the front yard, if he liked, since it was gated, but someone would have to watch him, since customers used that gate. We'd work it all out.

"Suit yourself," she said, spinning on her heel to face me. "And as for the will, I won't be back until this is settled. I want what is rightfully mine." She went around the counter, grabbed a bag, and put the bottles inside.

I snatched the bag from her. "You won't be taking these and you won't be back," I said, thinking of Aunt Claire's letter. "Besides indicating her preferences in the will, Aunt Claire left me a personal letter. Her intention was clear. I am to own and run the store and café. You are no longer needed here, Janice. You're fired."

Her face pinched even more as she narrowed her eyes. "I'm contesting the will. It will tie it up in probate for years. I hope you have lots of money to keep up with expenses. By the time things are settled and it's mine, you won't have a penny left. You'll see, this is an old building and it demands upkeep."

"Like the windows? Did you do this?" I pointed to the window. "And what are you planning to do with these ingredients, Janice?" I held up the bag. "Copy Aunt Claire's formula?"

"How dare you accuse me! I worked my fingers to the bone for your aunt. This is my store! You've got a lot of nerve." She clenched her fists. "And you're going to pay for it."

"So you're saying that Janice threw the brick through the window, stole the formula, and now is trying to re-create it." Detective Koren eyed me skeptically as he put the brick into an evidence bag, sealed it, and handed it to Detective Coyle. "And she threatened you."

"That's right." I'd told them what happened in the lawyer's office and this morning, too.

He listened while he watched the glass man measure the open space so he could replace the window. The locksmith also had arrived and was busy working. "Dr. McQuade, we can't conduct a murder investigation based on your hunches."

A few students, dressed in yoga attire and holding purple yoga mats, drifted past us, questioning looks in their eyes. "You can go upstairs," I said. "Nick will be here any minute."

Nick had called me early in the morning to let me know he'd be in. He told me he felt at peace in the yoga studio upstairs. Aunt Claire had spent plenty of time, money, and energy over the past year converting part of the second floor to his specifications, and the resulting space was welcoming and functional with its fresh, white walls, open floor plan, hardwood floors, and a wall of mirrors and windows that overlooked the street and harbor.

Detective Koren tapped on his notebook with his pen. "Right now we're just gathering information. For example, we've found out that you've come into quite an inheritance: the store, the café, twenty-two thousand dollars in the store's business account . . ."

"Which we've frozen, so you won't have access to it," Detective Coyle interjected.

Detective Koren nodded and said, "And the rights to your aunt's new anti-aging cream."

Another yoga student, dressed in a black unitard and shorts, came in. "Is the class still on?" she asked, and squeezed my shoulder. "I am so sorry about Claire." She was so empathetic that I thought I was going to lose it. But I snuffled away the tears. "Thank you. That's very kind. And yes, the class is still on. You can go on up."

Detective Koren cleared his throat, clearly not the sensitive type. "We were talking about your inheritance."

"You can't think I had anything to do with this," I said, suddenly unable to breathe.

Before he could answer, his cell rang and he plucked it out of his front pocket. After a moment, he said, "I'll be right there." Looking at me, he said, "We'll have to postpone our chat, Dr. McQuade."

"I'll be here," I said, trying to be cooperative.

"Good to know." He turned and headed out the door, Coyle and patrolman in tow.

Sucking in a breath, I stared after him. If he focused on me as a suspect, there was no way he'd find Aunt Claire's killer.

My thoughts were interrupted by the arrival of Nick, in time for his twelve o'clock yoga class. He said hello and kissed me on the cheek. Curiously, I could smell alcohol on his breath. Was it from a hangover, or had he drank this morning? I pointed to his yoga mat. "Are you sure you're up to this? You can still cancel, you know."

He headed for the stairs. "It's better if I keep busy. Claire was always an advocate of industry in good times and bad, and I think she was right."

I thought she was right, too. Fortunately, there was a customer in the herb and vitamin aisle who looked like she needed assistance, and I made a beeline for her. "Can I help you?"

The woman, dressed in a flannel shirt, jeans, and work boots, had an angular, weather-beaten, tanned face and bleached blond hair. She was probably forty-something, although she looked older. She turned to me and scowled. "You the new owner?"

"Yes, I am. I'm Dr. Willow McQuade, Claire's niece. Can I help you?"

"You could pay your bill." She pulled a sheet of paper from her bag and handed it to me. "Sorry about Claire."

This woman should work for the UN, I thought. She was quite the diplomat. I glanced at the total and felt my blood run cold: $5,962.56. That was about two thousand dollars more than I had in my checking account.

# chapter six

Dear Dr. McQuade,
What do you recommend for a cold? My head feels like it's the size of Idaho and my sinuses are running like a leaky faucet.
    Signed,
    Feeling Chilly

Dear Feeling Chilly,
One of my favorite remedies to help prevent a cold is matcha tea. It's like a super green tea filled with antioxidants that can help boost your immune system. Once you have a cold, zinc lozenges can help because they attack the rhinovirus that causes colds and coughs. Use a natural saline spray to keep your sinuses irrigated. Another good remedy is a teaspoon of honey and a vitamin C tablet. They work together to help you feel better fast.
    Signed,
    Dr. McQuade

Taking a deep breath, I tried to remain calm. "What's this bill for?"

The woman pointed to the top of the sheet. It read: *Helen's Organics.* "I'm your organic produce supplier. I haven't been paid in over three months. I think your aunt had other things on her mind."

You could say that.

"She was also supposed to help me with my ulcers and she didn't do much about that, either."

Maybe if I could help her with her stomachache, she'd stop being such a pain in my you-know-what. "I can help you with that. I'm a naturopathic doctor."

"I hope you know more than Claire did."

I bristled. I really didn't like this woman.

"Have you been tested for *H. pylori*? It's a bacteria that causes ulcers."

"Yes, but that's not what's causing it. They can't figure out the cause."

Probably her acerbic personality, I thought, but said instead, "Have you tried licorice?"

"Claire mentioned something about that."

I was sure she'd mentioned lots of things, but my feeling was that this woman didn't take direction very well. Aunt Claire knew her natural remedies, and I was sure she'd done everything she could for her. I went through the spiel anyway. "Licorice is anti-inflammatory. It stimulates the mucous layer in the stomach. This can help give you protection. Studies show that it can be as effective as prescription antacids." I reached for a bottle of deglycyrrhizinated or DGL licorice. "Take one thousand to fifteen hundred milligrams between meals or twenty minutes before meals. It could really help you feel better. You may also want to try mastic gum." I picked up a bottle with a bright green label. "Take one cap-sule a day."

She grunted, took the bottles from me, and read the ingredi-ents. "I'll think about it," she said, and then handed the bottles back to me. As I'd figured, she'd rather bitch than switch. This wasn't uncommon, especially when people made an identity out of their ailments. Without sickness and struggle, they didn't know who they were.

"Now, about that bill."

"I don't have this right now. But once the will is pro-bated . . ."

"I can't wait that long. I want my money."

"Leave the bill with me. I'll get it to you," I said, not know-ing how I would do so.

"See that you do," she huffed, and walked out the door.

With my decision to stay in Greenport, run Nature's Way, and find Aunt Claire's killer, it was time to cut city ties. First, I called William Cohen, my boss at the holistic medical cen-ter, and explained that I wasn't coming back. I also talked to Dr. Richmond-Safer in Arizona. Fortunately, both were very understanding about my change in life plans. Next, I e-mailed my editor, Katy Bloom, at *Nature's Remedy* magazine in New York, and within an hour, she'd replied, sending her condo-lences and giving her okay for me to continue to write my blog and any articles I wanted to contribute and send them in via e-mail. I'd done this from L.A., too, so there was no big change there. She did remind me that she needed four new question-and-answer pieces by next week, though, if at all possible.

As far as my living situation went, I was staying with my ex before I'd come out to Aunt Claire's, so I didn't have an apartment to vacate, just a few things to have shipped when I had time.

Okay, no job, no apartment, no L.A. Although I'd wanted to leave and this move felt right, suddenly I felt very alone. *Buck up, Willow, it's only going to get harder,* I reminded myself.

But could I somehow make the move easier on myself? I thought about the business and the building. The third floor housed Aunt Claire's bedroom, another bedroom where I had been staying, and two other rooms that were currently empty. If I could rent the two rooms to natural-health practitioners, it would not only draw more business to Nature's Way; it would help pay bills until the will was probated. I quickly ran through my mental Rolodex of people I knew who might be willing to pull up stakes and come out here to practice.

It didn't take long for me to think of my roommate from the Southwest College of Naturopathic Medicine. Allie Daniels, a certified massage therapist, was a small-town girl from Bennington, Vermont, now living in New York and who, like me, was always complaining about living in the city. We'd stayed in touch after graduation, and although she was doing well, I knew she longed for a simpler life. I immediately called her and explained the situation. Within forty-five minutes, not only was she on board but she'd suggested asking her friend Hector, an acupuncturist, to come in on the plan as well. I was thrilled with the suggestion.

The only fly in the ointment? I was worried about bringing them into this unsafe situation, and I told her so. She quickly reminded me that she had trained with me in self-defense. She also told me that Hector had a black belt in karate and had served in the marines when he was younger. After a fellow officer was killed by friendly fire, he turned to Buddhist teachings.

I blew out a breath. Having Hector here would make us all safer.

Next, I needed a new assistant. I went into the store and watched Merrily set up for lunch, nursing her cut hand. She had enthusiasm, was positive, and clearly had cared about Aunt Claire. I made a split-second decision and walked over to her. "Merrily, can I ask you a question?"

She put down a place setting and smiled up at me. "Sure, ask me anything."

"It's obvious that Janice and I can't work together. Would you like to be my new assistant? You can still work in the store and café."

She thought about it and smiled. "For Claire?"

I looked around at the store and café, her life's work. I knew I was doing the right thing, staying here. "For Claire," I said, and smiled back.

After Merrily and I went over what her duties would be, namely helping me with all aspects of the business, she went back to the café and continued setting up for lunch. As for me, I felt the grief encroaching again. So I closed the office door and gave myself over to it. Ten minutes later, I'd cried myself out.

When I'd finished, I decided to tackle the Q&A's my editor had asked for. To sharpen my attention before I got started, I fetched a bottle of distilled water from the store and added it to Aunt Claire's aromatherapy diffuser. As I scanned her aromatherapy essential oils, I recalled from my college studies that they nourished the body by carrying oxygen and nutrients to cells, including those of the brain. I chose frankincense, a powerful healing oil; rosemary, a bright, sharp scent that clarified the mind and emotions; peppermint, which boosts energy, creativity, and cognition; and vetiver, a mind tonic that eases stress. Just what I needed. I added a few drops of each to the purified water, and after a moment the warm, scented vapor emerged. I breathed it in and immediately felt much better.

In two hours, I'd created rough drafts for four new Q&A's. Satisfied with my work, I decided to check my favorite alternative health websites for new studies I should know about. Keeping myself up-to-date on natural medicines would come in handy when it was time to order new products for the store, and I'd also blog about them for *Nature's Remedy* readers.

On EurekAlert! I found a few new studies about natural remedies. One outlining how Chinese thunder god vine could help treat the symptoms of rheumatoid arthritis was very promising. I always got a secret thrill when research confirmed what I knew intuitively, that natural remedies worked extremely well to improve many common health conditions. I wrote up a brief blog entry and posted it. All in all, a very productive morning.

But my sanguine attitude about staying on the East End and taking over Aunt Claire's business was short-lived. As I headed for the kitchen to get a cup of herbal tea, the door swung open, and Simon Lewis, my ex-boyfriend from L.A., strolled through.

Simon was a skeptic of all things natural, so we had truly been an odd couple. Last I knew, he'd been in New York, researching his next novel. It had been nice to have the entire country between us. Now my buffer space had been reduced to a few feet.

Although not conventionally handsome, he had a broody demeanor and deep chocolate-brown eyes that were catnip to many women. Dressed in expensive-looking distressed jeans, a T-shirt I had given him that said Be.You, and Jack Purcell sneakers, he looked like a successful L.A. TV writer and author, and he knew it.

We'd parted two months ago when he left for the airport,

angry words still hanging in the air. We'd fought about his undermining attitude toward my work, dismissal of my difficulties with L.A. city life, and general lack of support in everything life had to dish out. Oh, and did I also mention he was a commitment-phobe?

"Simon? What are you doing here?" I said, feeling the knife enter my chest. The wound of our breakup had begun to heal with his absence but now felt raw again. I gave myself a pep talk to stay strong; this was not the time to fall back into old patterns or into his "love you, love you not" arms.

He pulled me into a hug. "I'm really sorry about your aunt," he said, releasing me and putting his hands on my shoulders to give me a searching look. "How are you?"

Pushing my grief out of sight, I gave him a brave face. "I'm fine, Simon. Who told you?"

"I found out when I arrived last night. The owner of the B and B where I'm staying for a few weeks told me."

I felt like I'd been socked in the stomach. "You're staying in town for a few weeks?"

"Yes. I'm on hiatus from *Parallel Lives*."

*Parallel Lives* was a hit TV drama, in the genre of *Lost* and *Fast Forward*. They had just been renewed for a third season. Simon, a writer and executive producer on the show, was now rich, and he acted like it.

"Last week I took a copter out to the Hamptons and did some hard-core partying. This week it's back to work on my novel." He reached into his pocket for a Kleenex and blew his nose. "Sinus infection. Got any natural remedies for me?" He gave me a sly grin. "A Vike would be great."

"Vicoden is not a natural remedy," I said, rolling my eyes. Simon had become too fond of the pills after he broke his leg while attending the Sundance Film Festival in January. The doctor had given him a generous supply, too generous, and he'd started to use them just to boost his mood. After, he crashed and became moody and irritable. It had been another reason I'd left him.

"That's your opinion," Simon replied, looking around at the market and café. "So this is where it all happens."

He knew how much I loved this place. I'd constantly talked about Aunt Claire and the store and café.

"Is it true that you're planning to take over?"

"Yes. I just gave my notice."

He frowned. "But you don't know anything about running a store and café."

Nice. "Supportive as always, Simon."

"I'm being realistic. You're a doctor, not a shopkeeper."

Instead of pointing out that my training as a naturopath made me extremely qualified to advise and sell natural remedies, I changed the subject. "So you're staying out here?"

He nodded. "My publisher is putting me up. You always talked about how it was so peaceful. She thought it was a good idea. It's what I need in order to meet my deadline. Peace and quiet."

"When is the book due?" I knew he was working on a novel about a TV actress who gets hooked on prescription drugs. Ironic, considering his own fondness for pain pills, although he'd never admit it.

Instead of answering me, he pulled out his BlackBerry and wrote a text.

"Simon," I prodded. "The deadline?"

He tucked the BlackBerry back into his pocket. "August third. Then it's back to L.A. to start the new season of *Lives*."

I sucked in a breath. Two months? This was not welcome news. I didn't want him here, especially not now. I had my hands full with the business and my new career as an amateur sleuth.

"Being in New York gave me plenty of time to think. I want to work things out with you."

His sudden desire to make up didn't come as a surprise, as we'd broken up and reconciled several times. But this time, after he'd left for New York, I thought long and hard about whether I really wanted him in my life. When I weighed the pros and cons, the cons won. I was officially finished with him, no matter how he felt.

"No, Simon." I headed into Aunt Claire's office and sat in the office chair. Qigong jumped on my lap, tail wagging.

Maybe Simon would take the hint, although I doubted it. Moments later he appeared at the office door. "Who's this? Now you have a dog?"

"Yes. His name is Qigong," I said as dismissively as I could. I was too busy to deal with Simon right now. This afternoon I wanted to write a story for *Nature's Remedy* about natural ways to beat allergies and blog about a silver nasal spray that was great for sinusitis. But most important, I wanted to search Aunt Claire's e-mail archives for any info that might help me figure out where the final formula was and who might have stolen it.

Simon approached the desk, leaned over, and tried to kiss me. I pushed him away.

He looked perplexed and definitely unhappy. "Willow, give me another chance."

I had to be strong. I knew ending our relationship was for the best. "Simon, we are so over." I opened the e-mail folder labeled *Fresh Face*. There were over two hundred messages. This was going to take some time, but finding out who had taken the formula was the most important item on my to-do list. Not only was this Aunt Claire's life's work but the murderer was still at large and might come for me next.

He shrugged. "I don't believe that."

I could see why; I'd folded before. But now, with my new mission to carry on Aunt Claire's work and find her killer, I felt bold and strong, like I was holding an Ashtanga yoga warrior pose. "Believe it," I said as I got up, pushed him toward the door, and began to close it in his face. "Now if you don't mind, I've got work to do."

# chapter seven

Dear Dr. McQuade,
I bumped my shin against my desk and now I have a
nasty bruise. I'm also achy when I finish my workout at
the gym. Is there something natural I can take to soothe
bruises and aches and pains so I can stay active?
Signed,
Feeling Sore

Dear Feeling Sore,
One of the best remedies for bruises and aches and
pains is *Arnica montana*. This herb from the daisy
family is super at moving fibrin, a blood protein that
forms at the site of an injury, out of your system, helping to reduce both swelling and inflammation. You can
put it on your skin topically or take arnica pellets. Find
them at your local health food store.
Signed,
Dr. Willow McQuade

Monday morning dawned like any other day, but this day was anything but normal. It was the day of Aunt Claire's memorial service. I'd been up until one o'clock going through old e-mails about Fresh Face, trying to find both the final formula and someone with a motive to steal it, but had learned nothing except that the development process had been tortuous.

Feeling bleary-eyed and bummed, I dragged myself out of bed and lingered in a hot bath with organic, fragrant rose bath salts and thought of Aunt Claire. As the tub cooled, I added more hot water. I was reluctant to get out and face the day. Finally, with the clock ticking, I dried off, dressed in my best black dress and flats, went downstairs, and made sure the Closed sign was in the window. We were definitely not open for business today.

At ten thirty Nick arrived to pick me up, wearing a sharp black suit and tie and looking mournful, his heart still broken into a million little pieces. As he bent over to give me a kiss, I caught the whiff of alcohol again. Had he always been a drinker? Or was this a response to Aunt Claire's death? I needed to talk to him about it, but now wasn't the time.

We arrived at the local church, which looked like it belonged in the English countryside, all dreamy spires and white clapboards. Pastor Wyatt, who was afflicted with seasonal allergies, was a faithful customer of Claire's. We parked in the back and headed inside.

The church was packed to overflowing with Aunt Claire's friends, customers, community members, and fellow activists. In the back row, I noticed my sister Natasha, dressed, natch, in a couture suit. Mother was at home recovering from her stay at the hospital. I nodded to Natasha and received a glare in reply.

Fine. I scanned the church for Simon to see if he'd had the nerve to show up. But whether he was respecting my wishes not to see him or had better things to do, he wasn't there.

The service began at eleven o'clock; it was brief and to the point. We sang "Amazing Grace" and "Ode to Joy," two of Aunt Claire's favorites that I'd recommended be included. In between, there was a lovely homily by Pastor Wyatt, and sobs and sniffles from the audience. After the benediction, Nick and I walked out in the procession behind Pastor Wyatt, the deacons, and the altar boys.

The mourners stopped one by one to give Nick and me their condolences. Aunt Claire's spirit definitely lived on in the lives of people she'd touched through her work at the store and in worthy causes. "She made my condition easier to live with," a woman with diabetes told me. "Never too busy to listen to my problems," said a man who struggled with depression. "Tireless in her commitment to animal rights," said one of her activist friends. "An inspiration," said a yoga student.

But then Janice trotted out, dressed head to toe in black, and hissed into my ear, "You're not going to get away with this. I've asked my lawyer to contest the will. Expect it to be tied up in probate for a very long time."

"This is not what Aunt Claire wanted," I hissed back.

"She wasn't in her right mind when she made out that new will. She was furious with Natasha and your mother. She wasn't thinking clearly. It's the only thing that makes sense. She wouldn't have forgotten me otherwise."

After reading Aunt Claire's letter, I knew that wasn't true. Her intention had obviously been for me to take over the business. That was definite. After all, we were family and she knew where my passion lay, in helping people and living here.

Nick realized we were fighting and pulled Janice away from

me. "Janice, thank you for coming." He gave her a hug and looked at me over her shoulder. *It will be okay,* he seemed to be telling me. He released Janice and pushed her toward Pastor Wyatt.

"But," Janice sputtered, "I'm not finished. She has to know she's not going to get away with this."

"Please, Janice, don't make a scene," Nick said.

Janice muttered something unintelligible as Pastor Wyatt led her away from the receiving line and counseled her privately.

Nick leaned over to me. "Don't let it bother you."

I couldn't help but take Janice's threat seriously, though. Not knowing how I was going to keep the business going until probate was settled, plus wondering if Janice was the one who may have killed Aunt Claire, I shook my head and replied, "If only it were that easy."

After a brief service at the cemetery and a post-memorial gathering at Nick's house, I returned to the store around 7 p.m., in time to discover another gathering taking place at Nature's Way. Although the café was closed, a half dozen women were grouped at two café tables they'd pushed together in the front of the store, chatting in low tones. Many of these friends of Aunt Claire's had been at the memorial service. Why were they here now? One of them, Elizabeth Olberman, waved to me.

Dressed in her mourner's attire, she looked the way I felt, depressed and tired but still trying to keep up appearances. She kissed me on each cheek, European-style, and said, "I hope you don't mind that we're here, but we have a protest planned."

"A protest?"

"These two miscreant business owners want to open a pet

store in town. They want to sell pure-bred puppies from puppy mills while the animal shelter in Southold is overflowing with strays. We're going to picket if the town board gives them a permit to run the business, and we should know in the next few days. It's bad timing, but I know that Claire would have wanted us to move forward with this. We have to be prepared."

One of Aunt Claire's passions was to shut down puppy mills that supplied pet stores with dogs. I'd learned from her that such mills were inhumane places where the owners treated dogs like products. They were kept in cages their whole lives, without companionship, exercise, or proper veterinary care. The females got the worst of it as they were bred relentlessly until they got too sick to provide the "product" read puppies, flowing to pet stores. When that happened, the dogs, both female and male, were thrown out like so much trash. Aunt Claire had given me a bumper sticker that read Stop Puppy Mills Now, with a photo of a miserable-looking dog trapped in a cage. I felt good about having her friends here tonight, carrying on in her name. "We have to do all we can to stop this. Please let me know how I can help."

Elizabeth patted me on the shoulder. "Keeping the store and café up and running is enough. She was very proud of you, Willow. I hope you know that."

I met her sad eyes and nodded. "I do, thanks." The store still fairly hummed with Aunt Claire's vibration and, looking around, I felt myself again near tears. Time for bed. "I'm going to go up, but please stay as long as you need to. It's important work."

"Thanks so very much," Elizabeth said, taking my hand. "And, Willow, please don't let the police worry you."

I stiffened. "What do you mean, worry me?"

Elizabeth seemed flummoxed. "I just meant that I heard the

police were taking an interest in you. But that always happens when you're first on the scene. That's the way it is on *CSI*." She turned back to the group of activists, who had obviously been listening to our conversation. "We'll vouch for you, won't we, girls?" The women at the table murmured assent.

Although it was a nice gesture, it didn't do much to loosen the knot of tension in my gut. Clearly, Detective Koren had made his "interest" known. I couldn't help but feel that he was marking his territory.

I went to bed but couldn't sleep so I went back downstairs to the office. After working my way through more Fresh Face e-mails, I finally drifted off to sleep around midnight. But early Tuesday morning, at 4:55, I awoke to a thumping noise coming from the kitchen. Qigong, who I'd carried upstairs to bed to play protector (Gingko and Ginger were nonplussed) jumped onto the floor and started barking.

Had my intruder from Saturday night returned? Should I call the police this time before I went downstairs and checked it out? Did I really want Detective Koren giving me a "You are my prime suspect" face if I called him and it turned out to be nothing? I decided to opt for the cautious approach and grabbed Aunt Claire's tennis racket from the closet before heading downstairs with Qigong.

When I got to the first floor, I stopped and listened. Yes, there were definitely sounds coming from the kitchen. What was going on? Qigong started barking frantically.

Quickly, I headed up the frozen-food aisle with Qigong close by my heels, past the refrigerators that held everything from organic mac and cheese to organic pizzas to organic enchiladas, and headed in the direction of the kitchen. Reaching the endcap of Pirate's Booty and blue corn chips, I peered to my right. Yes, there was a light on in the kitchen, which was divided into a prep area in the back and a counter to serve customers in front.

I could hear a rumbling, and then a crackling. Was someone cooking? Before I could find out, everything went black.

I woke up to the sound of Qigong barking, a crushing headache, and the smell of something burning. As I sat up I spotted a dented container of green food supplement powder nearby. It looked like someone had come up behind me in the frozen-food aisle and bashed me over the head with it. I didn't touch it, so the police could brush it for prints if they deemed it necessary. So far they weren't taking me very seriously, except of course as a person of interest. But that smell was definitely worth checking out. I was grateful Qigong had woken me.

Rounding the counter into the main prep area, I found the wall and the shelves next to the stove engulfed in flames. Panicked, I filled a bowl with water and threw it on the flames. The fire hissed back at me, reminding me of Janice at the memorial service. Did she do this? I ran to the checkout counter, grabbed the portable phone, and dialed 911, hoping the fire department would arrive before the entire business burned down.

Fortunately, the volunteer firefighters arrived in record time, put out the blaze, and cleared the area. As I stood anxiously on the front porch, they informed me that the damage was mostly cosmetic and it looked like the fire had been caused by faulty wiring in the stove. But I didn't believe it. I was sure it was arson and that Janice was behind it. And when Detectives Koren and Coyle arrived, I told them so.

"Just because she said she is going to contest the will and threatened you is not enough reason to arrest her for this,"

Detective Koren said, gesturing to the burned remains of the shelving next to the stove. "As we discussed before, doctor, you have more than enough motive for the two of you."

My blood ran cold, but I tried not to show it. "You need to check Janice out," I said, mentally adding that Detective Coyle should also check out a natural remedy for the adult acne on his cheeks. Some tea tree oil would do wonders. It's readily absorbed by the skin, which means it can help dry up and heal pimples. Calendula, from the flower petals of a marigold, with vitamin E, is also excellent for healing skin with acne, and lavender essential oil is a good antibiotic and antiseptic.

Coyle must have noticed me examining him, because he said, "What are you looking at?"

"Excuse me, but I notice that you seem to have a problem with acne," I said, sharing the tips about tea tree oil, calendula, and vitamin E with him. "You can also take retinol. I have some here."

"Thank you, doctor, I'll keep that in mind," Detective Coyle said with a distinct edge to his voice.

*Way to get on his good side, Willow,* I thought, chagrined.

"You might want to focus on yourself," Detective Koren said, pointing to the back of my head, where a goose egg was rising at the point of impact. "That bump on your noggin doesn't look too good."

"I'll take care of it," I said. "But aren't you going to find out who did this? If it's not Janice, then who?"

Not looking at me, Detective Koren scribbled something in his notebook and snapped it shut. "You don't need to tell us how to do our jobs, Dr. McQuade. We'll make the appropriate inquiries."

But in the meantime, I needed protection. I definitely didn't feel safe here now. "Is there any way you can have a patrol car cruise past the store tonight? This is making me very nervous."

Detective Koren put his hand on my shoulder. "Dr. McQuade, this is a very safe town. Our job is to keep it that way. Whoever did this was targeting your aunt. It doesn't feel like a random act. As I said, even you have motive."

"Yes, but . . ."

"Sit tight," he said, turning to leave. "We'll be in touch soon."

Oh goody, I thought. Not only was he not taking me seriously about Janice but he still considered me a suspect, and for that reason, wouldn't provide protection. I felt scared, infuriated, and helpless. How could I turn this around?

I knew one way to start. After feeling around the bump and doing a self-check in the bathroom, I decided that it didn't deserve ER attention. I didn't feel nauseous or disoriented. My only symptom was pain from the bump, which was bearable. I grabbed some arnica homeopathic pellets off the shelf near the counter and slipped some under my tongue to help the bump heal.

With that taken care of, I turned my attention to my psychic needs. One of the best ways I knew to get myself back on an even keel was to do yoga and meditate. I was sure meditation would lead to answers. So after the last of the firemen left, I went upstairs to the yoga studio to do just that. Qigong, whose wound was healing fast, padded happily behind me.

I opened the studio door to find sun streaming through the tall windows onto the wooden floor. As I breathed in the lingering smells of patchouli incense, I began to relax. I pulled out a sticky mat from the pile next to the wall and unrolled it on the floor. Qigong settled into a place in the sun and promptly fell asleep.

I started with mountain pose, or tadasana, which involves standing on your own two feet and staring straight ahead. I centered myself and moved to mountain pose with my arms overhead, reaching for the sky.

Feeling more expansive now, I spaced my feet four feet apart and moved on to the extended triangle pose, a position that gets its name from the triangle shape formed by one's legs. I reached one arm overhead and the other toward the floor, and then moved on to the warrior pose, with one arm extended to the front and one to the back, which always helped me feel strong.

Next, I did a standing forward bend pose, leaned over, and reached for my toes, since inversion postures are good for brain circulation and I needed to be sharp right now, and moved into downward-facing dog to stretch out my legs and arms. I wrapped up with a lying twist pose, with my feet wide apart, and finally corpse pose, where I lay flat on the floor and could feel the earth supporting me.

As I lay on the floor, I tried to let all the events of the past few hours go, but I kept smelling burning wood, and the bump on the back of my head kept throbbing. I decided to make a more conscious effort to meditate, so I sat cross-legged and began to focus on my breathing. Maybe if I could get myself calmed down enough, I could figure out what to do next.

I started my mindfulness meditation by focusing on the breath in my belly and continued to watch it as the thoughts in my mind began to calm and finally abate. It was good to feel peaceful, even though I knew it wouldn't last. Not with the fire damage, Simon's unexpected appearance, Janice, the missing Fresh Face formula, and Aunt Claire's murder. But right now, in this moment, I relaxed into the meditation and felt release.

# chapter eight

**Dear Dr. McQuade,**

I was helping a friend move this weekend and now my back is killing me. It's really difficult to even sit and stand. What do you recommend for a bad back?

Signed,

Feeling Like a Pretzel

**Dear Feeling Like a Pretzel,**

When you strain the muscles around the spine, you can end up with a backache. Some people take over-the-counter medicines for back pain, like aspirin and ibuprofen or what are known as NSAIDs (nonsteroidal anti-inflammatories), but I don't recommend doing that, because long-term use can lead to problems like stomach ulcers. Instead, to help your body repair itself, think about putting nutrients like glucosamine sulfate, chondroitin sulfate, and omega-3 fatty acids in your natural remedy toolbox.

Signed,

Willow McQuade, ND

Once I'd finished my yoga routine, I changed into jeans and a T-shirt and headed downstairs to grab some breakfast. I decided on steel-cut oatmeal, which is a good source of fiber and protein and helps reduce cholesterol, too, then topped it with organic salted butter, a dash of organic brown sugar, and lots of luscious blueberries bursting with vital antioxidants. Deciding to dine al fresco, I headed out to the porch with Qigong. The early morning air was fresh and clean. I took a few deep breaths of the salty sea air, abundant with negative ions that can improve one's mood. After the rough start to this day, I needed all the help I could get.

After breakfast, feeling refreshed, I faced the office. Not only did I want to find a contractor to fix the fire damage, I also needed to continue going through the e-mails about the Fresh Face formula and handle any managerial duties that might present themselves. The outstanding bill from Helen's Organics weighed heavily on my mind. I just had to hope that the will was probated in time to pay it, unlikely with Janice throwing a wrench in the works.

A few hours later, Merrily and Julian arrived. While they went to inspect the damage, I noticed an elderly man moving slowly around the aisles. Stooped over and walking like he was in pain, he was having a hard time getting from point A to point B. I went over to see if I could help him.

But as I got closer, I was surprised to see that he was not old at all. Tall, with close-cropped dark brown hair and a craggy, handsome face, he was dressed in jeans, a white T-shirt, and white Converse sneakers. His best feature? Sparkling greenish-blue eyes that reminded me of Aunt Claire's. I felt the knife twist. God, I missed her.

I tried to steady my emotions and focus on helping this customer. I might not be able to pay the supplier today, but I knew something about natural medicine. "Do you need help with anything?"

He turned to me holding a bottle of fish oil and said sarcastically, "Why, do I look like I need help?"

Okay, Mr. Defensive. Trying not to take offense, I pointed to the bottle of fish oil. "That's a good start. The omega-three essential fatty acids in the fish oil will help your back. It's your back that's bothering you, isn't it?"

He put his hand on the small of his back and brusquely answered, "What gave it away? The shuffling walk, or the stooping?"

"Can I ask what happened?"

He waved the question away like it was a pesky fly. "Occupational hazard. Happened on the job. I used to be a cop."

A former cop? Perhaps the Universe was sending me some help this morning. I sure could use some insider's knowledge, considering Detective Koren's interest in my inheritance.

"Did you get shot?" I asked.

"Direct, aren't you? Most people are too polite to ask right out like that." He seemed to like my approach, though, because he gave a crooked smile, which reinforced his Gerard Butler–type good looks, before adding, "Nothing so glamorous. I was chasing a suspect. He rounded a corner. I followed him and slipped on a huge patch of black ice. It happened last winter."

"Ouch," I said sympathetically. "And you've been out of work ever since?"

"Yes. It's put a real crimp in my style. Not only can't I work, but I can't do the things I want to do, like putting in an organic vegetable garden and tending to my roses. I've even had to hire a part-time gardener. I'm not a complainer, but it is discouraging. It's been six months since the accident, and it feels like I'm making progress by inches, not feet."

"Perhaps I can help you. I'm Willow McQuade—Dr. McQuade, actually. I'm Claire's niece." *And maybe you can help me by using your cop smarts to figure out exactly what I ought to do next,* I thought.

He brightened, then turned somber and held out his hand. "Jackson Spade. I'm so sorry. Your aunt was aces. She really helped me a lot. I'm doing better, if you can believe it. Before she put me on fish oil and glucosamine and chondroitin sulfate, I couldn't get out of bed. The pain is less now. Her advice did make a difference."

*Yes, I could tell by your happy countenance,* I thought. I plucked a bottle off the supplement wall. "Have you tried devil's claw? It's a plant from southwestern Africa that has anti-inflammatory and pain-relieving properties. Research shows that it can provide as much pain relief as prescription anti-inflammatories."

He took the bottle from me. "I think she mentioned this, but I hadn't gotten around to taking it."

"Try it," I said. "You should also be taking vitamins B1, B2, B6, and B12 for chronic back pain. Studies show that these vitamins can help block pain receptors." I plucked a good B-complex vitamin supplement from the wall.

"I feel better already," Jackson said, softening. He looked at me with gratitude and maybe something else. Was he checking me out? "How can I thank you?"

"Now that you mention it, since you are a cop and all . . ."

"Was a cop," he corrected. "I'm on indefinite disability now."

"Right, you were a cop. I could use your perspective on Aunt Claire's murder."

He took a step back and raised his eyebrows. "I thought it was an accidental death?"

"I don't think so." I related my theory and the series of disturbing events, including my conversations with Detective Koren, the broken window, the stolen formula, and the kitchen fire. I also told him about the insinuations Koren had made about my having a motive to kill Aunt Claire.

"Sounds like your brain is working overtime," Jackson said as he read the label on the B-complex vitamin bottle.

"I need to find out who did this."

He frowned and said, "It's best to leave these things to the professionals."

"Even if the professionals aren't doing their job?"

"I'm sure Koren is doing his best," Jackson said, reaching into his back pocket for his wallet. "You might want to cut him some slack."

"Is he a friend of yours?"

He drilled me with a look. "Everyone knows everyone. It's a small town." He turned and headed for the checkout stand, calling over his shoulder, "Thanks for your help."

The next morning, after I fortified myself with breakfast that consisted of an omelet made with free range eggs, a sprouted wheat muffin with ghee and homemade strawberry jelly and a cup of Chai tea, I headed back to the office. It was time to find out more about Jackson Spade. Who was this guy and how could I get him on my side in solving Aunt Claire's murder? I was desperate for help, and something about this guy told me he was the one. Aunt Claire appeared to have liked him, and he certainly trusted her.

My Google search yielded some newspaper articles about the accident. It was all as he had said, except for the fact that he had been married at the time and living in Great Neck. I hadn't noticed a ring today. The articles also confirmed that he'd been placed on permanent disability and had moved to Greenport in January. He might have some free time on his hands to help me find out who killed Aunt Claire if I could just get him to check the attitude. I'd have to work on him the next time he came in.

Next, I checked with Merrily, who gave me the name of the store's usual repairman. Turns out it was Bill Morgan of Bill's Building. I called him and told him what happened, although he already knew, small town and all. He said he'd be here in the morning.

That done, I grabbed a small bag of organic popcorn off the shelf (research shows it's chock-full of polyphenols, which are antioxidants that can help fight heart disease and cancer) and headed into the office to go through all the paperwork on Aunt Claire's desk. There was plenty of it.

I divided it into research for Fresh Face, PR from herbal and supplement companies touting their products, personal correspondence, and the dreaded bills. The last were formidable. Not only did we owe Helen, the supplier who had buttonholed me the other day, we also owed a good chunk of change to an organic snack company, an organic dry-goods producer who sold everything from cereals to pasta, and Shelly's Organics, which included garden burgers, pesto tortellini, and vegetarian lasagna. The store was well stocked, but obviously Aunt Claire hadn't been able to keep up with her suppliers' bills. I wondered if I'd be able to do so.

While mulling this over, I heard noises from outside the office door. Moments later, Allie's smiling face appeared. A tall redhead with model good looks, she was dressed in khakis, a flowered tank, and Keen sandals. She put her bags down and gave me a warm hug. "I'm so sorry about your aunt! How are you doing, sweetie?"

Having her there made me feel as though for the first time I could really be vulnerable. Tears streamed down my cheeks. Allie hugged me again and made soothing noises. After a moment, she reached for a few tissues and handed them to me. "We're going to get through this, don't worry. Hector is here, too. Hector?"

Hector, acupuncturist extraordinaire and Allie's best friend, rounded the corner and came into the office. Imposing at over six foot two, Hector was dressed impeccably in a tailored lime-green shirt that fit like it was painted on over his well-developed chest, shoulders and arms, a black tie, black pants, and black shoes. His smiling face immediately made me feel better. We had shared many good times, most notably when we took the *Sex and the City* bus tour of Manhattan a few years back. We ended the day with cosmos at the Stonewall Inn on Christopher Street in Greenwich Village and afterward walked arm in arm back to Allie's flat on Charles Street, talking and laughing. Life was good.

After he left the marines, Hector trained at the Southwest Acupuncture College in Santa Fe, New Mexico. Now he was one of the most sought-after acupuncturists in New York, especially among the celeb set (I was sure many of his patients would follow him here). Allie was a patient when he'd first opened his practice. She'd wanted to date him, but he was gay, so they'd settled into a solid friendship.

After ten years, he, too, was weary of city living, and he and Allie had talked often of leaving. It turns out I'd presented my idea at just the right time. June was the beginning of the summer season, and many of their clients kept weekend homes on the East End, so they would still be able to use Allie's and Hector's services. It was also the right place. They both adored Greenport and had visited with me many times over the years.

In addition, they could also still see clients in NYC by driving or taking the Hampton Jitney into the city.

Hector was unconditional in his support of Allie and, by extension, me. He put his two suitcases on the floor, wrapped me in a hug, and said in his singsong Jamaican accent that remained even after twenty years in the United States, "Hello, Willow darling. You hanging in there, my friend?"

Dabbing my eyes and blowing my nose, I said, "Guess so. It was quite a shock." I recounted the events of the past few days and my fears about being a potential suspect.

Hector rubbed his shaved bronze head and thought about this. "I have a friend who's an NYPD detective. He told me they always look at relatives first. I wouldn't panic about that."

"But Detective Koren keeps making these insinuations, like because of the inheritance I had motive or something. And I'm freaking out about the break-in and the fire. What if they come back? I feel bad about putting you guys in harm's way, but Allie said you would protect us, Hector."

Allie put her arm around me. "Hector can handle any situation. Can't you, love?"

Hector grinned at me, his perfect teeth looking extremely white against his coffee-colored skin. "Just let them try to get past me."

# chapter nine

Dear Dr. McQuade,

I feel like my blood sugar is on a roller coaster after I eat something sweet. I crash and burn and feel exhausted. Is there a natural way to keep my blood sugar in balance?

Signed,

Looking for Balance

Dear Looking for Balance,

Having low blood sugar is known as hypoglycemia. The first step? Stay away from sugary foods and white flour, which is converted into sugar quickly. The next step is to eat several small meals each day so you never get too hungry. Include foods that have complex carbs and protein. For example, if you need a snack, have a low-fat cheese on a whole wheat cracker, instead of that candy bar. Eat foods with fiber, too, which helps to control the release of blood sugar into your system. Taking chromium as a supplement can also help control your blood sugar, and taking glutamine can help curb those sugar cravings.

Signed,

Dr. Willow McQuade

It was nice to have a project to keep me busy, but my heart was still heavy with grief over Aunt Claire's death, and my skin was tingling with anxiety over what might happen next. After we ate lunch, I took money out of petty cash, and Allie, Hector, and I headed to the hardware store on Main Street. We picked up paint and painting supplies so we could give the two other bedrooms on the third floor a renovation worthy of *Extreme Makeover: Greenport Edition.*

We returned with a shade of lemony yellow for Allie's massage therapy room and a mellow seafoam green for Hector's acupuncture room. After we moved out the beds and furniture, we placed drop cloths on the floor, donned plastic gloves, and got to work. By the time we were ready for a break, we had put on a fresh coat of paint in each room and painted the ceilings. The transformation was nothing short of miraculous.

Allie's room benefited from a harbor view that boosted its appeal even more. Hector's room had a view of the back of the property, which was filled with lovely old trees, so it was nice as well. The plan was for them to see clients in the newly painted spare bedrooms and to live in my bedroom, which had two double beds, and I'd move into Aunt Claire's room. Once they'd relocated their respective practices to the East End, they'd find somewhere else to live. In the meantime, the rent money for the bedroom and their offices would come in handy, as would their clients, who would likely become customers of the store and café.

While we waited for the paint to dry before putting on a second coat, we went down into the café area for a limeade to refresh ourselves. It was warm upstairs but that seemed par for the course, since the main air-conditioning unit concentrated on cooling the bottom floor. Fans cooled things off on the second and third floors. But when we stepped onto the bottom floor, the place felt like the Amazon. What was up with the AC? I looked around for my new right hand, Merrily, who was bringing an order to a table of two sitting by the window. I waved her over.

When she reached us, I could see that perspiration dotted her hairline and her face was flushed. "Hey, Willow, I was just coming up to see you."

"Why is it so hot down here?"

She wiped her face with a napkin from her pocket. "I think the AC is down. It's been getting hotter and hotter over the past hour. I've been so busy I haven't had time to run up and tell you."

I looked around the café. Was she the only one on duty? "Is anyone else helping you?"

She shrugged. "It's Julian's day off, and Ron and Stephanie both called in sick. The two of them were tight with Janice, so I'm thinking it's a show of solidarity."

Great, now Janice's malice had extended to my staff? It was getting very difficult not to consider her the enemy. Had she tampered with the AC, too? That aside, Merrily needed help now. And the AC had to be fixed.

Hector, who had apprenticed as an electrician for his father when he was a teenager, and I headed out back to check the cooling unit behind the building. He studied the unit, flipped a couple of switches, turned it back on, and proclaimed it fixed. "Someone turned it off, that's all. But it will still take some time to cool everything off."

"But who would tamper with the AC on a hot day like this?"

"Perhaps it is a mischievous spirit," Hector said, his eyes twinkling.

"I'll bet it was Janice. She used to work here and has a grudge because she's not in the will."

"Yes," he said, considering this. "That's a possibility, too."

We went back inside. While Hector told Allie what had happened, I went to find Merrily in the kitchen. She was there all right, juggling two plates of food and scanning a third order. It seemed we were busy, which was a relief, despite the problems with the air-conditioning.

"Can I help?" I asked her.

She looked at me. "Are you sure?"

"Hey, we're all in this together. What do you need?"

"I need someone to man the checkout counter." She pointed to where a woman stood, a pile of bread, cheese, toothpaste, and assorted supplements, among other items, heaped in front of her. "And tables two and four have been waiting for me to take their order." She pointed out the tables in the brightly colored dining room.

"I'll man the counter and get Allie to help you. She's done it before." Allie had worked at a health food store very much like this one during college. I called her over and explained what we needed.

Merrily handed Allie her order pad. "Could you? I can make up the orders once you have them."

I considered this. "Does that system work? Where you have to make up your own orders?"

"It's pretty simple, actually, since most of the dishes aren't complicated. It works well." Could we serve more people and do it faster if we had a chef? I wondered. Something to think about.

Allie hustled over to the tables to take the orders. Hector tapped me on the shoulder. "Do you need me to help?"

"You've done enough by fixing the AC." I smiled. "Why don't you grab a drink and something to eat?" I pointed to the prepared sandwiches in the glass-fronted counter. "Then if you can, get back to painting. The sooner we get you set up, the sooner we can bring customers in." We all needed that revenue.

"No problem," Hector said, squeezing me on the shoulder and giving me a grin. "I'll be upstairs making it beautiful for you."

"I know you will. Thank you, Hector."

"It is my pleasure, truly. I am so happy to be out of the city. It is paradise here." He grabbed a sandwich and a drink from the refrigerator and headed back upstairs. I felt really lucky to have both of them here. It also tickled me that Hector appreciated the East End the way I did.

As I headed for the counter, the UPS man showed up with a package and left it in the hallway. I gave him a wave and turned my attention to the customer. "Did you find everything you needed?"

A slightly overweight woman with a severe haircut and dressed in a running suit, a toddler clutching her hand, gave me a baleful look. "Not really. I could use some energy." She looked down at her daughter, whose pretty face was framed with a wild tangle of blond curls. "With this one, I'm going twenty-four/seven."

"When do you feel tired?" I asked.

"I wake up tired. I have to push myself through the day."

I appraised her. First of all, she was about twenty pounds overweight. Second, her skin looked dry. She also seemed depressed. Classic signs of hypothyroidism or low thyroid function. "Have you been tested for hypothyroidism?"

She crinkled her nose. "What's that?"

"It's when your thyroid gland, located here"—I pointed to the base of my throat—"doesn't work the way it should. The thyroid gland is the master of your metabolism. So if you aren't getting enough thyroid hormone, you gain weight and feel sluggish and moody."

Her eyes lit up. "That sounds like me. How do you know about this?"

"I'm a naturopathic doctor. My name is Willow McQuade."

"I've heard of those. My name is Sammy Braff. This is Skye."

"Nice to meet you, Sammy and Skye." I walked around behind the counter. "Now, you'll need blood tests to tell if you are hypothyroid for sure, but you have all the classic signs. Your best bet is to see an integrative physician who can order the blood tests you need and interpret them correctly. Conventional doctors order a TSH or thyroid-stimulating hormone test, and it's just not reliable in many cases. An integrative doctor will test all aspects of your thyroid function. Once he or she confirms you have hypothyroidism, you'll be prescribed a natural thyroid replacement called Armour Thyroid. I think you'll be amazed at how much better you feel, how much more energy you have."

"Can I make an appointment with you?"

"I'm not set up to consult with patients just yet." Although that's the next thing I should be thinking about, I realized. "But you can locate some great doctors by visiting Mary Shomon's website on thyroid problems. There's a section called Top Docs where you can find someone on Long Island or in New York City to help you."

I tallied up her purchases as I talked: sprouted wheat bread, organic almond butter, paper towels, organic cheese, natural toothpaste, B-complex and super C vitamins, and tofu. I picked up the package of tofu. "You may want to stay away from this. Soy is what's known as a goitrogen, and it can suppress thyroid function. So do cruciferous veggies like broccoli and cauliflower."

"I won't buy it, then. Thanks for the advice. Would it be okay if I stayed in touch with you? I mean, if I had any questions?"

"Absolutely." I picked up a Nature's Way Market and Café business card and wrote my cell phone number on the back along with the Top Doc website address: www.thryoid-info .com. "Here you go. Good luck."

"Thank you so much." She handed me her credit card, and I ran it through the machine. "Mommy is going to feel better soon," she said, tousling her little girl's hair.

Treating her hypothyroidism would completely change her life for the better. "Yes, she is," I said, and smiled.

That taken care of, I checked out the package the UPS man had left. The label said it was from Green Focus, but it wasn't addressed to us. Instead, it was addressed to the health food store across the street, Nature's Best. I thought about what Nick had said concerning their efforts to sabotage Nature's Way and decided I needed to check them out. I told Merrily and Allie I'd be right back and headed across the street.

The day was hot but gorgeous, with an aqua sky that matched the water. I started down the crosswalk, the lovely breeze from the bay drifting over my skin, and headed over to Nature's Best. The outside of the building was dark and dingy. Their latest advertising circular was stuck up in the window along with announcements of Earth walks and yoga classes.

I pulled the door open and went inside. With the lack of quality lighting, the dark green walls, and the smell of mildew, the store wasn't very inviting. The cash register was crammed next to the front window, and the aisles were narrow and looked hard to maneuver. There were no signs telling you where to find what you needed, like we had in Nature's Way.

Stopping at a cash register, I put the box on the counter. A bored-looking, college-age guy glanced at it, half listened to my explanation, and thanked me for bringing it over. As long as I was in the neighborhood, I decided to check out the competition.

I browsed the center aisle all the way to the back of the store, scanning the shelves as I went, looking to see what products they offered and what they didn't. In the back, where the kitchen was located, a good-looking surfer type was putting together orders and handing them to customers to take out. I thought about our situation, in which the waitstaff had to make their own sandwiches and dishes, and considered again that there had to be a better and more profitable way to do business.

Halfway back to the front door, I stumbled on the cosmetic section, which was chockablock full of Green Focus products, and I saw what Nick meant about underpricing. The prices were ridiculously low, 30 to 40 percent less than what Nature's Way charged.

As I examined the selection, a short, forty-something man with bulging biceps approached me wearing a T-shirt that said "Nature's Best. Forget the Rest." Right.

"Help you?" he said in a way that was not friendly but, rather, perfunctory, like he really didn't want to help me at all. He reached into an open box on the floor that was full of Green Focus merchandise and grabbed a few bottles of hand cream and shoved them onto the shelf. The way he moved, slowly and with effort, led me to believe he had arthritis.

If this was the owner, former bodybuilder Gavin Milton, arthritis would make sense. Bodybuilding involves lots of bodily wear and tear, which is what osteoarthritis is known as, the wear-and-tear disease. Taking supplements such as glucosamine and chondroitin can help with pain and to rebuild cartilage. But I was not here to see a patient; I was here for information. "I'm just checking out your store," I said. "Are you Gavin Milton?"

He nodded, giving me a wary look.

"I'm Willow McQuade, Claire's niece?"

He gave me a questioning look and reached down to grab a handful of beeswax lip balms.

"From across the street? Nature's Way Market and Café?" I added. The place you want to drive out of business?

He grunted and put the lip balms in a lip balm holder. "Oh yeah. Sorry to hear about your aunt," he said, sounding anything but heartfelt.

"Thank you. I wanted to introduce myself, since I'm taking over my aunt's store." I stuck my hand out, and he shook it.

"Do you know anything about running a health food store?" he asked.

Was he hoping the answer was no so he could ease up on his efforts to drive us out of business?

"Not much, but I am a naturopathic doctor. I have plenty of experience prescribing natural remedies."

He harrumphed at this. "Oh, one of those."

His reaction surprised me, since he ran a health food store. I would have expected him to be more enlightened, but maybe he got into the business only for the money. Before I could tell him how misguided he was, my iPhone rang. I plucked it out of my pocket and looked at the display. It was a text message from Natasha, who was across the street. I loved my sister, and we had been very close our whole lives, which was why this estrangement was so painful. I did not look forward to yet another argument about my mother and Aunt Claire. I texted her back and returned the phone to my pocket. She'd have to wait.

Gavin kept talking. "I give you a month. I'm not optimistic about your chances. That store has been going downhill over the past six months. Your aunt's head was not in the game."

"We had a break-in and a fire this week. That didn't help," I said, wondering for the first time if he might know more than he was letting on. Why had he chosen to open his business right across the street from my aunt's in the first place? He had to have known just how well-established her business was. Maybe he was hoping to draft off her business. I had heard somewhere that when restaurants are close together, business actually increases for both. I didn't quite know why.

"Oh yeah, I heard about those accidents. Two in one week, huh?" He averted his eyes, picked up a stack of Kiss My Face soaps from the open box, and began to put them on the shelf.

I eyed him like Larry David does when he's determining guilt or innocence on *Curb Your Enthusiasm*. I couldn't say which category he fell into.

He grabbed another box and pulled out several bottles of peppermint and willow bark extract. I thought of the list of ingredients in Aunt Claire's formula. Was he the thief? He put six bottles of each on the shelf, leaving the rest in the box, and pushed the box aside.

He toed another box over in front of him, bent down, and ripped it open. From it he pulled several tubes of toothpaste and put them on the shelf. In another box was moisturizing cream.

I examined more closely the boxes strewn in the aisle. All of them, except for the peppermint and willow bark box, were from Green Focus.

"You do a lot of business with Green Focus," I said, hoping for some helpful information.

"So what?" That box empty of moisturizing cream, he

grabbed the box cutter, opened the next box, and turned his back, clearly dismissing me.

So nothing, but I was going to keep my eye on him from now on. I headed out the door and mentally prepared myself for my sister's visit. But when I hit the sidewalk, I noticed the cook had followed me out the door.

Nervously, he ran his hand through his spiky blond hair and said, "Hey, I couldn't help but overhear your conversation with Gavin. I was wondering if I could talk to you? I'm Stephen."

"I'm Willow. What do you want to talk about?" Maybe he was going to rat Gavin out, or maybe he wanted to defect and come work for me. Not a bad idea, depending on his skills.

He glanced back toward the store. "I'm kind of slammed today, but I could come over tomorrow after three. Is that okay?"

"Sure," I said. "I'll be there."

"Great," Stephen said, and darted back inside.

I hit the crosswalk and mulled over my conversation with Milton. He was obviously hiding something, and maybe Stephen knew what it was. As I walked up the path to the door, I noticed we had new customers seated outside. Smart, considering the AC situation and the wonderful breeze from the bay. Allie had already served them fresh lemonade and was now in the process of taking their order like a real pro. I opened the door, took a couple of deep breaths, and prepared myself for Natasha.

I found her in Aunt Claire's office, rummaging through the stacks of correspondence I'd organized. Natasha was so involved in what she was doing that she didn't even notice me come in. Qigong did, though. He hopped off the couch and came over. I scratched him behind the ears and noticed that his wound definitely looked much improved. I let Natasha search a bit more, and then I said, "What are you looking for exactly?"

Natasha jumped as if I'd poked her with a sharp stick. "Nothing," she said in a curt, clipped tone. "I was waiting for you." She tapped her expensive-looking watch, which went with her expensive-looking designer suit. "Where have you been?"

I decided not to push the matter of what she'd been looking for. My guess? The secret anti-aging formula. News traveled fast in a small town like this. Although Natasha didn't believe in natural medicine, she knew many other people did and that a product that keeps you looking young could be worth a lot. "So how's Mom?"

"You'd know if you ever bothered to call or go by," she snapped.

Now, I knew my mother was perfectly all right. I'd just spoken to her this morning before we headed out to get painting supplies, but no matter. Natasha was always out to play the "gotcha" game. "What can I do for you, Natasha?"

Natasha got up and walked to the door, pointing out into the store and café. "You really think you can run this business? You have no experience in retail. Aunt Claire must have been out of her mind to put you in charge."

Wanting to reclaim my territory, I went to the desk chair and sat down. Qigong hopped on my lap. "Who did you have in mind?"

Natasha sat primly in the guest chair and crossed her long legs. "Janice. That would placate her, and then she wouldn't be making this fuss about the will. It's embarrassing for the entire family. Can't you see you've handled this all wrong?" Natasha had a knack for pointing out my flaws, real or imagined, so she could feel superior.

"No, I don't," I said. "Aunt Claire made it clear that she

wanted me to be in charge." Plus I thought I'd made some good decisions so far, from making Merrily my new right hand to bringing Allie and Hector in to boost our revenue stream.

"From what I can tell, Claire just wasn't herself when she redid her will."

"Who told you that?"

"A little birdie."

"A little birdie named Janice, I presume."

"Okay, yes. I talked to Janice after the funeral. You've really treated her shabbily considering all she did for Claire. And you even told the police that she was involved in Claire's death. Just like you told the police about the rift between Claire and me and Mother. The police have actually questioned me. Did you know that? They came to my office yesterday. They're acting as though I have something to hide." Her purse buzzed. She opened it up, pulled out her cell, read the text message, and kept talking. "And of course I don't. I just told them about Aunt Claire's ways and how she could get on people's bad sides. I explained about the falling out and how it had been resolved, but I need you to back me up."

Well, it hadn't been resolved completely, considering Aunt Claire had cut both my sister and mother out of the will.

"Can't help you. They aren't listening to me, about anything. I've told them what I think, what I know, that Aunt Claire was murdered but—"

"That's crazy." Natasha stood up. "Yes, she may have rubbed people the wrong way, but murder? That's just ridiculous."

As she turned to leave, Detective Koren walked in, holding up a sheet of paper. "No, it isn't. Your aunt was murdered. And we have the tox screen to prove it."

# chapter ten

Dear Dr. McQuade,
What's the best thing to take if you ingest a poison by mistake?
   Signed,
   Scaredy-Cat

Dear Scaredy-Cat,
Keep charcoal capsules at the ready. If you or someone you love ingests a poison by mistake, take the capsules right away and call 911. You don't want to take any chances.
   Signed,
   Dr. Willow McQuade

The room seemed to spin like a carousel. I reached for the counter and leaned against it so I wouldn't fall. "Was she poisoned?"

He nodded. "Cyanide."

"So I was right. She was murdered."

Detective Koren nodded again. "That's what it looks like."

He tapped on his notebook with his pen. "Dr. McQuade, this changes things, especially in light of the fact that you've come into quite an inheritance." He tapped the notebook again and frowned. "This gives you what we like to call *motive*," he said with a penetrating look.

I thought about what Janice had said, that the first person on the scene was the prime suspect. Now, thanks to my inheritance, I had a motive. Means was the only thing left. It wouldn't be much of a leap for Koren to assume that I'd been able to obtain the cyanide. I dealt with natural remedies on a daily basis. I knew plants.

The cops had a search warrant to accompany the tox screen and used it to spend the next hour and a half going through the store and the rooms upstairs looking for the poison. Natasha had immediately left; so much for a show of sisterly solidarity. Merrily was there, though, cleaning up after the lunch rush, and so were Allie, Hector, and Qigong. We all waited together at one of the tables in the café, drinking Suntheanine green tea to keep us calm. L-theanine is an amino acid found naturally in green tea that helps relieve stress and anxiety. I often recommend it to my clients as a natural relaxant because it doesn't make one drowsy. As a bonus, L-theanine also helps to improve mental clarity.

Still, I had trouble thinking straight now. I kept worrying that they would find something to implicate me. After all, the store had been broken into before; it wouldn't be a stretch for someone to plant evidence, too. I patted Qigong on the head as I considered the possibilities.

Allie reached for my hand and held it tightly. "They can't possibly think you had anything to do with this."

"The first person on the scene is always suspect," I said. "At least, that's what they tell me."

"I know from my friend at the NYPD that they must prove motive, means, opportunity, and malice when it comes to a violent crime," Hector said. "How can they prove that you had malice toward your dear aunt? Clearly you loved her very much."

"I'll tell you how. Janice," I said. "She's out to get me."

"Why is this?" Hector asked. "Did she not used to work here?"

I explained to Allie and Hector the many sordid details of my dealings with Janice.

"She's putting out some very bad energy," Hector said.

I sighed. "Tell me about it." I heard footsteps on the stairs. "Speaking of bad energy," I said as Detectives Koren and Coyle and their crew came downstairs and went in to search the office. I got up and went over to the door, but one of the patrolmen asked me to step back. Inside, the team ransacked my office. "Hey! Take it easy in there, will you? I have to be able to work," I said.

Suddenly, Detective Koren focused on the bookshelf. He reached between *Ask and It Is Given: Learning to Manifest Your Desires* and *Money, and the Law of Attraction*, both by Esther and Jerry Hicks, and plucked something out. He turned to show it to me. "Now this is interesting. What is it?" He opened a small amber bottle and smelled the contents. "Cyanide," he said, waving to the patrolman to let me enter the office. When I did, he shoved the bottle in my face. "Now, what is this doing here?"

First of all, I wanted to know how he could be so positive it was cyanide, but perhaps he'd dealt with it before. "I-I don't know. Someone must have put it there."

"That sounds like a very convenient excuse." He put his finger in my face. "Let me tell you what I think. I think you had motive, your aunt's inheritance; means, since you know all about natural stuff like this; and opportunity, since you were the last person to see the victim alive. The one thing I'm not sure about is if you have malicious intent. I'm getting conflicting stories there. On one hand, I hear that you and your aunt got along as right as rain; on the other, I hear you and she went at it pretty good when it came to your mother and sister."

I figured Merrily or Nick had given me a thumbs-up, and Janice a thumbs-down. "I loved my aunt. I did not kill her."

He sat down in my office chair, in effect taking over. "Now, we're going to go over everything again. From the beginning. Start with when you got up Friday morning."

Coyle also sat down and flipped his pad open, while the patrolman pushed the door shut and stood guard. This wasn't going to be fun.

An hour and a half later, after being questioned repeatedly about every minute detail regarding the morning Aunt Claire was murdered, my relationship with her, and what he thought could be my motive for killing her, Detective Koren left. But I had a bad feeling that he'd return with an arrest warrant.

I opened the door to the store and found Allie, Hector, and Merrily waiting at the counter for the lowdown. As they entered the office, I sat down at the desk, almost collapsing into my chair. I quickly told them about Koren's questions and suspicions as they listened in rapt silence. When I finished, I said, "I'm afraid the next time I see him he'll have an arrest warrant in his hand."

"He can't actually think you did this," Allie said, her face scrunched into a frown. Yellow paint flecks dotted her forehead and cheeks.

"Obviously he does. He was coming at me pretty hard." And it had resulted in me feeling very anxious, so I swiveled in my chair to turn on the desktop fountain on the table behind me. As the water gurgled out of the top of the fountain and trickled down the metal leaves to the bottom, I felt myself relax just a bit.

"They were asking us some tough questions, too," Merrily said. "Mainly they wanted to know about your relationship with Claire. But I told them that you two were very close and that I didn't think you killed her."

"That's good, right?" Allie said, looking on the bright side, as usual.

"Not if he's got Janice in his other ear, but thanks, Merrily," I said.

Allie came around the desk and started to massage my shoulders. "You are really tight. Your muscles feel like granite. Take a deep breath."

I tried to, but the breath got caught in my throat. "God, I feel guilty. I should have done something to prevent this."

"But how could you have known what someone was planning?" Allie asked me.

I shook my head, frustrated. "I should have asked her why she was taking that remedy, period. Instead, I just left for my walk. If I'd asked her about it, maybe convinced her to try something else, she might still be alive. Instead she took that remedy and it killed her."

"It's not your fault," Allie said, and turned to Hector. "Tell her, Hector."

"She's right, Willow. You need to try to let it go. Just for now."

"I can't. Not when they want to put me in jail." Suddenly I

spotted Jackson Spade in the supplement aisle. "And I think I know someone who can help me."

As Allie and Hector headed upstairs to clean up and Merrily went to serve a few customers who had drifted in before closing time, I zeroed in on Jackson Spade. He still walked like a hunchback, so I had to conclude that the devil's claw hadn't done the trick. I did, however, like his royal-blue T-shirt, which made his eyes look gorgeous and had a great quote by Albert Schweitzer in white on the front: "Until he extends the circle of his compassion to all living things, man will not himself find peace."

"I like your T-shirt," I said. "As an animal lover, I can relate."

"I figured you could," he said.

Had he worn the shirt for my benefit?

"So," I said, changing the subject, "are you feeling better today?"

He shrugged. "I'm out of bed and out of the house, but beyond that, no, not really. Do you have anything else in that bag of tricks of yours, doctor?" He gave me a dazzling white smile that almost knocked me off my feet.

*Focus, Dr. McQuade.* In my mind I ran through my list of back-pain remedies. What might do the trick for Mr. Jackson Spade? "Did the devil's claw give you any relief at all?"

He put his hand on his lower back and looked at me. "It seemed to, but yesterday I went shopping and overdid it hauling groceries into the house. Now I feel like I'm back where I started. Like I said, frustrating. It's been a bad day."

I knew what he meant, as my life had been a series of bad days lately. Not the least of which was from losing Claire. But I had the feeling he could help me, if I offered the right incentive. I knew I was desperate, clutching at straws, but I had nowhere else to turn, and Jackson Spade was my only hope. At the very least, he might be able to give me advice as to what steps I should take to protect myself from what I saw as my imminent arrest.

Jackson reached for a bottle of an herbal supplement designed to help back pain and turned it around to read the label. "That's good," I said. "I know the doctor who created it. You know what else would help you? Massage and acupuncture. And I happen to have two new practitioners who've just joined the business. They're setting up shop upstairs on the third floor as we speak."

He put the pills back on the shelf. "I'm sure it would, but I'm a little cash-strapped right now, since I had to hire a gardener and a house cleaner to do things I can't."

"What if I told you that you could have treatments for free?"

He turned to me and gave me a bemused grin. "I'd say nothing is free, Dr. McQuade. What do you want in return?"

"Can we talk in there?" I gestured toward the office. "And please call me Willow."

He looked me up and down, this time definitely checking me out. "I think I'll call you McQuade. It suits you."

"That's a new one," I said, and went into the office. "But I think I like it just fine."

"Good," he said as he followed me in and gingerly lowered himself into the guest chair. "I'm glad." Qigong immediately jumped on his lap. He smiled and started scratching him behind the ears. "I love dogs."

"Do you have one of your own?" I asked.

"Been waiting until I feel better. I want to get a rescue. I had a dachshund when I was a kid. Thought I'd get two or three. You know, fill the house up. There's a great organization called All American Dachshund Rescue that does good work saving the dogs from kill shelters and breeders in the South."

"That sounds great," I said, distracted by a new e-mail

message Aunt Claire had received from someone named Sue Polumbo. But now wasn't the time to read it.

Instead, I turned to Jackson and laid out the facts of the case and everything that had happened, including the news of my inheritance, Janice's threats, the break-in and fire, and the fact that Aunt Claire's formula had been stolen. I also told him about Gavin Milton, my new neighbor across the street, the nasty organic-produce lady, and Aunt Claire's latest cause, preventing the opening of the new pet store. The news of the pet store definitely struck a chord with Jackson. He knew what dogs went through at puppy mills. Finally, I told him about the tox screen results, Detective Koren's questioning, and my feeling that I was definitely a suspect.

He listened without interrupting and, when I'd finished, said, "What exactly do you think I can do?"

I pointed to the computer screen. "I've been going through the e-mails she sent and received regarding Fresh Face, but so far I haven't found anything. It's essential that I find that formula; it was her life's work after all, not to mention the fact that the store and café desperately need the money to operate. Then there's the tiny problem of the murderer. What if he or she comes back again? I've already had two break-ins. If we work together, we can investigate her murder and find the killer and the formula."

He didn't say anything, but he didn't tell me to forget about it, either. Encouraged, I continued. "Free massages and acupuncture. We'll have you feeling like your old self in no time flat."

"Don't." He held up a hand and winced for good measure. "If you knew how many doctors, both conventional and alternative, I've been to see and how many products I've tried, you wouldn't make that assertion lightly."

"I'm not. I believe in what we're doing here, and I'm sure I can help you. Now, will you help me?"

# chapter eleven

Dear Dr. McQuade,

I've been feeling tired, so my doctor ordered blood tests, which showed that I'm mildly anemic. But the iron the doctor told me to take is really hard on my stomach. Is there something natural and gentler that I could take instead?

Signed,

Less Than Peppy

Dear Less Than Peppy,

Anemia is a common problem (it affects up to 80 percent of the world's population, according to the World Health Organization) and often runs in families. Women need 18 milligrams of iron but often get only 6 milligrams. So supplementing makes sense. For someone who is severely anemic, it's a good idea to eat red meat (choose beef that has been raised humanely) two times a week and take an iron supplement combined with vitamin C for better absorption. In your case, since you are only mildly anemic, you may want to try a liquid extract herbal remedy supplement called Floradix Iron & Herbs. It's a combination of herbs such as African mallow blossom and nettle wort that provide iron naturally and is easy to digest. It's good for vegetarians and vegans, too. You'll need to take it twice a day with meals.

Signed,

Dr. Willow McQuade

Jackson said he needed time to think about whether he would help me. But in the meantime, I knew there was something I could do to keep the ball rolling. After Jackson left, I plucked from the top desk drawer the piece of orange cloth that Qigong had found when he chased the intruder out of the store, and examined it again. Tomorrow morning, I'd head to the organic clothing store to see if I could find a customer who'd bought a T-shirt like it.

The next day, after I did my yoga and meditation routine in Aunt Claire's room, Qigong and I headed downstairs to grab breakfast before the store opened. I found Allie already there, sitting at one of the café tables nursing a cup of herbal tea. Her face brightened when she saw me. "How are you doing this morning?"

I sat down next to her. "I feel calmer, less anxious, thanks to yoga and meditation."

Allie nodded. "No better time to keep up your practice. If you're relaxed, you'll be able to handle everything better."

"I also feel incredibly sad. I can't believe she is really gone." I felt tears well up at the edge of my eyes. I brushed them away.

Allie put her hand on mine. "It will get better," she said. She took a sip of her tea and bit into a muffin. We sat together in silence for a few moments before she said, "What are you planning on doing today?"

"I'm going to the organic clothing store in town." I told her about what Qigong had found and that I wanted to check it out.

"Want company?"

"You bet."

A few minutes later, sugar-free muffin and banana in hand, and with Qigong accompanying us on a leash, Allie and I left Nature's Way Market and Café and headed for the Good Green

Earth, an organic clothing store on Main Street. The town was slowly coming to life, with people window-shopping, running errands, and enjoying the waterfront. We found the Good Green Earth nestled between an insurance office and a T-shirt store.

The owner, Viv Colletto, an attractive woman in her forties with a pixie-like face, wearing an organic lime-green top and matching skirt, greeted us with a smile. The store, which had a minimalist feel, featured bright white walls and dark hardwood floors accented by all types of colorful organic T-shirts, yoga wear, dresses, shorts, pants, and pj's from companies like Life is good, Earth Creations and SYNERGY. Viv also carried a wide selection of colorful Crocs and quirky Keen shoes. I found myself wanting to update my wardrobe. But now was not the time.

As Viv bent down to pet Qigong, I made introductions and small talk, but I soon got to the point of our visit. I pulled the piece of orange fabric out of my hemp carryall and handed it to her. "Do you carry this brand of clothing?"

She pulled down reading glasses from the top of her head and closely examined the tag. I noticed that her fingers were red and knobby, gnarled like old vines, a classic sign of rheumatoid arthritis. "Sure, we carry this line. I just got tees like this in about two weeks ago. I've got them in aqua, salmon, lilac, salamander, and orange."

Good news. She hadn't carried it for long, so she might be able to pinpoint who bought it. Of course, the intruder could have bought it anywhere, but I was playing out a hunch. "Have you sold many of the orange tees?"

Viv pushed the glasses back up on top of her head and went around to the counter. She pulled a book out from under the counter and started to flip through it. She seemed to have difficulty moving her fingers. "Can I ask why you want to know?"

I explained what had happened the night of the break-in and what I was hoping to find.

"Playing detective, huh?" She continued to flip through the book.

"Something like that," I said. "Viv, do you have RA?"

She held out her hands to show me. "Yes, and it's dreadful. My hands ache all the time. I've tried everything."

"I was just reading about a new study in the *Annals of Internal Medicine* that shows that a Chinese herbal remedy *Tripterygium wilfordii,* or thunder god vine, can help to ease joint tenderness and pain. The people who took sixty milligrams of the Chinese herbal extract three times a day found greater relief than the people who took sulfasalazine."

She brightened. "That's what I take. Do you think this thunder god vine might work for me?"

"It's worth a try. We have it at the store if you want to come over."

"That sounds good. Thank you. Now let me see what I can find here." She flipped through a few more pages and stopped at one, put her glasses back on, and ran her finger down to the bottom. "It looks like we sold three in orange."

My pulse quickened. I looked at Allie, who held up crossed fingers for luck. "Do you have a record of who you sold them to?"

She pursed her lips. "I'd have to go back through the credit card receipts. It might take a while."

"I hate to ask, but would you mind checking it out?"

She raised her eyebrows. "It's that important to you?"

"I think it could lead to Aunt Claire's killer if I'm right."

She pushed her glasses up onto her head. "Say no more. I'll do what I can to help."

"Thanks," I said, grateful. "And, Viv? The thunder god vine is on me."

Before we headed back to the store, I took Allie on a quick tour of the town. We started by heading down to the south end of Main Street, past quirky boutiques and a new cupcake store, which was tempting, but I was off sugar. While we walked, I filled her in on the history of the village. Greenport was first settled in 1640 and eventually became well known for its whaling, oysters, and later, commercial fishing. Now it was a popular tourist mecca, especially for New Yorkers, who only had to take a relatively short two-hour ride to reach the East End, and those from Connecticut, who either came here by boat or on the Cross Sound Ferry to Orient Point.

We stopped outside a small gallery with a display of watercolor landscapes. I recognized one of my favorite beaches and was tempted to buy it, but I had too many other economic worries to think about acquiring art right now.

Arts are an important part of Greenport. We've been host to many famous writers and artists, including Walt Whitman, the playwright William Gillette, the painter Whitney Hubbard, and many other writers and artists. Galleries occupied numerous storefronts in the village and gallery walks and openings helped to expose artists and their work to the community. When we got to the end of the street, I showed Allie and Qigong the docks, the harbor, and the view of Shelter Island across the bay.

As we walked up Front Street, we passed the new location

for the pet store. I felt my heart drop. This was not right. A guy sat on the bench outside smoking a cigarette and looking disgruntled, mean even. I glanced past him into the store. It was all empty space. So, nothing yet.

He appraised us. "You need a dog?"

I pointed to Qigong. "I have a dog."

He looked at Qigong. "That's not a dog. That's a mutt. You want a purebred. That's the way to go."

I sucked in a breath. "Where are you getting these purebreds from?"

He shrugged. "Someplace in Pennsylvania."

Allie touched my shoulder, warning me to go easy. But it didn't stop me. "It's probably a puppy mill. They supply ninety-nine percent of pet stores."

"So?"

I proceeded to tell him about the horrors of puppy mills. After I was done, he seemed completely unaffected. In fact, he shrugged and said, "I gotta make a living, lady."

"Off the backs of these animals? You should be ashamed of yourself."

He stood up and gave me a suspicious look. "You with those broads who are planning on protesting this store? Those friends of Claire Hagan?"

"Yes, I'm with them. Claire Hagan was my aunt, and she was murdered. You know anything about that?" I was feeling angry and bold.

He ground out his cigarette and snarled, "Nope, and you got one helluva nerve asking me that question." Then he mumbled, "Bitch."

"I don't think so," I said. "You've certainly got a motive."

"Who are you, Jessica Fletcher? Get lost."

"We'll leave when we're ready." Qigong was straining on his

leash. Guess he wanted to get away from the mean man with all the bad karma. So did I.

"I'm warning you. Back off," he said. "Or else." He gave us one more mean look and headed back inside.

We tried to shake off his bad vibes on the way back to the store. I knew he had to be stopped. Aunt Claire would have wanted it that way. But before I could dwell on it further, my iPhone rang. I looked at the display. Randy McCarty. The development executive at Green Focus. Wonderful. I had no good news to share. I took a deep breath, pushed Answer, and said hello.

"Dr. McQuade, Randy McCarty here. I'm checking to see if you've found the Fresh Face formula."

"Not yet."

There was a long silence. "I can't impress on you enough how much we need to find that formula before it gets to our competitors."

We entered the store and Qigong and I headed for the office, while Allie went back upstairs.

"Dr. McQuade? Do you have any idea who might have taken it? It's extremely urgent."

I found Jackson Spade waiting for me in my office, and I offered a silent prayer that he would say yes to helping me unravel this mess. "I may have an idea of something I can do to help."

"Well," he said. "Please get back to me right away."

"I will. As soon as possible. Good-bye." I ended the call and let Qigong off the leash. He quickly jumped onto Jackson's lap and gave him a good, slobbering kiss.

"He really likes you," I said.

He scratched Qigong behind the ears. "The feeling is mutual."

I sat behind the desk and folded my hands on top. Taking a deep breath and trying to be calm, I asked, "So, have you made your decision?"

Before he could answer, we heard shouting outside in the store and hurried outside to see what was going on. We found a trim, track-suit-wearing forty-something brunette standing at the counter, screaming at Merrily.

"But she said this could work!" the woman screamed.

"I'm sorry, ma'am," Merrily said calmly. "There is nothing we can do."

"Perhaps I can help?" I said. "I'm the new owner, Willow McQuade, ND. I'm Claire's niece."

The woman, her cheeks flaming with anger, pushed a bottle of supplement pills toward me.

"You can shove this where the sun doesn't shine!"

I looked at the bottle of pills. It was an herbal supplement intended to improve overall health and fertility. "You want to return these?"

"I told you what I want to do with those. Your aunt told me to buy them, since I was trying to get pregnant. Well, big surprise, I got my friend this morning. So this is all a bunch of crap. My husband, Eric, and I have been trying for over a year now. This was my last hope."

Pointing to the bottle, I said, "This doesn't guarantee to get you pregnant. Just to give your body a helping hand. It's not a cure-all. Perhaps if you're having trouble conceiving, you and your husband need to be tested."

"Why don't you mind your own business?" She turned her back to me, held out her hand, and said impatiently, "I want my money back. Now."

I motioned to Merrily to do as she asked. She credited her card and the woman turned and left, huffing her way out the door in disgust. I looked at the receipt, which told me her name was Jane Marsh.

"Nice lady," Jackson said. "Do you get a lot of satisfied customers, McQuade?"

"Very funny," I said, not liking his implication.

"Seriously," he said. "A dissatisfied customer could be your best suspect."

I turned to Merrily. "Are there any other dissatisfied customers that were angry at Aunt Claire?"

Merrily fiddled with the money in the cash register and wouldn't look at me.

"Merrily? It could help us solve Aunt Claire's murder. Are there any other customers like Jane Marsh?"

She took the receipt, put it under the money tray, and pushed the drawer closed with a sigh. "There was this one lady, her son was having problems with allergies and sinus infections. What she didn't tell Claire was that he also had asthma and wasn't under a doctor's care. Claire tried to help by suggesting several natural remedies, but then her son had an asthma attack and almost died. She blamed Claire. She used to come in here every few days, ranting and raving, until we had to get an order of protection against her."

"Who is she?" I asked. "Someone local?"

Merrily nodded. "Yes, her name is Sue Polumbo."

The woman who had sent Aunt Claire the e-mail I hadn't yet opened.

I dashed into the office and clicked on the e-mail icon. The e-mail program seemed to take forever to open, and in the meantime I told Jackson what I was doing.

Jackson agreed. "What's taking so long?"

"Unfortunately, I think her computer has a virus." I made a mental note to get a new, superfast computer when I had the funds. I needed it for my writing, the store and café, and my eventual practice here as a naturopathic doctor.

Finally, the e-mail program opened. Sue's e-mail was right there on top, unopened. "Okay, here it is." I clicked on it.

Jackson leaned next to me. The smell of his sandalwood aftershave was intoxicating, and I could feel his warm breath on my neck. *Cool it, Willow. Focus,* I told myself. We both read the e-mail. The subject line was blank, but the message was loud and clear: *This IS NOT over. SP.* I did not like the sound of that.

"What isn't over?" Jackson asked.

"I don't know, but it's giving me the creeps. And who is she writing to, Aunt Claire or me? Is it possible she doesn't know she was killed?"

"Hard to say," he said, circling the desk and sitting in the guest chair.

I put my head in my hands. "I hate this. I'm the kind of person who likes to feel in control. Now everything seems to be spinning out of my control." I grabbed a tissue just in case.

Jackson saw that I was getting upset and said softly, "You need to calm down, McQuade, okay?"

I nodded.

"Take a deep breath."

I did.

"All right, now tell me about your suspects."

I told him about Janice, Gavin Milton, my trip to the Good Green Earth, and what Mr. McCarty had just said to me on the phone. "I really think Aunt Claire's murder is connected to the formula." I rolled my chair back and put my feet up on the desk to ponder this further when there was a loud *c-r-u-n-c-h!*

"What was that?"

I picked up the item I'd just rolled over. It was a Zip drive, amazingly still intact. I handed it to Jackson.

"It's possible that this was Claire's and it got knocked to the ground when the police searched the office. But thinking outside the box . . ."

"Yes?"

"The murderer may have used another one like it to copy documents off Claire's computer and left this one behind by mistake," he said. "The question is, did he make two copies?" We looked at each other. He got up, came around the desk, and handed the portable drive back to me. "Plug it in."

I held my breath, plugged it into the USB port, and waited. And waited some more. It was pure agony since so much was at stake. If we found the Fresh Face formula, Aunt Claire's life's work could be produced, the store could stay afloat, and we might be able to find the killer and keep him or her away from me.

I forced myself to take a deep breath, afraid I'd pass out from the stress. A moment later, the window for the drive opened. I clicked on the icon. "Now, let's see what's on it."

A second later, the folder opened. Unfortunately, it was blank. I felt the same way.

Jackson put his hand on my shoulder. "Hey, you okay, McQuade?"

"Definitely not. I don't know what to do," I said, and looked up at him. "Jackson, I need your help now more than ever. What do you say?"

But before he could reply, we heard a *big* crash.

"Okay, now what was *that*?" Jackson said.

We ran for the back door, where we found our answer. Our salamander-green delivery van, which had lavender plants painted on it along with *Nature's Way Market and Café,* was now wedged next to the stockade fence that separated Nature's

Way from Nan's Needlework. Merrily apparently had been trying to back out when things went haywire. She spotted me and jumped out of the van.

"I don't know what happened. I had the car in reverse and I was maneuvering my way out when the brakes stopped working."

"It's a good thing you weren't driving on the Main Road, if that's the case," Jackson said.

"Where were you going?" I asked her.

"Betty's Organic Bake Shop. She makes the breads we serve. And we're almost all out."

I hoped we didn't owe Betty money, too.

Allie shouted to me from the upstairs window. "What's going on down there?"

"The brakes on the van gave out!" I shouted back.

"We'll be right down," she said, closing the window.

A moment later, Allie and Hector appeared on the back porch. I introduced everyone quickly, and Hector and Jackson went over to the van. Jackson released the hood latch; Hector lifted the hood and examined the engine.

Jackson walked around to the front of the van. "What do you think?"

"The brake lines were definitely cut," Hector said. "It looks as if someone is causing trouble for you, Willow."

"That's awful! Who would do this?" Merrily said, looking on the verge of tears. Allie put her arm around her shoulders to comfort her.

"I don't know," I said as I walked over, leaned in, and looked at the cleanly snipped brake lines. "First the break-in, then the fire, the clonk on the head, the AC, and now this." I felt that cold shiver of fear snake down my spine again. This stunk. I turned to Jackson. "See? Someone is out to ruin the store."

Jackson rubbed his chin. "I admit it does look suspicious."

Merrily, meanwhile, continued in meltdown mode. "What am I going to do about the pickup from the bakery?" she cried.

"Calm down. I can give you a ride," Allie said, and pointed at her sunshine-yellow VW Beetle, which thankfully hadn't been involved in the accident.

"Actually, I think you should stay put, Merrily. You've had enough excitement for one day. Make yourself a nice cup of herbal tea. Not an energy drink," I added. I definitely had a sugar addict on my hands. I pointed to Aunt Claire's red PT Cruiser. "Allie, you and I can take Aunt Claire's car. It really holds a lot of stuff."

"No problem," Allie said.

"It's in Southold, right on the Main Road," Merrily said. "Here's the address." She grabbed a brown paper bag from the passenger seat, scribbled on it, and handed it to me. "But hurry, we are really, really low. Oh, I'll have to call the mechanic, too."

"Merrily," I said. "The important thing is that you're okay. We'll take care of the bread run. Go on inside and get that cup of tea."

"Okay," she said, sniffling and going inside.

"That's a different side of her," Allie commented. "She's always so chipper."

"True. I think the stress and strain of Aunt Claire's death and all the crazy comings and goings have just worn her down. Once she rests, she'll feel better," I said.

"If you want to go, first we have to get that van out of the way," Hector said. "Willow, why don't you steer the van? Jackson and I will push you."

"No, not Jackson," I said. "I don't want him to hurt his back again. Jackson, why don't you take the wheel?"

"That'll work," Jackson said, slowly climbing up into the

van. He put the car in neutral and took the wheel as Hector, Allie, and I pushed it into the corner of the yard.

Jackson got out of the van and came over to me. "I don't know what I can find out, but I'm going to get started."

I felt a surge of hope. "So you'll help me?"

"Yes. Claire was tops in my book. She listened to me complain more times than I can count. I owe her." He gestured to the van. "It's also obvious someone is out to hurt you. From what you've told me, the police don't seem to be taking the threats seriously. Probably because they consider you a suspect. Regardless, I'm going to look into it. Claire would want me to. Besides, you're growing on me, McQuade. I like your style. You don't take no for an answer."

I felt myself blush. He definitely seemed interested in me, and the feeling was very mutual. "Thanks, Jackson. I really appreciate your help."

"No worries," he said, heading to the porch. "But watch yourself, okay? Until we find out what's going on, you're in danger."

"I think I'll be okay," I said, quickly filling him in on Hector's background and the fact that Allie and I had taken courses in self-defense.

"That's all good," he said as he opened the door and stepped inside, "but you still need to be extra careful. Call me or the police if you see anything suspicious. Okay?"

I nodded. "Thank you, Jackson."

He waved as he closed the door. "No problem."

"Did he agree to help you?" Allie said as she came over, headed for the Cruiser.

"Yes," I said, blowing out a breath.

"That's good news."

I followed her and opened the driver's door. "Yes, and we desperately need it right now."

# chapter twelve

Dear Dr. McQuade,
I just got back from a camping trip and I have a bad case of poison ivy. Can you recommend a natural remedy that will help?
Signed,
Awfully Itchy

Dear Awfully Itchy,
Poison ivy produces urushiol, which irritates your skin and causes an itchy rash. Typically, it lasts about a week. To get better faster, natural cures can help. If your poison ivy is itchy and oozing, apply a paste of baking soda and apple cider vinegar or oatmeal. Leave it on until you take a shower. If you need to, apply it again. You can also find good poison ivy treatments at your health food store. Choose formulas that contain gumweed, jewelweed, and plantain to calm the itch and remove toxins. The homeopathic remedy *Rhus toxicodendron* can also help you heal faster by stimulating the immune system.
Signed,
Dr. Willow McQuade

Getting to Betty's Organic Bake Shop was a quick trip, only about seven minutes out of town, along scenic Route 25. We passed the pond, with geese congregated all about, the Lutheran church, the miniature golf course, and several craft stands, then went up a hill with a peekaboo view of the wet-lands below. Once over Mill Creek, with its vista of the bay, we passed the fish market, the organic vegetable stand, and the animal hospital, and then eased into Southold. We drove with the windows down, and the fresh breeze was delightful, salty and tangy.

We found Betty's Organic Bake Shop wedged between a pottery studio and doctor's office on the Main Road. A bright, welcoming place, the building was painted white with navy-blue trim and navy-blue awnings. I pulled into the parking area in front and we hopped out.

I opened the door to the delicious scent of fresh-baked bread and immediately began to salivate. A few people were queued up to the counter, but other than that, it didn't seem too busy. When we reached the counter, we were greeted with a smile from an apple-cheeked, pear-shaped woman wearing a baker's apron that said Betty's Organic Bakery.

"Can I help you?"

I scanned the bins behind her, which were full of breads, pastries, and doughnuts, and wanted it all. My stomach was empty and it was very close to lunchtime. But I tried to remain focused. "I'm Willow McQuade from Nature's Way Market and Café. I'm here to pick up our bread order."

The woman frowned. "You haven't paid for the last one yet. I'm sorry about your aunt, but business is business."

My stomach lurched. Allie and I traded an "uh-oh" look. Luckily we were now the only ones in the store. I didn't need the whole East End to know we had financial troubles. "How much how do we owe you?"

She pulled over a ledger and flipped it open. "Two hundred sixty-two dollars and fifty cents."

I blew out a sigh of relief. Now that amount I could handle. "Check?" I asked, opening my checkbook.

"Wonderful. Make it out to Betty Evans. You want the usual?"

"Sure," I said, writing out the check. I wanted to get to the bottom of my aunt's finances. I needed to know why the business was in such bad shape. "Did you regularly have a problem with payment, Betty?"

She grabbed five loaves of freshly baked bread and put them into bags. "Just lately. Claire was really good about paying me when we first started doing business together last year. But in the past two months or so, I think things must have gone wrong. She was always late with payment and carrying a balance. Whenever Janice came to pick up the bread order, she seemed stressed out to me. Although, let's face it, she isn't exactly Ms. Mary Sunshine on a good day. You know what I mean." She rolled her eyes.

I sure did. I nodded in agreement. "Was she complaining about my aunt? Or her job?"

"Not in so many words, but I got the impression that she wasn't happy with how business was being done. She was always saying they didn't have enough money." She popped two dozen yummy-looking rolls into another bag. "I do remember her saying once that Claire seemed distracted."

"In what way?"

"Janice said she was always holed up in her office, out of the shop, or off to New York for meetings. I used to see Claire next door sometimes, at Dr. Neville's. Arnold is a dermatologist. About what I don't know."

I thought maybe I did.

We thanked Betty for her bread and left the store, and I headed next door while Allie waited in the car. I figured I'd have better luck alone. I stepped inside to find a pretty twenty-something receptionist wearing a flower-print dress, who gave me a once-over for any zits or other blemishes. Her skin was clear, natch.

"We're about to close," she said, not being helpful. "Can I help you?"

"Is Dr. Neville around? He treated my aunt Claire, Claire Hagan?"

She made a show of looking at the appointment book on the desk in front of her. "I can't talk about other patients. But if you'd like, you can make an appointment for yourself."

Did I look like I needed to see a dermatologist? To my thinking, my complexion was one of my best features. I always got compliments on it.

The door opened behind her and a man I presumed to be Dr. Arnold Neville came out. He put a file down on the desk, told the receptionist he'd see her in the morning, and turned to go. But I had other plans for him. "Dr. Neville?" He turned back to look at me. "I'm Willow McQuade, Claire Hagan's niece. Can I speak to you for a minute?"

He made a big show of looking at his watch, and then sighed. I guessed I was making him late for his golf game. Regardless, he opened his office door and said, "Please come in."

I followed him inside and he closed the door. The office

was bare-bones, just a desk, a bookcase, filing cabinets, and an unhealthy-looking aloe vera plant on the windowsill. Two diplomas had been placed on the wall along with some generic seascapes. I walked past a door that opened into a small adjacent room that looked like a lab, filled with test tubes and equipment and smelling of ammonia. I wondered if he, too, was making up a version of Fresh Face. He gestured to the guest chair and we both sat down.

"I was so sorry to hear about your aunt. My deepest condolences."

"Thank you so much. It has been a difficult time." Especially since it had become increasingly clear that Aunt Claire hadn't been keeping a close eye on her business before she died. I had a strong feeling I was playing catch-up and whoever had killed her and/or stolen the Fresh Face formula was way ahead of me. Case in point, his lab. "I was wondering why Aunt Claire came to see you."

"She had some problems with her skin."

Problems with her skin? Aunt Claire, like me, had skin like a baby's bottom, even considering her age. He wasn't being straight with me. "I think there was more to it than that. Did she ever mention her new herbal face cream, Fresh Face?"

He shifted in his seat. "We talked about it, yes."

"Was she looking for advice? Were you working on it together?"

He held up his hand in a "whoa" gesture. "Now wait a minute. I don't think this is any of your business."

"I am her sole heir and someone stole that formula from the store. I need to find out who it was."

He pointed to himself and said, "Surely you can't think that I broke into your store and took the formula."

"Who said anything about breaking in?" I questioned him.

He shifted uncomfortably in his chair again. "I must have read something about it in the paper."

The phone on his desk buzzed. He grabbed the receiver as if it were a lifeline. "Yes, Penny?" He listened for a moment to what I was sure was a lame excuse to get me out of his office. "Thank you for letting me know." He hung up the phone and stood up. "I have to be going. Office emergency."

Was there a really big zit that had to be dealt with? I thought not. He obviously wanted me gone.

"No problem. I'd like to talk to you again, if that's all right."

"My schedule is completely booked for the next month. Besides, I've told you all I know," he said, going to the door and opening it for me.

I didn't believe that for a second.

"So what did he say?" Allie asked.

"It's what he didn't say," I replied as I nudged the car out onto the road and headed east, back toward Greenport. "He definitely knows more than he's telling. If he worked on the formula with Claire, he might have a motive. He could have killed her and then come back for the formula."

"But if they worked on it together, wouldn't he have a copy?"

"Not if she just went to him for general advice," I replied. "Maybe he got hip to what she was working on and wanted it all for himself, so he killed her."

"That makes sense."

"I just don't know why she'd go to see someone like him. He doesn't have great credentials," I said, telling her where he went to college. "It's not like he went to a top-tier medical school."

We passed the animal hospital where Qigong had been treated. "Claire was an expert. She knew how herbs worked on the skin. If she had any questions, wouldn't she have tapped a more well-known dermatologist, someone with real weight?"

"Like an MD in New York?"

"Yes."

"But how are you going to find out who that is?"

"The answer may be in her e-mail folder; I have plenty more to wade through." And I needed to do it immediately. I increased my speed. A light rain had started to fall, so I switched on the wipers.

We drove up and over the hill and headed for Greenport. As we passed the eco-friendly building-supply place, I took a quick glance in my rearview mirror. Right on my bumper was an old black Ford truck that had seen better days. "I hate it when people do that."

"What?"

"Tailgate." As I watched in the mirror, the truck sped up and tapped my bumper. "Hey! What does he think he's doing?"

Allie turned around and looked back at the truck. "I can't get a good look at the driver."

Squinting into the mirror, I tried to see the face of the driver. Whoever it was had on a baseball hat and sunglasses, so it was next to impossible to identify him. The truck zoomed up again and tapped my rear bumper. I pressed the gas pedal, but within moments, the driver increased his speed and tapped me again, even harder. Panicked now, I punched the gas pedal.

"You're going almost eighty!" Allie said, glancing at the speedometer.

"I know!" I cried, pressing the pedal to the floor.

"There!" Allie pointed to a turnaround in front of the

Lutheran church up ahead. "Make a left! He won't follow us into a church parking lot."

I glanced into the rearview mirror and saw that the truck was gaining on us again. I wasn't too sure Allie was right. If this person was connected to Aunt Claire's death or was the one who had thrown the brick with the note that said to get out, he might follow us. Clearly, he wanted to get rid of me. Why, I didn't know.

"Turn!" Allie yelled, pointing at the church.

I cut over the road and aimed for the turnaround. But as I did so, the truck caught my bumper again, and thanks to the slippery road, we headed for the drainage ditch. "Hold on!" I yelled, fearing for our lives.

I gripped the steering wheel and Allie grabbed the dashboard as we spun into the ditch. We landed with a thud, but right side up, facing in the opposite direction. The Ford truck turned and burned rubber, heading west. It was gone so quickly, I didn't get the license number.

I unbuckled my seat belt and leaned over to look at Allie, who now had a gash on her forehead from the dashboard. "Allie, you okay?" I gave the cut a close inspection. It was superficial, but head wounds always bleed profusely, and this one was no exception. I reached into the glove compartment and grabbed a wad of Kleenex and pressed it into the wound. I replaced my hand with hers. "Keep the pressure on."

Allie gave me a concerned look. "Are you okay?"

Good question. I did feel some discomfort in my left hand. I flexed my wrist and felt a sharp bolt of agonizing pain. "I think I broke my wrist. But we're lucky it wasn't worse."

# chapter thirteen

Dear Dr. McQuade,
I went for a walk today and sprained my ankle when I stepped into a hole. Is there anything I can use to feel better faster?
　　Signed,
　　Feeling Sore

Dear Feeling Sore,
With any sprain, you'll first want to follow PRICE—protect, rest, ice, compression, and elevation. As soon as possible, start taking homeopathic *Arnica montana*. We call it homeopathic aspirin. It helps to relieve pain and swelling and speed healing. You can also apply arnica topically to the injured area. Be careful, though, not to apply it to broken skin. Hawthorne is another helpful herb. It contains anthocyanidins and proanthocyanidins to help reduce inflammation. To stimulate the repair of tissues, supplement with glucosamine sulfate, which comes from shellfish.
　　Signed,
　　Dr. Willow McQuade

After waiting in the ER for an hour, we were finally seen, assessed, and treated. The doctor put a neon-green cast on my severely sprained wrist and a bandage on Allie's head wound.

When we pulled into the parking lot of the store, Merrily ran out through the raindrops to meet us. The van was gone.

"Are you two okay?" she asked, worry furrowing her brow. I'd called her on the way to the hospital and told her what had happened.

"We're okay," I reassured her, and grabbed a bag of bread, the original purpose of our wild ride, out of the backseat with my good right hand.

Allie picked up another bag. "We're alive. That's what counts. I do, however, have one heck of a headache."

"I'll bet," Merrily said, and took two bags of rolls from the back. "The mechanic took the van. It'll be back in a few days."

Inside, the dining room was empty except for Stephen, the chef from across the street who had made good on his promise to visit, albeit a day late. There was also a huge delivery of products next to the counter that would have to be dealt with.

Merrily nodded in his direction. "He's been waiting for you."

"Thanks. Can you get started on the orders that came in?" I asked, pointing to the boxes. "I'll help in a minute."

"No problem." She put the bag of rolls on the kitchen counter. "Just let me get these trays of raspberry and blueberry muffins out of the oven. I started baking when you guys didn't get back right away, just in case. And I need to finish clearing off a table."

I thought again how lucky I was to have her. "Merrily, you're amazing."

She smiled, clearly pleased by the compliment. "Just doing my job."

Giving her the bag of bread I was holding, I waved to

Stephen and grabbed two vials of arnica to help minimize the swelling and inflammation from my accident. I handed one to Allie, who said she was going upstairs to lie down. Since she had a head injury, I'd check on her in a little while to make sure she was okay. I headed over to Stephen.

He checked out the cast. "Whoa! What happened to you?"

"We got into a car accident," I said as I twisted open the bottle of homeopathic pellets and put four under my tongue. I'd need to repeat the dose three more times in the next twenty-four hours.

"That sounds nasty," he said.

"It was pretty bad," I agreed, wondering if Gavin Milton had been in that truck. "Did your boss go out this afternoon?"

"No, he was in the store. We had a lot of new inventory to unpack, like you do." He glanced at the boxes on the floor. "Why?"

So much for that theory. Still, Gavin might be guilty of breaking and entering or of knocking me on the noggin. I dug a little deeper. "Did you ever hear Gavin trash-talking Aunt Claire?"

He rolled his eyes. "All the time. Sometimes he just stands at the front window and stares over here and bitches about the fact that we have you as our main competition."

"Do you think he was out to get Aunt Claire?" Or me, I thought, feeling my wrist ache from our near miss.

He looked out the window, in the direction of Nature's Best. "He definitely wanted her out of business."

"I don't know if you're aware, but someone threw a brick through our front window and started a fire. Someone also stole a new face-cream formula my aunt was working on. I'm thinking it could have been Gavin."

"I wouldn't put it past him," Stephen said as he fiddled with a fork on the table. "He's got kind of a shady past. When he was a trainer and nutritionist in New York, he was involved in fight fixing. He's not a good guy, which is why I want out."

I nodded to Merrily, who was clearing dishes at the table next to us, and said, "The servers here make their own dishes." Even though I had been thinking about adding a chef for better efficiency, with all the new bills flowing in, now was not the time to take on a new hire. "I don't have the budget to add a chef right now."

"I wasn't thinking of being a chef. I know you guys don't work that way. I want to be a server. I could use the tips. Figure I'll make out better, especially in the summer."

I wasn't sure about that. Business seemed to be picking up, but we were by no means really busy. Still, I needed one more person to help out now that Janice and the rest of the crew was gone. (I'd fired Ron and Stephanie when they called in sick again.) Stephen seemed motivated, and he had a good attitude, a far cry from Janice the grouch. He also was a cook, which would make it much easier for him to learn how to serve our dishes. In addition, he didn't seem bothered by the recent series of weird and dangerous events around here. I decided he would be a good addition to the new team I was building. I put out my hand to shake his. "Welcome to Nature's Way Market and Café."

While Stephen went across the street to tell Gavin the bad news, I joined Merrily in unpacking the orders.

She sliced open a box and glanced over at me. "Are you sure you can do this with your wrist?"

"I'll just use my right hand. This is a lot of stuff to get through." She handed me the box cutter, and I cut open the top of a large box. Inside, I found a cod-liver oil supplement with vitamin D that I liked to recommend to my patients. It was an important supplement that helped to boost overall health, especially brain health, and was also good for depression. Vitamin D can prevent many chronic diseases, but too many people, lacking sun exposure, are deficient. We need the sun to manufacture vitamin D, so the key is to get sun, not sunburn, as I always told my patients. Everything in moderation.

Merrily gave me a smile. "You're a champ, Dr. McQuade," she said, pulling out several bottles of vitamin C and putting them on the floor, followed by a good B-complex vitamin, including magnesium, selenium, and folic acid.

"I try," I said, lifting out a bottle of the fish oil. "And please call me Willow." I pointed to the bottle. "Do you know what we charge for these?"

Merrily pulled a thick green binder from a cubbyhole underneath the counter. She flipped through the pages for a minute and said, "Twenty-five ninety-five. Do you mind marking them?" She handed me a pricing gun.

"No problem." I adjusted the price on the gun to $25.95 and started to slap the labels on. The smell of the newly baked muffins drifted over to us from the kitchen and for a moment I felt content. I only wished that Aunt Claire were here.

I was getting into a nice rhythm with the labeling when I heard Merrily gasp.

"What is it? What's the matter?" I stood up and went over to her.

She pointed to a box she had just opened. Inside was a dead bluefish. I guessed someone was trying to give us a message, mafia-style, although I didn't think the mafia had anything to do with it. There was no return label, so who it was remained a mystery. "Looks like someone doesn't like us, or me," I said, pointing to my wrist. "I don't think our mishap before was an accident, either."

"No, not after the break-in and the fire. Someone is definitely out to get you. Did you tell Detective Koren what happened?"

I had called the police on the way home from the hospital, and Koren said he'd try to find out who had tried to run Allie and me off the road, but I wasn't holding my breath. I thought about the fact that Gavin Milton had an alibi and returned to my default suspect mode. "Do you think Janice would do these things?"

Merrily thought about it but quickly shook her head. "I just don't think she would. Yes, she was a workaholic and she can be bitter and mean, but running you off the road? No."

"Who ran you off the road? Do you know?" Jackson asked as he walked into the dining room holding a beautiful bouquet of roses in gorgeous shades of pink. Raindrops dripped off his windbreaker and onto the floor. The storm must have worsened. He took off his coat and hung it on one of the colorful hooks by the door. When he handed me the flowers, they were also dotted with translucent raindrops. "It's a get-well bouquet from my organic garden. Figured it would cheer you up. You okay?"

"Appearances to the contrary, yes," I said, relishing the delicious scent of the roses. "This is very sweet of you." I noticed he had stubble on his chin, which gave him a nice rugged look. It suited him.

He took a look in the box and made an "uh-oh" face. "Someone sending you a message, McQuade?"

"Yes, and I don't think it's 'eat more fish.'"

His green-blue eyes drilled me with a look. "I heard about the accident on the band scanner. I went to the ER, but they said you'd already left."

I held up my arm and pointed to my cast. "This is what I got for my trouble. Want to sign it?"

"And ruin that great green color you have going? Not a chance," he said as he pulled out a chair and slowly sat down next to us. "Did you tell the police?"

"I did, and they said they'd check it out. But Koren didn't seem too interested."

Jackson nodded. "He may think you staged it to avoid looking like a suspect." He crossed his arms in front of his chest and looked thoughtful. "Did you get the license number?"

I headed for the kitchen to get a vase. "No go. And it wasn't an accident. Someone forced us off the road."

"Did you get a good look at the driver?"

I shook my head. "But it wasn't Gavin Milton. Stephen, my new server, told me he was in the store all afternoon."

Jackson flipped open a small notebook. "I've got news about him, too. Seems he was running a betting scam in the city, fixing fights and things like that."

I grabbed a vase and filled it with water. "Stephen mentioned that."

Jackson tapped the notebook on his knee. "So if it wasn't him in the car, who do you think it was?"

I came back out and put the vase on the counter. The roses were truly lovely, and I was touched by his gesture. "I don't know. I say Janice, but Merrily says no."

Merrily shrugged. "I just don't think she would do that."

Jackson flipped the notebook closed. "Sue Polumbo, your e-mail admirer? Jane Marsh, the lady who was complaining before?"

I labeled a few more bottles. "Actually, I was thinking it might be Dr. Neville, the dermatologist." I related what had happened at his office.

Jackson stood up and winced. "I can check him out. Could be your aunt went to consult with him, he got wind of what a moneymaker the formula might be, and he decided to steal it. Then decided he wanted you out of the way. And we still don't know if Gavin was involved in any of these other pranks, so I say he stays on the list. This may be more complicated than we originally thought. I'd like to talk to this Stephen."

"He'll be here in the morning," I said.

"I'll come by and see him then." Jackson gingerly put his coat back on. Clearly, he was still in pain.

I put down a bottle of fish oil I'd tagged and went over to talk to him before he left. "How are you doing? Feeling any better at all?"

He shrugged. "On a scale of one to ten, I'd say I'm a five. The devil's claw helped, but I'd still like to take you up on the offer of massage and acupuncture."

I smiled at him. "As soon as Allie and Hector are set up, you'll be the first patient, gratis. Especially after those roses."

He smiled and squeezed my arm. "They weren't a bribe, McQuade. I thought they would make you happy."

"They did," I said, still smiling at him. "And we will help you with treatments. It'll make a big difference."

Allie appeared at the counter and headed toward us. "That may take longer than we thought."

"We've got a problem," Allie said. "The roof is leaking in the workrooms."

"Oh no," I said, immediately seeing dollar signs. "What about the bedrooms? The studio?"

She shook her head. "I checked. It's not leaking anywhere but into our rooms. You'd better come up and see."

The four of us went upstairs and found Hector trying to place empty paint cans under the drips coming from the ceiling in his room, but he didn't have enough. Water dribbled down from multiple places in the ceiling. I groaned. Another problem. Lately they seemed endless.

Allie pointed at the ceiling. "It just started up a few minutes ago, when the storm got worse. If you look in my room," she said as she led us next door and pointed at the drips coming from her ceiling, "you can see it's almost as bad."

What a disaster! I didn't have the money to fix this section of the roof, but if I didn't correct it, Allie and Hector couldn't see clients and bring in more income. Not to mention that this part of the roof might fall in, a small consideration.

"I'll go down and get some buckets," Merrily said. "I know we have a few in the kitchen."

I thanked her and studied the ceiling in Allie's room. "Why did this have to happen now?"

"I know," Allie said, putting her arm around me. "The timing stinks. We really wanted to be up and running by next week."

"You still will be," I said, determined to fix this as soon as possible. But how?

"You might want to call Mike Bowden," Jackson said, surveying the damage. "He's a good roofer, and I think he'd work with you on payment."

"You do?"

Jackson shrugged. "He did some work on my house a few years ago and I've recommended him to a half a dozen people. I can put in a good word for you if you like."

"That would be great," I said, relieved.

"Okay, then, I'll give him a call." He pulled out his cell phone and walked to the window at the end of the hallway that overlooked the bay. Rain still came down in sheets. Mother Nature definitely was not playing nice.

Allie watched him walk away, then leaned over to me and whispered, "He is so cute. Yummy."

"He's just helping me with the case," I said, although it did feel like something was starting between us. "In exchange, I promised him your services, and Hector's, too. His back is bothering him. He took a slip on the ice while chasing a suspect."

"No problem," Allie said, watching him talk on his cell phone. "So, are you interested in him?"

I was attracted to Jackson, but I felt too preoccupied with worries about the state of Claire's business, all those overdue bills, the repairs that needed to be done, who Claire's killer was, and the location of the Fresh Face formula to really turn my attention to a potential love interest. Not to mention the fact that Simon had reappeared in my life. I wanted to keep the promise of a relationship between Jackson and me private, for now. It felt like a tender sprout that needed to be nurtured. Rather than share my feelings, I said, "I think my plate is full."

She nudged me as he clicked off the phone and headed over to us. "Willow, for a man like that, you make room."

# chapter fourteen

Dear Dr. McQuade,
I ate at a new restaurant last night and now I have food poisoning. I've been spending most of my time in the bathroom. Is there something natural I can take to feel better?
    Signed,
    Bad Tummy Ache

Dear Bad Tummy Ache,
Food poisoning is a result of bacteria such as *E. coli* and salmonella in food. That's why it's important to store and cook meat, chicken, and fish correctly. To treat the symptoms of food poisoning try umeboshi, pickled Japanese ume plum. You can also try a nice cup of peppermint tea. Make sure you stay hydrated! You'll find a ready-to-make electrolyte mix at your health food store.
    Signed,
    Dr. Willow McQuade

Luckily Mike, Jackson's roofer, was available and would be able to come over the next morning. I went to bed at eleven, after making sure all the buckets in Allie's and Hector's rooms had been emptied, since it was still raining. I'd trolled through a hundred more e-mails but didn't find anything that referred to Sue Polumbo or Dr. Neville or looked suspicious.

I also had to put out a few fires in L.A. Dr. Richmond-Safer had questions about my treatment plans for several patients. We conferred and decided on the best course of action for each. Otherwise, he said things were going pretty smoothly and that he'd call me with any questions and concerns. I was asleep before my head hit the pillow, but my mind didn't stop working, and I dreamed about Aunt Claire's murder.

When I woke up at eight o'clock Thursday morning, I felt exhausted. I did my yoga, did a short seated meditation, showered, and headed downstairs to find Merrily and Stephen already in full server mode, taking care of early morning customers.

Since everything was under control, I headed into the kitchen to grab a muffin and some coffee. As I did, Stephen came up next to me. "Hey, boss!" he said, sounding like the excited newbie he was.

Pouring the dark liquid into a mug, I checked in. "How's it going so far?"

He grabbed two purple ceramic Life is good mugs from the shelf next to me. "Really well, although Gavin wasn't too happy about my leaving without giving him any notice." He frowned. "Actually, he was really pissed."

I hoped that didn't mean more trouble. I had my hands full. My cell rang, and I looked at the caller ID. Koren. Speaking of trouble. I said hello and held my breath.

"It's Detective Koren. Just calling you to update you on that hit-and-run. I think we found the car in question up by the dump, but it had no ID. The VIN showed it belonged to Frank Stafford of Riverhead, but that seems to be a dead end. Stafford is a retired cop from Queens. Can you remember anything else about the driver?"

I thought about the man in the truck. I hadn't been able to see his face, but I remembered that the baseball cap he'd been wearing had some sort of insignia on it. I told Koren this.

"Okay, if you think of anything new, let me know. And, Dr. McQuade?"

"Yes?"

"Please don't leave town."

I said good-bye feeling nauseous. I was still on the suspect hit parade and it really, really scared me. How many innocent people were in jail, I wondered. I did not want to be one of them.

Stephen arched an eyebrow and gave me an inquiring look. Before I could reply, the front door opened and Jackson came inside. The rain must have been coming down really hard because when he shook out his coat, water droplets splattered on the entryway rug.

"Speaking of Gavin, a friend of mine, Jackson Spade, wants to ask you a few questions about him. He's here now." I gestured in Jackson's direction and Stephen turned to look.

"Don't know what I can tell him that I didn't tell you. But sure, I'll talk to him. Let me just serve these two coffees." He quickly poured two cups and headed for a table where two men sat, chatting.

Jackson hung up his coat and came over to me. "Good morning," he said, and nodded in Stephen's direction. "That the guy?"

"That's him." I caught Stephen's eye and waved him over. "Do you want to talk in my office?"

"Sounds good," Jackson said.

As Stephen headed to the office, I pulled Jackson aside and told him about Koren's call and how it had freaked me out. "Please try to find out something, anything, that can help us," I said. "I'm really scared."

Jackson took my hand. "McQuade, it's early days yet. Try to remain calm. I know it's not easy." He motioned to Stephen that he'd be right there. "I promised I'd help. Let me try, okay?"

I nodded. "Okay, I'm calm."

Jackson laughed. "Sure you are." He squeezed my hand and went to meet with Stephen.

Meanwhile, I switched gears and dealt with Mike, the roofer. After we went upstairs and he surveyed the damage, he gave me his assessment. Then he pointed to the ceiling in Allie's room, and said, "You're gonna need to fix this. You're lucky it hasn't fallen in."

Oh no! Another problem. I struggled to find a solution. "Can you just fix the roof over these two rooms?" I asked him, hoping to save money. "The other side isn't affected."

"Let me get up there and take a better look. You might be able to do a patch job, but my feeling is, when these types of things start to happen, it's time to replace the whole thing."

I was afraid of that.

The rain let up a bit so, a few minutes later, he was able to go up onto the roof and check it out. I could hear him tromping around. I hoped he wouldn't come crashing through into the room below, but I had to think he knew what he was doing. Heading downstairs to check on Jackson and Stephen, I spotted Stephen back at work and, when I looked into the office, found Jackson on his cell. He held up a finger for me to wait.

Students started arriving for Nick's eleven o'clock yoga class. A pretty blonde with a dancer's body, wearing a Nature's Best T-shirt and leggings and holding a hot pink yoga mat, had stopped to talk to Stephen. I couldn't remember seeing her here before, and the fact that she was wearing our competitor's T-shirt made me curious. She finished her conversation with Stephen and headed past me to the stairs and the yoga studio. As she did, Stephen started back into the kitchen. I drank the last of my coffee and went that way, too, hoping to get some information about the mysterious blonde.

Putting my cup down, I reached for the coffeepot. Stephen was at the adjacent counter reheating vegetable quesadillas. He put three on a tray and slid them into the toaster oven.

I filled my cup and turned to him. "Can I ask you a question?"

"Sure, boss, what do you need?" He leaned in and checked the quesadillas, then pulled a plate off the shelf above the counter.

"That woman who was talking to you, does she work across the street, too?"

"You mean Polly Milton? She's Gavin's wife. I mean ex-wife."

Aunt Claire's chief rival's ex-wife took yoga classes at Nature's Way? I definitely needed more info. I decided to start with the basics. "How long has she been taking classes here?"

Stephen thought about this. "For a while. When I started working for Gavin, she was over here two, three times a week. He definitely didn't want her to do it, but we didn't have classes so . . ."

"When did they get divorced?"

He reached into the small refrigerator under the counter,

pulled out ready-made cups of salsa and sour cream, and put them on the plate. "About six months ago. I think it had something to do with that yoga instructor named Nick. Gavin got it into his head that they were having an affair."

Nick having an affair behind Aunt Claire's back? And with the wife of Aunt Claire's chief rival? This didn't sound right. I took a sip of coffee and mulled it over.

Stephen pulled the quesadillas out of the toaster oven. "Is that it? I need to serve this."

I waved him on. "Go ahead." I headed for the office to talk to Jackson, but just then the front door opened and Nick entered. He looked exhausted. His eyes were red and his color was off.

"How are you doing, kid?" he said, drawing me into a bear hug, then pointing at my neon-green cast. "What happened to your arm?"

"I had a little accident," I replied, appraising him. He hadn't shaved, and he smelled of alcohol again. "You don't look so good."

He shrugged. "Can't sleep. I'm not used to . . ."

"Being alone?"

"Yes, that's it. We weren't together every night, since Claire had her apartment here, but most nights we were. I can't get used to it. It feels strange and wrong."

"It is wrong. But I've been trying to make it right." I told him what I'd been up to, investigating Aunt Claire's death.

"You've been busy," he said. The door opened and more yoga students headed upstairs. "Let me know how I can help," he said, and checked his watch. "I'd better go up."

I pulled on his arm to stop him from leaving. "I just found out one of your students is Gavin Milton's ex-wife."

"Polly, yes."

"Has she been taking your class for a long time?"

He gave me a puzzled look. "About a year, why do you ask?"

Infidelity wasn't an easy subject to broach, but I had to know. "Stephen, my new server, used to work for Gavin, and he told me Gavin was jealous of you two."

"Jealous, why?"

I blurted it out: "He thought you were having an affair."

Nick rubbed his chin. "That was all in his mind. Nothing happened," he said brusquely. "I've got to go up." I watched as he hurried down the aisle and upstairs.

Nothing happened? Nothing happened when? I had an unsettled feeling I didn't like. Was it possible there had been an incident between Nick and Polly? And if so, when? Thoughts swirled around in my head like a swarm of bees. I made my way to my office, and fortunately, Jackson was off the phone.

"Mike get you taken care of?"

"I guess so. He hasn't come down from the roof yet." I flopped into the guest chair and blew out a breath. I felt guilty talking about Nick, but I had to confide in someone. "I've come across something kind of disturbing."

Jackson leaned across the desk, folded his hands, and gave me a 100-watt stare. "So spill."

"Gavin Milton's ex-wife is a yoga student here."

"So?"

"So it seems Gavin thought that Nick and Polly were having an affair. I asked Nick about it, and he said, 'Nothing happened.' What I want to know is, what almost happened? Did they almost have an affair? Did Claire know?"

"If they did have an affair and Gavin knew about it, it would be more likely that he'd go after Nick, not Claire," Jackson said, and leaned back in his chair.

"But if she wanted Nick, maybe she killed Claire," I said.

"That's a stretch," Jackson said. "But you never know. Let me look into it."

After Jackson filled me in on his interview with Stephen, which hadn't resulted in any new information, he left to do some digging about the Milton divorce. Mike came down from the roof and gave me the bad news: the entire roof needed to be replaced. I took a deep breath and told him to go ahead, even though I had no idea how I was going to pay for it. Maybe once we had a new roof and Allie and Hector started to generate income, it would all take care of itself. I held on to that good thought.

I decided to go upstairs and spy on Nick's yoga session. I felt bad about doubting him, but I had to know everything in order to figure out who had murdered Aunt Claire. She was my top priority.

The door to the yoga studio was open and I was able to see into the room. There, ten students sat cross-legged on yoga mats. Nick was leading a meditation to begin the session. I spied Polly in the front row and noticed that she didn't have her eyes closed in concentration. No, her eyes were open, watching Nick. She had a peculiar look on her face, smug and satisfied, like the cat that ate the canary.

Nick must have felt her eyes on him, because he opened his and looked at her. Something passed between them, a connection, then Nick shook his head at her and closed his eyes again, settling into his meditation. Suddenly, Polly spotted me in the hall, and a look passed over her face, like a storm cloud, as if she'd been caught doing something wrong. She quickly readjusted her posture and closed her eyes.

Moving away from the door, I tried to get a grip on the anger I felt bubbling up inside of me. That witch. How dare she? Aunt Claire didn't deserve this. I took a couple of deep breaths, headed down the hallway, and pulled out my cell phone to call Jackson. Unfortunately, he didn't answer, so I left word for him to call me.

Allie and Hector were going to try to finish painting today, and I decided now would be a good time to check on them. They were busy painting the trim in their respective rooms. Buckets were still catching the raindrops that dripped from the ceiling, but it looked like they were making progress just the same. The positive vibes that flowed from them made the place seem brighter somehow. "It looks really good, guys."

Allie put her brush down and surveyed her room. "I'm almost done. My massage table should be delivered today. But I was wondering about other furniture. Is there a thrift shop or something like that around here? Hector needs stuff, too."

"I could use a rug and a desk, maybe a vase, too," Hector yelled from the green room.

I thought about our options. There was a thrift store that donated its profits to the local animal shelter, but I hadn't seen any furniture there. Antique stores would probably be too pricey, but yard sales were right in our budget. "I'll get the paper and check the yard sales. There are always a ton, and you can get some great stuff. We could go tomorrow."

"Sounds good," Allie said, dipping her brush into the can of white paint. "I like yard sales. It's like a treasure hunt."

"Me too," Hector said, coming in to join us. "You never know what you might find."

I left them there to finish up, and when I got to the second floor, my phone rang. It was Jackson. "Thanks for calling me back," I said as I descended to the bottom floor. "I've got news." I told him what had happened in the yoga studio.

"It's not enough to prove something is going on between them," Jackson said. "But something definitely was bad in the Milton marriage. Seems the police got a few calls from the neighbors about domestic disturbances. They got into it pretty good."

"Did he hit her?"

"No, nothing like that. They were just disturbing the peace. The cops gave them a warning, but then it happened two more times. Neighbors were worried it was going to get violent."

"Maybe they were fighting about Nick," I said, hating the fact that I was doubting his devotion to Aunt Claire.

"Maybe. Listen, I've got to go. I'll call you later when I know more."

"Thanks, Jackson." Now I definitely had to include Gavin and Polly Milton in my pool of suspects. I headed up the dry-goods aisle to the counter to check the paper for upcoming yard sales and found Gavin Milton, his face beet red, tearing into Stephen. He wore a Powerhouse Gym T-shirt with the sleeves cut off and looked tough.

"You're working here? For the competition?" He glared at Stephen like he wanted him dead.

Stephen took a step back and put his hands up. "I don't want any trouble."

"Gavin," I said. "I think you should leave."

He sneered at me. "You've got a lot of nerve, lady." He shook his finger at me. "It's not bad enough that your family wrecked my marriage; now you're stealing my help."

"Wrecked your marriage?"

He scowled. "Don't pull that innocent act with me. You know."

"I have no idea what you're talking about."

"Ask Nick about his little project with Polly."

Several yoga students walked past us. The class must be over. I said a silent prayer that Gavin would leave before Nick or Polly appeared. Fortunately, Gavin's phone rang. He plucked it out of his pocket and answered it. "What?" he snapped, and headed for the door. "I'm coming. Hold on." He turned around and glared at Stephen. "You owe me. I want payment in full."

"What was that all about?" I asked Stephen after Gavin had banged out.

Stephen looked sheepish. "I did some betting on the side and lost. I owe him three thousand dollars."

Gulp. It looked like I had complicated my life considerably by hiring not only the competitor's employee but one who also owed him a big wad of cash. "Can you pay him back?"

"I'm working on it, but he keeps complaining that it's not fast enough." He glanced at the tables in the dining room. "I'd better get back to work. I don't want to lose this job."

"You're doing fine," I said, ignoring the red warning light about him and his situation. "Don't worry." Worrying was my job. And I had plenty to keep me busy.

I turned to head back upstairs to talk to Nick when I spotted him by the back door with Polly. He opened the door and they walked outside. I zoomed down the aisle to try and talk to him before he left, but by the time I got there, he was down the stairs and opening his car door. Polly was already in her car. I waved to him, but either he didn't see me or he was ignoring me. He started the engine, backed out, and drove down the driveway, with Polly following him. Time to play detective.

# chapter fifteen

Dear Dr. McQuade,
I have irritable bowel syndrome and suffer from abdominal cramps. I alternate between constipation and diarrhea. Are there any ways to make my digestive system work more efficiently?

Signed,
Coming and Going

Dear Coming and Going,
If you have irritable bowel syndrome (IBS), you are not alone. One in five Americans have it. The first step is to remove fatty foods and beverages, such as coffee and sodas, which irritate and inflame the bowel. Allergies to wheat, dairy, or corn can also aggravate IBS. I suggest adding fiber slowly to your diet and choosing whole wheat grains and breads. You can also put a tablespoon or two of flax-seed powder on a salad. Research shows that enteric-coated peppermint-oil capsules can help ease IBS, especially taken with clown's mustard. Using probiotics or so-called friendly bacteria can also improve bowel health. Take coated probiotic "pearls" for best effect. Yoga can also ease the effects of IBS.

Signed,
Dr. Willow McQuade

The rain had stopped, which would make my job easier. I hopped into Allie's Bug, since her keys were in the ignition and my car was still in the shop, and followed them out of town to the North Road, headed east. Nick lived in a tiny cottage on the water in East Marion, a small town on the way to Orient. I wended down the road, past the public golf course, the Hellenic Snack Bar, various developments, and Sep's Farm. Nick took the right before the Lavender by the Bay farm and drove south into Gardiners Bay Estates, a small enclave on Gardiners' Bay with summer cottages and year-round residences. Polly remained close behind. I took the right and followed them.

Nick continued down the country lane, past a farm field, fallow with rich, brown earth. A tractor moved back and forth, turning the ground for planting. When the road forked, he headed south toward the water. A few moments later he pulled up in front of his house, an old-style Craftsman located on the dead end, facing the pristine, blue bay. Polly pulled up behind him and they both got out and entered Nick's cottage without speaking.

Pulling over to the side of the road, I turned the engine off. Now what? Did I go inside and confront them? Or sneak around the house and try to see inside? I decided to spy first and confront later. I scurried toward the house, sidled up to the window of the small sitting room in the front, and peeked in.

Nick and Polly were already in the middle of a heated conversation. Nick's face was red, and I wondered if it had to do with the alcohol he'd been drinking. He had a tumbler of what looked like Scotch in his hand. But maybe he was just angry. Nick strode toward Polly, who sat on the couch, and jabbed his finger into her face. "We agreed to keep this between us. Why did you tell Gavin?"

Polly pouted. "I didn't think I was doing anything wrong. I was just happy you were going to help me."

Nick's face screwed into a frown. "Can't you see? This just feeds his insane jealousy. And if he tells anyone, it will look like I was disloyal to Claire. I just can't have that, Polly."

"What's the big deal? All you said was that you would teach at my studio."

"I was thinking about it. I would have had to clear it with Claire, but I never got that chance." He downed the drink and refilled his glass at the bar.

Polly got up and went over to him. "But now you can do whatever you want." She put her hand on his shoulder.

Nick shrugged it off. "I have to think of Willow. She needs my clients. The store needs the business. Now that you're open in Greenport instead of Riverhead, I can't work with you. You're the competition now."

"But you have to!" Polly whined. "I was counting on you."

"I can't."

Polly headed for the door. "Just think about it, please, Nickie?"

Nick took another swig of Scotch. "I have, Polly. The answer is no."

Polly left the house, plucked out her phone, and punched in a number. When whoever she was calling answered, she began to rant, gesturing wildly. She jumped into her car and took off. Although I did need to talk to Nick, including regarding his drinking, I knew where to find him. I decided to stay on Polly.

Turning my car around, I followed Polly back onto the main road and into town. At the intersection of East Front Street and Main, she made a left, drove a few yards, and parked in front of Polly's Peaceful Yoga, a store tucked between an embroidery shop and a travel agency.

This was the business Nick was talking about. But he wasn't going to help her now. Would her desire to have Nick teach at her studio have been enough to push her over the edge and cause her to kill Claire? Or was she in love with him as well? That would certainly give her motive to continue to take classes from him at Nature's Way when she had her own studio right here.

I drove past, turned around, and parked on the opposite side of the street. Inside, Polly was chatting with, of all people, Janice, who wore a bright white apron with Polly's Peaceful Yoga written on the front. So she'd joined up with a competitor of Nature's Way. As they talked, Polly got more and more agitated, probably relating the events at Nick's house. Janice gave her a concerned look and patted her on the back.

I had to admit, the store was a nice space. To the left was the studio, with bright white, mirrored walls and dark teak floors; to the right, where Janice and Polly stood, was a small store chock-full of supplements and other natural remedies. So she was in competition not only for my yoga clientele but for my health food store customers as well. Greenport had such a huge influx of visitors from May to December that ordinarily this wouldn't be an issue, but since Nature's Way was in debt, I needed to make as much money as possible right now.

My first instinct was to jump out of the car, run across the street, and confront them, but I didn't think that would end well. Before I got to my second big idea, my iPhone trilled in my pocket. I plucked it out and looked at the display. The store. "What's up, Merrily?"

"Uh, Dr. McQuade, it's Stephen. Your mother is here and she's pretty upset. She says she needs to talk to you right away."

"Is she okay?"

"I don't know. She's seems mad about something."

Uh-oh. "Please put her in my office. I'll be right there."

Outside Nature's Way, I found Stephen holding Qigong. "Don't tell me. My mother kicked you both out."

He shrugged. "I guess she doesn't like animals?"

*You got that right,* I thought. My mother did not have child-hood pets and had never become fond of them. My father, on the other hand, loved our furry friends and had grown up with a procession of black labs, assorted mutts, and lots of cats. So did I. My mother tolerated them, but it wasn't a warm and fuzzy relationship. "Where is she?"

"In your office."

I reached out for Qigong, and Stephen put him in my arms. "Wish me luck."

"Will you need it?"

"Oh, yeah."

We headed inside, and Stephen peeled off for the kitchen while I went into my office, where I found my mother sitting in my chair, a disgusted look on her face. "There is dog hair everywhere!"

"I'm fine, how are you, Mother?" I put Qigong on the floor and he hopped onto the sofa.

"Why did you bring *that* back in?"

"This is Qigong. He's my dog. He lives here. And so do I."

She huffed. "So it's true. You are staying here. Nick told me about your plans." She crossed her arms over her chest and gave me the death-ray look. "Have you completely lost your mind?"

I sat in the guest chair and took a deep breath. Eckhart Tolle, the author of *The Power of Now,* says situations like this can trigger the pain-body, a part of you that lives on negative energy, takes over your thinking, and makes you miserable. Kind of like that cloud of dust that follows Pig-Pen around in the *Peanuts* cartoons. I'd been with my mother for only a minute and already I wasn't feeling too optimistic.

My mother drilled me with another look. "Well? What do you have to say for yourself? Now you're going to run Claire's store? You don't know anything about how to do that. This is so typical of you, Willow. Always making the wrong choice."

I realized in that moment how much my mother reminded me of Simon. Both of them made me feel bad about myself, which is probably why I chose him. It felt familiar.

My pain-body was having a field day. Anger, guilt, and shame rose to the surface. I took another deep breath, but it hurt, it really did.

"And what about Simon? You ruined that, too. A successful writer and producer and you dump him." Her cheeks flushed bright red, and I became worried she'd have another "incident."

"Calm down, Mom. Please."

"I can't calm down. He was perfect for you." My mother was, let's be blunt, a snob, so she actually liked Simon. She thought he was witty, urbane, and handsome, not to mention charming.

"Mom, Simon is actually out here. He's working on a book. He stopped by a few days ago to offer his condolences."

My mother smiled and clapped her hands with glee. "So it's not over? You two are going to get back together? I knew you would come to your senses, eventually. I'm sure he can help you figure out what to do with your life. God knows I've tried."

Shaking my head, I said, "No, Mother. Not at all. We are *not* getting back together and I *am* staying in Greenport. I'll be helping people here. It's what Aunt Claire wanted. It's what I want."

She pushed herself away from the desk and got to her feet. As usual, she was dressed impeccably, in a lime-green sheath, pearls, and heels. "I wish your father were still alive. He'd know what to do. He could reason with you, at least." She picked up her yellow Kate Spade bag. My parents hadn't been wealthy by any means, but my father had indulged her tastes as much as he could. Now that he was gone, her preferences hadn't changed, and she indulged herself. Putting her hand on the doorknob, she turned to me and said, "I just hope you know what you're doing." She opened the door and walked out.

Considering all that had happened, that made two of us.

# chapter sixteen

Dear Dr. McQuade,
I just came back from a visit with my doctor. He told me that my blood glucose level was 104, making me prediabetic. Is there anything natural I can take to control my blood sugar levels?
    Signed,
    Too Sweet for My Own Good

Dear Too Sweet,
A good remedy to help control your blood sugar naturally is cinnamon. This exotic spice assists the body's conversion of glucose into energy (rather than ending up as stored potential energy in the form of fat deposits), which can contribute to a healthy weight. Take one capsule after each of your two largest daily meals.
    Signed,
    Dr. Willow McQuade

I sat at my desk and took a couple of deep, cleansing pranayama breaths. No one, and I mean no one, could push my buttons like my mother. Qigong licked my face and gave me a quizzical look. "No, Qigong, you can stay right here; the nasty lady is gone." He took this at face value, jumping onto the couch and snuggling up in the corner, his eyes closed.

I, however, had work to do. I just had to find that formula, Aunt Claire's life's work and the key to the success of the store and café. I was also really scared that whoever had tried to run me off the road would try again. I dialed Nick to see if he might have any new ideas about who took the formula and heard his phone ring. A moment later, he walked into the office.

"You rang, my dearest Willow?" Nick said, clicking his phone shut. He still didn't look like his usual self. He hadn't shaven and even now smelled like alcohol. He flopped into the guest chair and put his feet up on the edge of the desk.

I put the office phone down, surprised he was back in Greenport again. Had he gone to see Polly? I put that aside for now. "I'm still on the hunt for the Fresh Face formula. I was wondering if you knew anything about this Dr. Neville in Southold she went to see."

"Not much, but it's all bad," Nick said.

"What do you mean?"

"Claire went to see him because he practiced at one of the top dermatology institutes in New York City. But pretty soon she just saw him out here. What he didn't tell her is that the New York practice let him go because of patient complaints. She must have sensed something wasn't right, though, because she did some checking, told him what she found out, and ended their professional relationship. He wasn't happy. He'd call at all hours telling her that he wanted in on the formula, that he'd helped her and she had no right to cut him out."

"Did he help her?"

Nick shook his head and took his feet off the desk. "No. They only met once or twice. Why, what are you thinking, that he stole the formula?"

I shrugged. "He's a likely candidate." I told him about the office visit.

"I know he was deeply unhappy at being cut out of the process. My advice? Follow your gut," he said as he got up and headed for the door.

"Did you need something from me, Nick?" I asked, wondering why he was in the store.

"I came to get something for dinner, but not much appeals."

"Try the homemade chicken soup. Merrily outdid herself. It will comfort you."

He blew me a kiss and headed out the door.

Time to go through more Fresh Face e-mails. Were any from Dr. Arnold Neville? I clicked on the e-mail icon and the in-box flooded. The little envelope in the lower right corner opened and closed repeatedly. When it dinged to say it was done, I took a look.

Most of it looked like spam, but there in the middle of the new mail was another e-mail from Sue Polumbo, with a subject line that read: *I hate you!* I took a deep breath and opened it.

*I'm taking the next step. SP,* I read.

What the heck? What next step?

Scanning the rest of the e-mail, I soon realized that it was part of an ongoing e-mail correspondence that had begun in January, after her son became so ill. I scrolled down. In the first e-mail, dated January 29, she said: *You are a hateful woman. This is all your fault and you are going to pay! SP.* Claire e-mailed back that she needed to calm down. The next exchange was more vitriolic, with Sue calling Claire a few choice words and telling her she had gotten in touch with her lawyer. A few months went by and Sue was in touch again, saying that her lawyer had told her it wasn't reasonable to sue but that she was going to get Claire somehow. Claire replied that she hoped she would consider getting professional help. Sue responded by telling her to mind her own damn business. Claire didn't answer. The next e-mails were Tuesday's message of "It's not over" and now the one I'd just received.

While I was considering all this, a phone rang, but it wasn't the office phone. What was it? It rang again. Qigong got up and put his nose in between the seat cushions. Turning to me, he gave me a look like, *Are you going to get that?*

I dug between the cushions and plucked out Aunt Claire's iPhone. I realized then that it had been missing. The battery was almost dead. "Willow McQuade."

There was heavy breathing on the line, and then the call was disconnected. Sue Polumbo? I considered calling Jackson. Perhaps he could trace the call? But if she was smart, it was a disposable cell. I placed the phone on the desk, thinking, when the office phone rang. Hesitantly, I pushed Answer. "Willow McQuade."

"Dr. McQuade, it's Randy McCarty at Green Focus."

"Did you just try to call me?" I asked.

"No, I'm calling you now," he said, sounding frustrated. "The police contacted me because they needed to ask me some questions. They told me that Claire was murdered with cyanide. I'm absolutely shocked. Why didn't you tell me?"

"It's been hectic here," I said, putting it mildly. Not only was I trying to find Aunt Claire's killer, I was also trying to locate the Fresh Face formula and run the store and café, not to mention dodge attempts on my own life. "I apologize for not calling you personally."

This seemed to pacify him. "I understand," he said. "You have my condolences."

"Thank you," I replied.

"The formula seems so insignificant in light of this."

I took a deep breath to stop the tears I knew would come. Finally, I said, "The formula is important. It was the culmination of Claire's life's work. I'm making every effort to find it. Yesterday I talked to Arnold Neville, the dermatologist Claire consulted with. And just now I learned that they had a falling-out. I think he felt she owed him something for his help."

McCarty pooh-poohed this. "Nonsense. Claire only met with him once or twice. Once we found out about his background, we let him go as a consultant. Any other leads?"

"Like I said, Mr. McCarty, I'm working on it." I clicked on the Fresh Face e-mail folder.

He sighed. "Dr. McQuade, I can't impress on you enough that we need to find that formula. This could be a case of industrial espionage. I'm beginning to think I need to send an operative out there to look into this."

The office phone rang and I looked at the caller ID. Simon calling from his B and B. Wonderful. I let it go to voice mail. "I'm working with a retired cop already. He's very smart and capable. I think someone else would just get in the way."

McCarty was silent for a moment and finally said, "We are planning on launching Fresh Face in September. That's why we need to know that the formula is safe. I don't want anyone scooping us. Do you understand?"

"Completely. I'll be in touch soon." Before he could suggest sending his rent-a-cop out here again, I hung up. I thought for a moment and then picked up Aunt Claire's phone. What if one of the contacts listed in her phone had stolen the formula? I found the charger in the top drawer and plugged it into the power strip behind the desk so I could use it, opened the application and scrolled down. The usual names—me, Nick, Merrily, and Janice—were there, along with various vendors and suppliers, such as Betty and Helen and Randy McCarty. I checked for texts from him to her but didn't find any. Perhaps Claire had purged her messages.

Next I scrolled to the N's but didn't find Neville. I did see several texts from someone named Sean Nichols about mowing and trimming the front lawn and walkway late last week. Not too exciting. Under P, I found Sue Polumbo. I switched over to the texts, most of which were short and sweet, like F U; that had been sent six months ago. I was interrupted by a knock on the door. "Come in," I said, fearing what was next.

It was Mike, the roofer. "Miss, I'm all done up there. Didn't take as long as I thought. Once I got a closer look at it, I realized that I could patch it in the places where it needed it most. You will have to think about replacing it before winter though."

"That's great, Mike. Thank you so much." Then I asked the dreaded question. "Any idea about how much it'll be?"

He pulled out a pad and checked some figures. "Fifteen hundred oughta do it."

Oh, boy. "Mike, I'm having a little trouble with cash flow right now. Any chance I can pay you installments?"

He considered this. "If it was anyone else, I'd say no, but you know Jackson and he got me sober, so that's fine by me." He made a face. "Uh-oh, I'm not supposed to say that. I'm not allowed to say who is in the program. Please forget what I said." He looked really embarrassed.

So Jackson was a recovered alcoholic? If so, he might be able to help Nick, who seemed to have a problem. "I'll keep it between us if you'll do the same about our payment plan." I went over to the desk and wrote out a check for five hundred dollars. I now had just fourteen hundred left in my account to carry me over. Very scary, indeed. "Will this work for now?"

He took it and looked at the amount. "Right as rain. I'll bill you for the rest."

I finished going through the address book but found nothing interesting. Next, I checked her notes but there was just one that said, "Tell Neville no." This confirmed what Nick had said. There were no voice memos. I checked Safari and found the last few websites she'd visited were pretty innocuous: The New York Times, Mother Jones, and Newswise.

Finally, I checked the photos. There were several of her and Nick, one of her and Janice in happier times and, of course, photos of her prized cats, Ginger and Gingko. I also found several shots of the bay and sound where I knew she liked to take her evening walks. The next to last photo was blurry. It looked like some sort of garden, but the flowers were reduced to swirling colors of red, purple, and blue. All in all, not much to go on.

Discouraged that I hadn't made any progress on finding the formula, I turned my attention to a few administrative things that needed doing. First I paid a few small bills and next I ordered a few new products for the store, which thankfully were COD. One in particular, for migraines, called Migralex, which contained magnesium and aspirin in a special formulation, seemed especially promising. I decided to write a short blog about it.

After lunch, I finished up the piece on natural remedies for allergies, printed it out, proofed it, made a few changes, and e-mailed it to my editor, Katy. That done, I opened the *Suffolk Times* and checked to see which yard sales looked promising for tomorrow. I circled a few and mapped out a rough route. By that time, it was just about four o'clock, and my stomach was grumbling. I went into the kitchen to grab a snack.

But before I could, Allie came downstairs, a huge grin on her face. "My table is here! I'm so excited. So is Hector's, and all of our equipment, too. Looks like we'll be able to open next week after all!"

This was good news, as I needed to pay for the new roof pronto. "Good timing. Mike the roofer is done with the job."

"Great!" She clapped her hands, still smiling broadly. "Want to see?"

"Lead on." I grabbed a box of organic fish-shaped cheese crackers and popped a few into my mouth as we headed upstairs.

Allie's massage table was in place in her room, along with unopened boxes. I appraised the space. "You definitely need a few more pieces of furniture."

Hector came out of his room. "So do I."

I went over and looked in. His table was in the middle of the room, and he'd pinned up a chart about acupuncture on the wall. It did look a bit bare. "I checked the paper and found quite a few yard sales that have some good stuff. I'm sure you guys will be able to find what you need."

"I can't wait," Allie said, ever enthusiastic.

Suddenly, my cell phone rang. I plucked it out of my pocket and looked at the caller ID. Simon, Mr. Impatient. I hadn't called him back. I decided to get it over with and pressed Answer. "What is it, Simon?"

He groaned. "You got to come to the B and B. I'm hurt bad."


Picking up my mobile first-aid kit, I jumped into Allie's Bug and headed over to the B and B. From the way Simon sounded, though, I suspected he needed to go to the ER. The picturesque two-story white-clapboard B and B was located on upper Main Street, with a wraparound porch and verdant gardens lush with lavender, cosmos, sunflowers, and roses. I parked around the corner, trotted to the front door, and rang the buzzer. After a few moments a plump fortyish woman with blond hair came to the door. "Can I help you?" she asked, giving me a nice smile.

"Hi, I'm Willow McQuade. Simon Lewis called me. Can I see him?"

She tsk-tsked. "He needs to see a doctor. But he said he needed to see you first." I wanted to say I was a doctor, but before I could, she opened the door and pointed to the stairs. "First door on the right."

I climbed the stairs, past framed Degas prints and assorted antique knickknacks on various shelves, to the second floor and knocked. Simon came to the door pressing a Kleenex against his bloody nose. "You came," he said.

"Of course," I said, trying to sound officious and keeping my professional distance. If I knew Simon, and I did, he'd use any excuse to try and wheedle his way back into my life. "Are you okay? That looks bad. What happened?"

He flopped into a comfy-looking overstuffed chair, pulled a new Kleenex from a box on the end table, and put it to his nose. "I was defending your honor."

Sir Lancelot. "Come again?"

"I went downtown to Claudio's and had a couple of drinks. Then I went to that bar by the water."

I nodded. "Go on."

"I get to talking about why I'm here and that I know you. And this guy starts in on me. He tells me that your aunt is the reason that his son almost died. I told him that just couldn't be true and we started arguing. He just got madder and madder.

Next thing I know, he knocks me off the bar stool and onto the floor and he storms out. I caught a cab back here and called you. I didn't want to just show up at your place."

Simon being considerate? How strange. "Did he say what his name was?"

He pressed the Kleenex harder and thought about it. "Dan Polumbo."

# chapter seventeen

Dear Dr. McQuade,

I've had eczema for the past three months. My skin is dry, hot, and itchy, but sometimes I have no symptoms at all. What is going on?

Signed,

Itchy and Twitchy

Dear Itchy and Twitchy,

Eczema affects over 15 million Americans, so know that you are not alone. You may have a family history of allergies or hay fever. Detergent, fabric, and cleaning products (another reason I say go natural) can all irritate the skin and cause eczema. To eliminate any food allergies, try Doris Rapp's Multiple Food Elimination Diet (*www.fibroandfatigue.com/files/elimination_diet.pdf*). You'll also want to add omega-3 essential fatty acids, found in cold water fish like salmon and mackerel, to ease inflammation. Oatmeal baths also soothe inflammation because oatmeal contains beta-glucan, which forms a gel that keeps moisture in the skin. It's also important to learn how to ease stress, since it can cause eczema flare-ups. Try the Relaxation Response, created by Herbert Benson, MD, which can be found at www.relaxationresponse.org.

Signed,

Dr. Willow McQuade

Saturday morning I woke up with a vague sense of dread, like something bad was going to happen. Something new and different from what had already gone down. Last night, I'd taken a good look at Simon's nose and determined that it was broken. We'd gone to the ER, where he was x-rayed, bandaged, and given an RX for hydrocodone. Obviously, Simon didn't tell the doctor about his addictive tendencies.

We picked up the prescription and he popped two at the checkout. By the time we grabbed a sandwich and a Coke for him—he missed dinner because he'd been drinking—at 7-Eleven and returned to the B and B, he was just starting to feel the effects. This led to him trying to kiss me, but I nixed that and left.

I wished he hadn't called, although as a doctor I felt I had to be available whenever I was needed. The only good thing about last night was that it confirmed for me that I'd made the right choice in dumping Simon. He was immature, with poor impulse control. Jackson, on the other hand, was a man, and I liked that. But I pushed those thoughts aside. Romance was the last thing I was interested in right now.

Ginkgo, Ginger, and Qigong slept peacefully at the foot of Aunt Claire's bed while I mulled over Simon's interaction with Sue's husband, Dan. Obviously, they had a whole lot of hate for Aunt Claire, an emotion that could lead to very bad things, maybe even murder. I thought about the possibility that Dan had turned his anger toward me, and I shivered.

I reached over to the dressing table, grabbed my iPhone, and called Jackson Spade, intending to leave a message, but he picked up.

"It's Willow. Did I wake you? I was just going to leave a message."

"I was just dozing. The muse struck last night, and I was up late painting."

My, my, Jackson was a man of surprises. First, the organic gardening, then the rescued dachshunds, and now this. "I didn't know you were a painter. What are you painting?"

"A table."

"A table? A painting of a table?"

"Nope," he said, and chuckled. "I hand paint furniture I find at yard sales and on the side of the road. I sell them in Annie's Antiques on the North Road. It doesn't add up to much, but it keeps me busy."

"What about your back?"

"I can't explain it, but I lose myself in the process. Time just zooms by. It's good therapy."

"You are a true Renaissance man," I said, liking him more and more by the minute.

"Thanks for noticing, McQuade. So what's going on?" His voice sounded husky. Sexy.

*Stop it, Willow. Focus.* I told him about the anonymous phone call, Sue Polumbo's e-mails and texts, and Simon's incident. He listened and then went quiet.

"Jackson?"

"Just thinking," he said.

The world rotated on its axis. Moments moved by at a glacial pace. Finally, I said, "And?"

"What are you planning to do today?"

"Speaking of yard sales, Allie and Hector need some furniture, so we're hitting a bunch. They want to open next week. You'll be their first client."

He grunted. His way of saying thank you, I guessed.

"I'll do some checking," he said finally. "Call me later. And, McQuade?"

"Yes, Jackson?"

"Watch your back. I'd miss you if you were gone." He hung up.

Gulp. So he *did* like me. After that, it was difficult to focus, but I reached over to grab the *Suffolk Times* from the night stand and turned to the yard sale section. *Concentrate, Willow.* I'd circled the ones that looked most promising in Orient, East Marion, Greenport, Southold, New Suffolk, and Cutchogue. We had a lot of ground to cover. If you wanted to get the best bargains, you had to be an early bird. We'd agreed to be out the door by no later than 8 a.m.

I got out of bed, which disturbed Ginger, Ginkgo, and Qigong. Although initially the cats were skittish around Qigong, once they realized he wasn't a threat, they'd warmed to him. Now they were best buddies. Ginger and Ginkgo jumped off the bed, and I helped Qigong down. The three of them immediately began to play, the cats rolling over on their backs while Qigong tried to give them little kisses.

I went to the window and looked out at the harbor. Over the water, the sun glinted from behind a tumble of white, fluffy clouds. Usually the clouds would clear, but they could also mean rain. You never really knew on the East End. I opened the door, padded across the hall to my old room, and knocked gently. Allie mumbled, "We're up." I told them I'd meet them downstairs.

We ate a breakfast of organic apple pancakes with lots of butter and turkey bacon on the porch. Eating right doesn't mean it can't be yummy. It was also comfort food, which I needed because my grief was still painfully fresh.

As we were finishing up, Viv Colletto, the owner of the Good Green Earth, waved to us from the street and headed up the path. "I've got that list you wanted. I was just going to leave it in the mailbox, but since you're up . . ."

I went down the stairs to meet her. "We were going to hit some yard sales," I said. But that might change now, depending on what she told me. "What did you find?"

She unfolded the piece of paper and pointed to the three names. "They all have local addresses. But they could be summer people or weekenders, I'm not sure."

I glanced at the list, feeling my heart go pit-a-pat. Was Aunt Claire's murderer's name there? I quickly read the names: Walt Scott, Timothy Milton, and curiously, Sean Nichols, Claire's lawn man, all from Greenport. I had to call Jackson right away, especially about Nichols. It's possible that his T-shirt ripped while he was working here, but what if he was the one who broke in and stole the formula, not to mention hit me on the head and set the fire? He may have used the ruse of taking care of her landscaping to learn where she stored the formula.

Before I called Jackson, though, I thanked Viv and walked her inside to the herbal supplement shelf. I found a bottle of thunder god vine pills and plucked it off the shelf.

"Thank you so much, Viv. I really appreciate it."

She took the bottle, then looked at me, a serious expression on her face. "Tell me you aren't going to do anything dangerous with that list."

I patted her on the arm. "Don't worry. I've got people for that." We said our good-byes and she headed out the door. As she did, I grabbed the office phone and quickly called Jackson. When he answered, I told him I had three new possibilities, based on a piece of orange T-shirt fabric I'd found. "I'm particularly interested in Nichols, because he did some lawn work for Aunt Claire just last week."

He whistled. "Wow, McQuade, you are something. Talk about playing a long shot. But give me all the names. I'll check them out this a.m."

I rattled off the names and said, "I want to go with you."

"You have yard sales to attend to."

"This is more important." I needed answers.

"Yes, McQuade," he said, "but it's also more dangerous. Let me handle it. I'll call you later."

"Jackson . . ."

"Later." He hung up.

Allie, Hector, Qigong, and I headed out for our yard sale/ treasure hunt. We picked up the fixed Cruiser and Allie drove, since I still was incapacitated by my severely sprained left wrist. We decided to start in Orient and work our way west. The first yard sale was being held at a house on Navy Street owned by an artist who had advertised household goods, furniture, canvases, and artist's tools. Most of the action was out back in a big, rustic-looking red barn.

After putting Qigong on a harness that Merrily had thoughtfully purchased and that didn't touch his still sore neck, we followed the signs there, dodging a man on a ride-on mower. The smell of the freshly cut grass was fantastic. We poked our noses into the barn, the aroma dusty and damp.

Allie immediately spotted a cupboard she liked, and Hector a small table. They bargained with the owner, a man with paint smudges on his clothes and in his hair and a bad cough that sounded like bronchitis. He sipped on a glass of juice, but I knew he could do better.

I pointed to the glass. "Is that helping with the bronchitis?"

He shrugged. "Not really. I'm hoping the antibiotics I'm taking will kick in soon."

"You know, a great way to coat and soothe mucous membranes and ease inflammation and congestion is by sipping warm licorice tea. Licorice is a powerful herbal demulcent. And cherry-bark tea can help with that cough."

Hector smiled. "Dr. McQuade is a natural doctor. She knows these things."

The man arched an eyebrow. "A natural doctor? You mean a naturopath?"

"Yes," I said.

He smiled. "I used to see an ND in New York. He was very helpful. Thanks for the tip. I'll have to try that."

As a thank-you, he let Allie and Hector have the two pieces for thirty bucks. Used to city prices, they were elated, both feeling as if they'd struck it rich. We told him we'd pick up the cupboard and table that afternoon.

We carried that good momentum (and karma) to three more sales in East Marion and Greenport, finding a desk/hutch for Hector, a small love seat for Allie, and two lamps. By ten o'clock, we'd reached yet another sale in New Suffolk, an area just south of the Main Road with an interesting mix of year-round and summer residences. We stopped at a quaint yellow cottage on 1st Street that looked promising even at this late—for yard sales—hour. The four of us crossed the street and started the hunt.

It wasn't long before Hector found two big glass vases for flowers, one for himself and one for Allie, and she, in turn, scored two colorful area rugs. This was shaping up to be one heck of a yard sale cache.

Qigong and I followed them over to the front of the house to pay the owner, a trim brunette with a severe chin-length haircut, dressed in capris and a bright white sleeveless blouse.

As we waited, I noticed the name on the mailbox next door: D. Polumbo. Pointing to the disheveled house, with a rotting roof and front porch, I asked, "Is your neighbor related to Sue Polumbo?"

She gave me a quizzical look and then nodded. "Yes, it's her ex-husband, Dan. They divorced after all that business with their son, Tad. Him being sick and all."

I cocked my head, gave her a questioning and concerned gaze, and played dumb. "Sick?"

"He almost died," she said impatiently, like I didn't get it. "He had asthma and developed pneumonia. Sue went to see Claire Hagan at that natural food store. She gave them some bad advice. He ended up in the emergency room."

I wanted to say that Aunt Claire was unaware of Tad's asthma but instead said, "Where does Sue live?"

She narrowed her eyes. "You ask a lot of questions." Allie shoved some money at her, but she ignored it. "And you are?"

Allie looked at me and shook her head. The "don't tell her who you are, we won't get a good deal" look.

"Willow McQuade." Since my last name was different from Claire's, she didn't make the connection. But at that moment, a dented, ancient red Chevy crunched into the Polumbo's driveway. A big, muscled, angry-looking man wearing a Powerhouse Gym T-shirt cut off at the sleeves clambered out. I remembered that Gavin Milton had been wearing a shirt just like it and immediately wondered about the connection. Were they workout buddies? Or partners in crime?

I worried that if this woman told Dan I'd been asking about him, things might change, and fast. Especially after what had happened with Simon last night.

Knowing all of that, Allie quickly handed twenty-five dollars to the woman and gave her a smile. "Will this cover it?"

The woman's narrowed eyes swiveled between me and Dan. Allie, Hector, and I held our collective breath. This could get ugly. Finally, Dan entered the house and closed the door.

Making her decision, the woman took the money, and the four of us scuttled off to the car with our booty.

"Don't look at her," Allie said as she shoved the rugs in the back and put the vases on top of them, then closed the door and climbed into the driver's seat. "She's still checking you out."

I climbed into the passenger seat and put Qigong on my lap.

"She does not seem very happy," Hector observed.

"No, she sure doesn't," Allie said as she put the car in drive and pulled away from the curb.

We were halfway back to Greenport when my iPhone buzzed. I pushed Answer and said hello.

"It's Helen, from Helen's Organics. I'm calling about that bill."

Oh, boy. "Sorry about that. Things have been hectic here." I rolled my eyes at Allie.

"I'm sure they are, but can you drop off payment today?"

Gulp. I mentally calculated how much I had left in my checking account after paying Betty at the bakery, the glass man, the locksmith, Mike the roofer, and to have the PT Cruiser and the kitchen repaired. Luckily the store had been busy enough for me to cover the staff's salaries and even a little extra. I figured I could give her just under 20 percent of what she was owed. After that, I might have to cash in a CD I'd saved for an emergency. When I told her how much I could pay her, she harrumphed and said, "Better than nothing. But I'll expect the rest soon. I'm on the North Road, just past the light in Mattituck, on the right." She ended the call.

"See, aren't you glad you took care of that?" Allie looked at me.

"Thrilled," I said. "You'll need to turn around."

Allie pulled into the IGA parking lot, went around back, took a right at the light, and headed west. Ten minutes later, we pulled into the dirt driveway of Helen's Organics. The spread was impressive, with several acres of cultivated land and four greenhouses, along with abundant flower beds and fruit trees. Several day laborers were busy moving plants and watering.

A ramshackle white farmhouse perched on a small hill next to the greenhouses. Several fat-bellied cats sunned themselves on the porch. Allie tucked the PT Cruiser between two trucks and turned off the ignition. I quickly wrote out a check for a thousand dollars, put Qigong on Allie's lap, and hopped out of the car. "I'll be right back," I told them, and strode toward the back of the house. I knocked but received no reply, so I headed toward the greenhouses. Now that I was ready to pay, I wanted to get it over with.

I walked across the grounds and came to a collection of what looked like new beehives. Opposite that was the third greenhouse. Helen was potting plants inside. The smell of moist loam and budding plants was intoxicating. The space was also crammed with equipment, gardening materials, and lots of bottles of yummy-looking organic honey.

I pointed to the bottles. "Is the honey something new? I thought you just sold herbs."

"I just started making it this week. People like it."

"I'd love to carry it in the store."

"When you pay your tab, we can talk." She continued potting plants.

Although I didn't care for her attitude, I wanted to keep this nonconfrontational. I had enough stress in my life right now. I pointed to the plants she was working with. "What will these be when they grow up?"

Without looking up, she said, "Organic peppers." I noticed

she wore jeans and a green Life is good T-shirt with a flowerpot on it, although her attitude seemed anything but good. Maybe part of the reason was the bad sunburn she had on her face, neck, and arms.

"Looks like the sun got the better of you."

She potted another pepper plant. "Forgot sunscreen. Today, I pay."

"Have you tried aloe on it?" Aloe is one of the best natural remedies because it's an anti-inflammatory plant that contains compounds similar to aspirin. This means it helps ease the pain and redness of sunburn. Aloe also stimulates blood flow, improving healing time.

"It looked worse before I used the aloe."

A cat jumped up onto the table and nudged Helen's face. She picked it up and put it back on the ground. I spotted three more at the end of the greenhouse and more milling outside.

"You've got a lot of cats," I said.

"Barn cats. A new one shows up every day."

I thought about the cat overpopulation problem on the East End. "Are they spayed and neutered? If not, you could call SAVES." SAVES stood for Spay, Alter, Vaccinate Every Stray.

"Yes," she said, exasperated. "Your aunt Claire told me about them more than once. But I let nature take its course." She potted another plant.

That was a backward attitude, but I didn't want to get into a big thing with her. Better to call SAVES myself and alert them that there were a lot of cats in this area that needed to be trapped, spayed or neutered, and hopefully found homes.

I turned my attention to the large assortment of colorful herbs in the greenhouse, hot-pink echinacea, red yarrow, and several different types of lovely smelling lavender. The latter prompted a thought. "You can also make a compress with lavender for sunburn. Have you tried that?"

"I hadn't thought of it," she said absently.

On Helen's worktable were pouches of dried herbs and herbal essences in glass bottles with toppers. I thought about the Mimulus Claire had taken. Could Helen have swapped it with a potion that included cyanide? But killing Aunt Claire would prevent her from getting paid. Still, maybe there was something going on here that I didn't know about.

"Did Aunt Claire buy fresh herbs from you as well?" I hadn't noticed any in the store.

"She used to. But she wanted better, more exotic, herbs for that formula she was making," she said bitterly. "That I helped her with."

"You helped her with the Fresh Face formula?" I smelled Motive with a capital $M$. The same one that Dr. Neville had.

She frowned. "Yes, in the beginning. She consulted me. But then, when it looked like it was really going to happen . . ." She rubbed her face with her hand, leaving a smudge of dirt on her cheek.

I prompted her: "What?"

She put the seedling in a row with a dozen others. "I just didn't hear from her."

"Did she mention any problems she was having with it? Did she ever mention a Dr. Neville?"

She considered me and my questions, grabbed another handful of potting soil, and put it into a new container. "I just know that she was under a tremendous amount of pressure from New York. From that guy McCarty. He'd call her every day, sometimes two or three times. E-mails and texts, too, sometimes a dozen a day."

I thought about Aunt Claire's iPhone and the fact that there were no texts from McCarty. She'd probably cleaned them out because there were so many. Still, they could be helpful now.

Helen continued. "She was working as fast as she could, but she wanted it to be just right. I told her that she needed to cool it with the stress, but she didn't listen to me. About anything." She put the seedling in the pot and, it seemed to me, angrily pressed earth around it.

Yes, definitely some bad blood here. I hadn't realized how much. Before a seedling bought the farm, I handed her the check. "Thanks for the info and your patience. I'll get you more as soon as I can."

"See that you do," she said, not looking up as she shoved potting soil into a new container. "I'm not waiting forever for what is mine."

# chapter eighteen

Dear Dr. McQuade,
I'm in menopause and I have so many hot flashes each day that I'm constantly changing my clothes. I'm either hot or cold. But either way, I'm miserable. Can you help?
    Signed,
    Running Hot and Cold

Dear Running Hot and Cold,
They call menopause "the change" for a good reason. When you're in the middle of it, what with the hot flashes, brain fog, muscle aches, and mood swings, your whole world seems in flux. One of the best natural remedies is black cohosh, which is a member of the buttercup family. And research shows that Remifemin is especially effective. You can find more about it at www.enzymatictherapy.com. Another good remedy for hot flashes is dong quai, an aromatic plant from China. And chaste tree can help balance hormones during menopause, increasing the level of progesterone while reducing the level of estrogen. Homeopathic remedies for menopause include belladonna and *Gelsemium*.
    Signed,
    Dr. Willow McQuade

We returned from our yard sale adventure to the store and unloaded our goodies. After we'd brought everything up to Allie's and Hector's offices, the two of them headed back out to pick up the van. Aunt Claire's mechanic, Rick, had left a message on the office phone that the brakes were fixed. No questions asked. After that, Allie and Hector would pick up the rest of their purchases.

As for me, I planned to take a nice nap with Qigong on the couch in the office, because the events of the past week and grieving Aunt Claire's death had left me exhausted. I am a firm believer in the restorative power of naps. Not only do naps improve energy and make you more alert, research done by the Harvard School of Public Health shows that regular napping can even be helpful in lowering your risk of coronary heart disease by 37 percent. Amazing.

But my nap idea was nixed the minute I turned into my office. There I found a middle-aged man dressed in an expensive navy-blue suit, running his hand through his hair and pacing. Qigong ran up to him, sniffed him, decided he was okay, and jumped on the couch. I still wasn't sure.

"Hello, can I help you?"

He put his hand out. "Randy McCarty. Green Focus."

Oh, boy. This was getting serious. "I'm Willow McQuade. I didn't expect you."

"I know that, and I'm sorry. My boss called me in late yesterday and demanded answers. I thought I'd better come out and see for myself. Okay if I sit?" He pointed to the chair. "It's been a heckuva day."

Didn't I know it. "I'm sorry you came all the way out here, Mr. McCarty." I sat down behind the desk.

"Randy, please. And I'm so sorry about your aunt. We all are."

"Thanks, Randy. But I don't have anything new to tell you."

"Can you show me where she kept the formula?" He scratched his head and several flakes of dandruff floated through the air to the floor. He looked at me. "Well, that's embarrassing."

"You know, you can use a eucalyptus rinse to treat dandruff. It fights infection and tones the skin."

"A eucalyptus rinse? Can I buy it here?"

"You can get the dried leaves here. My friend Brigitte Mars, a master herbalist, has a great recipe. You put four heaping teaspoons in a quart of boiling water, stir, cover, and let it steep for an hour. Then you just strain the liquid and put it into a plastic squeeze bottle and add a tablespoon of apple-cider vinegar. After you take a shower and wash your hair, you pour it on. But don't rinse it out. Let it dry. You'll see the difference."

"Okay, I'll try it. Now, the formula?"

I stood up and pointed to the area in the wood floor that looked uneven. "See that spot? She kept it in there."

He craned his neck to see. "You're kidding, right?"

I shrugged. "Aunt Claire was very trusting. To a point. For her, that was a real security measure."

He put his head in his hands. "I'm toast. I've got a kid who is applying to NYU and I'm going to lose my job."

"Now, we don't know that. I've been busy trying to find some answers. A local retired cop named Jackson Spade is helping me."

"I think I need to bring in my own man." He pulled out his phone and began scrolling through numbers.

The last thing we needed was someone else gumming up the works. My major focus was finding Aunt Claire's killer and the formula, in that order. Randy's operative, whoever it was, would be intent on finding the formula, period. But I didn't say that. Instead, I said, "I don't want a stranger hanging around here. It might make customers nervous." Which was also true.

Randy stopped scrolling. "I understand that, but I need to find this formula."

"There's no record of it at all? I find that strange."

Randy sighed. "We do have a copy of the formula but not the final version. Claire was supposed to send that to me last week. But then . . ."

"She was murdered before she could finish," I said.

"Yes." McCarty spread his hands, and then nervously wiped his palms on the tops of his trouser legs. "Can this Jackson person help? If someone who stole it was, let's just say ambitious, they could sell what they found to a competitor who could beat us to the punch."

"We've got several suspects," I said, and ran down the case against Janice, Gavin, Polly, Dr. Neville, and the Polumbos. I also told him about my conversation with Helen of Helen's Organics this morning and my suspicions about the pet store owners.

McCarty blew out a breath. "You've done a lot, but I still think I need to bring a man in."

Jackson chose this time to walk into the office. He seemed a little less hunched, but very stressed. Qigong jumped off the couch and went over to him. Jackson stooped over as far as he could and petted him on the head. I could tell from his expression that he had something big on his mind.

"Jackson, this is Randy McCarty. He's the development executive at Green Focus. He's here about the missing Fresh Face formula."

Randy got up and shook Jackson's hand. "Terrible business, this."

"Yes, Claire was the best," Jackson said, and looked at me. "Willow, something has happened."

"Something bad?" Had my feeling this morning come true?

"Yes, something bad. I ran down those names you gave me. I cleared the first two, Scott and Milton. Both had alibis for the night of the break-in."

"And Sean Nichols?"

He shook his head. "He's dead, Willow. Someone strangled him."

Randy McCarty and I sat in stunned silence. Jackson came over to me. "You okay?"

Dazed, I nodded. "I'm okay."

Qigong didn't think so. He trotted over, hopped onto my lap, and licked my face. I gently scratched his ears and turned to Jackson. "What happened?"

"I did the rounds of the other two guys, and when I got to Nichols's house, it was past twelve. Sean's place was in Driftwood Cove, corner unit. I knocked hard, but no answer. I pushed on the door just to check and found it was open, so I walked in and he was lying on the kitchen floor. You could see the bruises around his neck. I checked for a pulse, but he was gone. Nothing to do."

"Oh, God." I shook my head. What next?

"Before I called the cops, from a pay phone, anonymously, I did take a good look around. I found an empty manila envelope that had *Fresh Face Formula* written on the front, so that connects him to Claire's murder. But no cyanide."

"What's going on?" Randy asked nervously. Jackson quickly explained Nichols's connection to the store.

"Did you know him, Jackson?" I asked.

He locked eyes with me. "No, Willow, I'd never met him. But my sources tell me he was a petty thief. He'd been arrested once for B and E."

I placed my palms on the desk and tried to quiet my nerves with some deep breathing. "So is he the guy, or not? Did he kill Aunt Claire?"

Jackson shrugged. "Maybe. More likely? The real murderer hired him to get close to Claire and then steal the formula. Once he had it, Nichols was dispensable."

I felt shook-up and suddenly scared. Someone out there had been ruthless enough to kill Aunt Claire, hire someone to steal her formula, and then kill that person when he no longer proved useful.

McCarty began scrolling through the names on his phone again. "I've got to get someone on this asap."

Jackson held up his hand. "I'm on it, McCarty. I'm doing all that can be done."

He thought about this and put his BlackBerry back into his pocket. "I suppose you are, but perhaps I can help in another way. I'm going to hire someone to do some digging at our competitors to see if they're working on anything new. Will you update me on your progress?"

"Yes," Jackson and I said together.

"Good." He stood and checked his watch. "I can just make the next bus." He reached over to shake my hand and then turned to Jackson. "I'm leaving this in your hands."

Jackson gestured to me. "We're both on this."

He nodded to me, said, "Okay, then," and left.

Jackson took a seat in the guest chair. "He's tightly wound."

"We all are," I replied weakly, and stared at a painting of London's Clock Tower on the far wall. Suddenly I wished I were anywhere but here.

Jackson cocked his head like a bird listening for worms in the garden. "McQuade? You okay?"

I pulled my attention back to the present moment. "Fine. Let me tell you what I found out about Dan Polumbo." I proceeded to relate how I had run into Dan this morning, his possible connection to Gavin Milton, and my conversation with Helen of Helen's Organics.

He scribbled down everything I said onto his small notepad. "I'll get a time of death on Nichols from the coroner, and then we'll know if Polumbo or Helen could have done this. I'll also have to run down alibis for Milton, his wife, those pet store owners, and Janice."

"Speaking of which," I said, and nodded to Janice as she entered the office. She had on the apron from her new job at Polly's Peaceful Yoga. I was sure she'd worn it just to give me a dig. Without a word, she dropped a fat legal-sized packet on the desk. My stomach clenched. "What is this?" I picked it up and started to open it.

"I'm contesting the will," she said.

# chapter nineteen

Dear Dr. McQuade,
I'm a waitress and I'm on my feet all day long. I wear support hose but my varicose veins still make my legs ache. Is there anything natural that can help give me some relief?
    Signed,
    Achy, Breaky Legs

Dear Achy, Breaky Legs,
One of the best remedies for varicose veins is horse chestnut cream. Research published in the medical journal *International Angiology* in 2002 shows that taking horse chestnut seed extract orally helps to relieve pain, itching, fatigue, and swelling. You can also apply it topically. Just rub it on gently, especially if you are prone to blood clots. You'll find horse chestnut seed extract and horse chestnut cream at your local health food store. It's also helpful to eat foods that are rich in bioflavonoids, such as apricots, blackberries, cherries, and cantaloupes, because they contain potent antioxidants and help reduce inflammation.
    Signed,
    Dr. Willow McQuade

Janice stood there looking smug, like she'd backed me into a corner. I decided to do the same to her. "We were just talking about you, Janice."

She narrowed her eyes and glared at me. "I'll bet."

"Where were you this afternoon?" I arched an eyebrow.

She pointed to her Polly's Peaceful Yoga apron. "What does it look like? I was at work. What business is it of yours, anyway?"

"Sean Nichols was murdered today," Jackson said, and tapped his notepad on his knee. "Know anything about that?"

Janice drilled me with a look. "Who's he? Why would I have anything to do with his murder?"

"We think it may have something to do with Aunt Claire's death."

"I know you're trying to pin that on me." She put her hands on her hips and glared at me some more. "You've got a lot of nerve. Who was here to help Claire build the business for the past ten years while you were out west? I was. Who held her hand through the whole development process of Fresh Face? I did. That's why I'm contesting the will. I put my heart and soul into this place. And I did it for her."

I took a deep breath and tried to remain calm. "She left me a letter . . ."

Janice waved away my comment, and said, "I know all about that," which was a surprise to me. Had Claire told her about her intentions? Had Nick told Polly, who then told her?

Janice huffed. "That was just Claire being Claire. So dramatic. So unpractical. You don't know anything about running a health food store."

"I think she's doing a pretty good job," Jackson said.

Janice gave him a sour look. "That's not what I hear." She pointed at the packet. "This will effectively shut you down. This is what you deserve." She walked to the door, stopped, and turned back to us. "And if you hassle me anymore about Claire's murder, you'll be sorry."

Before I could say something smart, the office phone rang and I glanced at the caller ID: Southold Dermatology. Picking up the phone, I watched Janice go and said hello.

"Ms. McQuade? It's Penny at Dr. Neville's. I need to see you."

Jackson left to follow up on Nichols's time of death and check the alibis of our suspects while Qigong and I hopped into the Cruiser and headed to Southold. I called the estate lawyer, Mr. Matthews on my way, and left a message about Janice contesting the will, asking him to call me back right away.

When I got to Dr. Neville's office, the place seemed deserted, with only a red Nissan Sentra that had seen better days in the parking lot. While Qigong stayed in the car and worked on a bone that he liked, I went into the office to find Penny red-faced and crying at her desk. She wore a T-shirt and jeans, not exactly office attire.

"Penny? Are you okay?"

She looked up at me and grabbed a tissue from the box on the desk and blew her nose. "No, I'm not okay. That bastard just fired me. On the phone!" she said as if it was one of the world's greatest injustices.

"Fired you? What happened?" And what's that got to do with me? I wondered.

She blew out a big sigh. "Oh, he got mad because I took a few two-hour lunches. Okay, maybe more than a few. But big deal. He can answer his own damn phones."

I thought about Sean Nichols's murder and wondered where Dr. Neville was.

"You said he called you. Where exactly is he?"

"He's in Chicago at some stupid dermatology convention."

"When did he leave?" Depending on when he left, it might make him a suspect in Nichols's murder.

"This morning. He called me and fired me from the airport!" She started crying again. "I need this job. I'm going to Suffolk Community College. I'm in my first year."

"I'm sure you'll find another job," I said. Especially with that work ethic.

"Right," Penny said, and dabbed her eyes.

I needed to get back to the store, so I got to the point. "Why did you want to see me?"

She fished out a file from under the blotter and slapped it on top of the desk. "I know you want this," she said, and pushed it toward me. "Serves him right."

"What is it?"

"It's Dr. Neville's file on the work he did with your aunt. I think he was trying to do something with it. Every time I went into his office, he was on the phone with this file in front of him. It sounded like he was trying to sell something."

My hands shook slightly as I picked up the file, opened it, and pulled out a few pages. It looked like some sort of formula with an extensive list of ingredients. Was this the missing Fresh Face formula? I looked more closely. No, it had been written by Neville, not Claire. Had he been cribbing notes on her formula when they met? Was he trying to sell the information? I had to get this to Randy McCarty at Green Focus. And fast.

I left Penny a small bottle of Rescue Remedy to help calm her nerves and headed back to base. I could have called McCarty from the car, but I wanted to do it back at the office, where I could focus. I did call Jackson and leave a message, updating him on the latest development.

I reached the store, and Qigong and I met Hector at the back door. He bent down to pet the dog. "Willow, we're just setting up. It's going to look beautiful. The yard sale finds were indeed treasures." His eyes sparkled with glee.

I smiled at him. "That's wonderful, Hector. I'll come up in a minute." Qigong and I went to the office, where he hopped up on the couch and I hopped into the office chair and grabbed Aunt Claire's iPhone. Before I could call McCarty, Merrily walked in and flopped in the guest chair. Stephen followed and stood in the doorway, keeping an eye on the shop. I looked out past him and watched Nick head toward the stairs. He wore his workout clothes, loose-fitting pants and a Kripalu Center for Yoga & Health T-shirt, from a retreat in the Berkshires of western Massachusetts that he visited at least two times a year. I planned to go up there this fall, if things went back to normal. Whatever that was. Nick threw me a wave. Strange that he didn't stop in.

"We've got a problem," Merrily said.

Another one? I put down the phone and blew out a breath. I really missed my nap.

"The register is short. I think Janice may have done it."

"What makes you think that?"

"Because when she first came in, she didn't go right to your office. She was prowling around the aisles."

"We couldn't keep an eye on her because we had people to serve," Stephen said.

"After she left, I noticed that the five hundred dollars that was stuffed under the drawer, our just-in-case money, was gone," Merrily said.

"Just-in-case money?"

"Claire always kept five hundred dollars in the cash drawer. Just in case there was an emergency. She started doing it after 9/11. Said we needed to be prepared."

That sounded like Aunt Claire. Taking precautions, sort of. Like the hidey-hole in the floor. But unfortunately, she didn't take them far enough.

"Okay, I'll look into it," I said. "Right now, I've got to make a call."

"We just thought you should know." Merrily got up and headed to the door. "I hate thinking she did this, but no one else was around. Unless it was a customer," she added, and raised her eyebrows.

"Don't worry. We'll find out what's going on." And put a nice pair of handcuffs on light-fingered Miss Janice.

She nodded and the two of them went back into the store. I scrolled through Aunt Claire's iPhone for McCarty's number and called him. When he answered, I told him what I'd found.

"This is great! You've found the stolen formula," he exclaimed.

Not so fast. "No, I don't think so. These notes weren't written by Aunt Claire. They were written by Neville. But I do think he might be trying to sell his research. Right now, he's at a dermatology conference in Chicago; I thought you could send your man to check him out." I gave him Neville's hotel address. Penny had been only too happy to oblige.

"Right away. And, Dr. McQuade, thank you."

# chapter twenty

**Dear Dr. McQuade,**
I've heard that yoga can help keep you young. Are all forms of yoga good for this, or are some more helpful than others?
    Signed,
    Looking for the Fountain of Youth

**Dear Looking for the Fountain of Youth,**
All forms of yoga are beneficial to mind, body, and spirit. But if you want to try something new, consider laughter, or hasya yoga, created by an Indian doctor, Madan Kataria, MD, which is gaining in popularity in the U.S., India, and other countries. It not only boosts immunity but also helps depression. Research shows that twenty seconds of a good belly laugh equals three minutes on a rowing machine! Visit www.laughter yoga.org for more information. Laughter is indeed good medicine!
    Signed,
    Dr. Willow McQuade

Before I could head upstairs, I got a return call from Mr. Matthews. I told him about Janice's visit.

"She just delivered a copy to me," he said. "This is definitely going to delay settling the will. And I know you have operating expenses."

"Yes," I said. "I need the estate to be settled so I can pay for the roof and keep this place going."

"Let me talk to her lawyer and see what I can do," he said. "Try to remain calm."

I put the phone down and took a few deep breaths. I'd missed my yoga and meditation practice this morning. I decided to head upstairs and do some light stretches to try and focus. I also wanted to check on Nick.

I found him sitting in the lotus position, facing the window that overlooked the bay. The low afternoon sunlight glinted off the water. People walked their dogs in Mitchell Park. A small boy flew a kite with his dad. The Shelter Island ferry plowed through the water, headed for the Greenport dock. Life as usual. But life without Aunt Claire was anything but.

"Oh, Willow. Hi, honey." Nick untangled his long legs, stood up, and gave me a kiss on the cheek.

As I hugged him, I tried not to let my imagination get the better of me, but I definitely smelled liquor on his breath. His eyes were red-rimmed and rheumy-looking, and he seemed suddenly old, which made me sad. "Nick, you okay?"

"I don't think you could say that, no."

"You're having a hard time, I know." I wasn't going to tell him that I'd seen Polly at his house or overheard their conversation.

He sighed. "I could have done more."

I felt the knife twist. "We all could have done more." I could easily go to the dark side myself, but I'd been focused on finding answers. Now that blackness threatened to descend again. Going to bed seemed like a good idea, but I didn't have that luxury.

Nick sat in the lotus position again. "I'd like to be alone if you don't mind, Willow."

I put my hand on his shoulder. "Okay, but if you want to talk, I'm here."

I left him, thinking about how I could help him, and headed upstairs, as I told Hector I would.

The bedrooms had been transformed. Allie's work space was now bright and inviting, with her massage table pushed up next to the window that overlooked the harbor. She'd lit several candles, and the scent of magnolia blossoms filled the air. Miniature yellow roses bloomed from the vase Hector had found. The pink-and-yellow-flowered rug on the floor and the pink love seat fit in perfectly.

"Oh, Allie, this is a treat," I said. "It's so you! Are you happy with it?"

Allie hugged me. "Yes, yes! I'm so glad to be here. Hector is, too." She took me by the hand and led me next door. Hector's space was equally as inviting, with the mellow green walls, his treatment table, the new desk, a tan throw rug, and a vase filled with hot-pink gerbera daisies. Outside the windows, the canopy of trees infused the space with even more green.

Hector smiled. "This is just perfect. Thank you, Willow, for the opportunity to practice here."

"I'd say this calls for a celebration," Allie said. "Vine Bar, anyone? My treat."

That sounded like a great idea. But I needed to make a stop first. "I'll meet you there."

Polly's Peaceful Yoga did look peaceful. A class was in session, led by Polly, but I didn't see Janice. Summoning up the nerve to confront her, I crossed the street and walked up the steps. As I entered the store, the class ended and Polly headed to the back of the studio. I craned my head around the corner. Gavin Milton, wearing a Powerhouse Gym T-shirt, stood at the back door, along with Dan Polumbo. Connection made.

Polly went over to them and they began talking. I expected fireworks between her and Gavin, but the conversation seemed amiable, which was surprising considering their contentious divorce. Now everything seemed hunky-dory between them. Polly, who wore a skintight purple leotard that emphasized her breasts and butt, twirled her ponytail on the tip of her finger and gave him a big smile. Gavin leaned over and said something, then kissed her, and the two men left. A quick but telling visit.

Polly spotted me, frowned, and came over to the counter. Along with herbs and supplements, I noticed that she also sold bee-based products, mostly soaps and candles. I wondered if she got them from Helen's Organics. "I'm surprised to see you here."

I'd been surprised to see Polly and Gavin acting so friendly. "I thought you two were divorced."

"So that means we can't be friends?" She crossed her arms protectively over her chest. "Besides, it's really none of your business."

I moved on to my next question. "So Gavin and Dan Polumbo are friends?"

"That's none of your business, either, but yes, they're friends. They met at the gym when the Polumbos moved out here a few years ago. They were big fans of your aunt Claire. Until she almost killed their son."

"That was not her fault," I said.

"Of course you'd say that," Polly replied, rolling her eyes.

"But if it wasn't for Gavin, Sue would have given up on natural remedies entirely. He made her a convert, despite what happened with Tad."

I wondered if Gavin had taught Sue well enough so she'd known how to poison the flower remedy that killed Aunt Claire.

"So what do you want?" Polly said, impatient. "I'm busy."

The yoga studio was empty, and she had no customers. Okay.

"I want to talk to Janice."

She narrowed her eyes. "I thought she came over to see you this afternoon."

"She did. This is about something else. Where is she?"

She shrugged. "Her shift is over. She went to the Vine Bar. But she's not going to want to talk to you, I can tell you that."

I headed for the door. "I'll take my chances."

When I reached the Vine Bar, Allie and Hector had already commandeered a table outside on the patio. The place had a really nice energy despite the fact that Janice sat at the end of the bar. Rich reds and rustic browns dominated the decor, along with lots of green, leafy plants and flowerpots on the windowsills. Along the walls were framed colorful labels from various wineries, including brands from California and New Zealand. Of course, East End brands were represented, too, everyone from Pindar to Bedell Cellars to Paumanok.

Outside, the patio featured black wrought-iron tables and chairs surrounded by a white picket fence covered in vines and twinkling white lights. Before it became the Vine Bar, the place had been a shambles, a house long since fallen into disrepair, but had been reborn, as many businesses in Greenport had been, thanks to the economic boom years past. Now tourism kept things going.

Allie and Hector, who had staked out a large table on the patio, spotted me and waved. I waved back and walked over to Janice, who nursed a large glass of red wine.

I ordered a glass of local pinot noir and sat down. "Janice."

She groaned. "I'm trying to relax. I don't want to talk."

"We have a problem at the store."

"Another one? I'm surprised it's still open, given that you know nothing about running one."

"Some money was stolen from the register. We noticed it after you came in."

Her face twisted into a frown. "Well, I didn't take it. I don't steal what's not mine. Unlike you."

"The store is mine. This is what Aunt Claire wanted."

Her face became beet red as she shook with fury. "It's my store! Stop saying that!"

"I won't, because it's the truth. And you have to accept it."

"Accept this!" she said as she spilled the wine all over my jeans. She got up and stormed out.

After I got a towel from the owner and dabbed off my pants, I went outside and updated Allie and Hector. They decided food was the answer and ordered a cheese platter, with bleu, Camembert, goat-milk Gouda, and crisp crackers. Eventually, I was able to relax, and talk turned to our future plans for the business. Yes, Janice, Aunt Claire's murder, and the missing formula were still at the forefront of my mind, but just for a moment I wanted to put it aside. I tuned in to what Allie was saying.

"I've put our new location on Facebook, so people can 'like' us, and on LinkedIn," Allie said. "And I'm tweeting about it, too."

"We can do a YouTube video about our services at Nature's Way as well," Hector said. "It's easy to do."

"Great," I said. "On the low-tech front, I think we should go to the local chamber of commerce meetings."

"That's a good idea," Hector said. "We need to get to know everyone here."

We talked about the services they wanted to provide. Hector would be offering traditional acupuncture, which balances yin and yang and unblocks chi, the vital life energy. Acupuncture is also effective at reducing pain, inflammation, stress, and chronic conditions and even elevating mood. Allie had been trained in Swedish massage, developed in Stockholm hundreds of years ago and known to be fantastic for boosting the level of oxygen in the blood, releasing toxins, and improving circulation.

"I'd also like to offer clients deep-tissue massage for knots and chronic muscle tension," Allie said. Deep-tissue massage uses strokes across the grain of the muscles, rather than with the grain, as in Swedish massage. "It really helps to tamp down inflammation and eliminate scar tissue."

She sipped her cabernet. "I can do trigger point and hot stone therapy, too." Trigger point massage therapy focuses on a tight area that refers pain to other parts of the body. A trigger point in the back, for example, can cause pain in the neck. Trigger point massage gets rid of toxins and releases those feel-good endorphins, which helps decrease pain. Hot stone therapy reduces muscle tension and stiffness and boosts circulation. Not to mention it feels so good.

"I think this all sounds excellent for one Mr. Jackson Spade. I'm convinced you two can help him get better. You'll just need to talk him through it, although he's obviously open to the alternative healing route."

"I want to tell him about that new study in the *Archives of Internal Medicine* last year that showed acupuncture helps back pain better than pain meds and physical therapy," Hector said. "It will give him more confidence in the method."

"Good thinking, Hector," I said. The door to the patio opened and Jackson appeared. He headed down the stairs and over to us, looking a little less hunched but still uncomfortable.

"We were just talking about how we can help you," I said.

"I hope you can," Jackson said as he sat down next to me. "Merrily told me where you'd be." He flipped open his pad.

I looked at all his scribbling. "You've been busy," I said. "Would you like a drink? Soda, seltzer?" The minute I said it, I realized my mistake. I knew Jackson was an alcoholic thanks to Mike. But he didn't know I knew, and he probably didn't want anyone else to know, either.

But he just kept his head down and flipped through the pages. "I've still got more work to do, but from what I can tell, all of our suspects are still viable: Janice, Gavin, Polly, the Polumbos, Helen, Dr. Neville. The time of death was between ten and twelve last night. You dig up anything new?"

I told him about the possibility that Janice was a thief and my visit to Polly's Peaceful Yoga, where I saw Polly and Gavin together. "They may be divorced, but they aren't enemies."

Jackson chewed the end of his Bic pen. "It's possible they were working together to drive Claire out of business. When that didn't happen fast enough, they killed her. And stole the formula."

"Exactly." I sipped the pinot noir. "Plus, Polly gets the extra bonus of ending up with Nick. At least in her own mind."

Jackson pointed to my wrist, still in the cast. "Whoever it is, now they're after you. The note telling you to get out, hitting you on the head, cutting the brake lines, running you off the road, even that fish in the box. You're going to need to continue being careful. We don't know what's going on here. Nichols may have been behind all of this or just some of this. So don't let down your guard. Period."

"He's right," Allie said, taking a swallow of her wine. "You shouldn't be alone. Ever."

The front gate opened and two men entered. One of them was the unpleasant man from the puppy store, and the other was a rough-looking guy who seemed vaguely familiar. I lowered my voice as they walked past us. "This guy should be on the list, too. We had a kind of run-in the other day. They're trying to open a pet store, and Aunt Claire and her friends were against it." We watched as the two men went inside the bar.

"Stay here," Jackson said. "I'll see what I can find out."

Allie nodded toward Jackson as he walked away. "Not to repeat myself, Willow, but yum-*my*."

She was absolutely right, of course. His butt looked fantastic in his jeans, and his broad shoulders were to die for. I felt a buzz of electricity as I watched him climb the stairs and go inside. Allie gave me a pointed look and I felt myself blush. "He's very helpful. And very nice."

"He's nice all right," Allie said, and drank some of her wine.

Hector nodded and gave me a knowing smile. "Yes, very nice."

We continued our discussion about the ins and outs of our new business venture until Jackson returned five minutes later carrying a glass of what looked like seltzer and lime.

"That was quick," I said as he sat down again.

"They gave me lots of attitude but no info," Jackson said. "I'll have to go another way."

"Another way?" I asked.

"Let me worry about it," he said.

I was about to say that I'd shared all my info with him and he needed to reciprocate so we were on the same page when Simon rounded the corner.

"Willow!" he yelled as he came through the gate. Dressed in a Greenport T-shirt, khaki shorts, and Jack Purcell sneakers and wearing retro Ray-Bans, he made a beeline for our table, carrying a thick sheaf of papers. His nose was black-and-blue and still swollen, but he seemed in good spirits, surely due to the painkillers he was taking. He dropped into a chair on the other side of me, pushed his sunglasses up onto his head, and put the manuscript and a copy of the *New York Times* and *Newsday* down on the table.

"You come here to work?" I said. "Starbucks seems like a better idea."

"That's what you say," Simon said. "This is more fun." He said hi to Allie, whom he knew from her visits to L.A., then looked at Hector and Jackson. "So, introduce me."

"Simon, this is Hector Solo and Jackson Spade," I said, gesturing to them. "Jackson's helping me look into Aunt Claire's murder."

"Oh, that again," he said. "I hope you can convince her it's not her job to get involved. She doesn't know anything about running a store, let alone solving a murder."

"I think McQuade can do whatever she sets her mind to," Jackson said.

I savored the gooey, warm feeling his compliment gave me. The fact that he believed in me was definitely a huge plus in his favor.

Simon, on the other hand, didn't seem to like it at all. Instead of responding, he pointed to the newspaper. "That cop

Koren told a reporter that they didn't think the events were random and that there was a personal motive. He said that the public shouldn't be alarmed. That they had it all under control. It sounds like they know what they're doing."

"We're not sure about that," Jackson said. "As a former cop—"

"You said it, buddy, *former,* as in not now," he said in a snarky tone. "You two better leave it to professionals." He opened the wine menu. "So, what are we having, kids?"

I pointed to my glass of wine. "We're all set. And I'm not sure you should be drinking while you're on those painkillers."

He waved that suggestion away and called over a short, stocky busboy with a peach fuzz beard who was clearing an adjacent table. His name tag read *Tad* and I wondered if this was Dan and Sue's son. I'd pictured him as a young, innocent boy, but he was anything but. He looked dark and brooding, menacing even.

"Excuse me," I said anyway. "Is your last name Polumbo by any chance?"

The kid shoved the cleanup rag into the front pocket of his apron. "Yeah, I'm Tad Polumbo. Who's asking?"

Simon stiffened. "Is your father Dan?"

"Yeah, so?" He started to clear the table next to us.

"You see this?" He pointed at his nose. "Your father did this to me."

"You're lying!" Tad yelled, throwing the rag on the table. "He wouldn't."

"He did," Simon said, gesturing to me. "I was trying to defend her aunt Claire."

"Oh, her," Tad said, like he was describing the dregs of the earth. "Serves her right she ended up dead. She almost killed me!"

I shook my head no. "My aunt didn't know your entire medical history. Your mother didn't tell her you had asthma. She would have been more conservative in her approach. I know that."

"That's BS. My mom and dad said it was all her fault!" His voice got even louder, and I wondered if he should be on the suspect list, too. He was big enough and angry enough to have killed Aunt Claire.

"Let's all calm down now," Jackson said. "Take it easy, Tad."

"Yeah, kid. Get me a waiter," Simon said, waving him away. "Make yourself useful."

"I oughta slug you, too." He lurched toward Simon. "My old man had the right idea."

Simon put his hands up to defend his nose, and Hector jumped up and grabbed Tad. Hearing the commotion, the pet shop boys exited the Vine Bar and marched over to us.

"You got trouble, Tad?" the unpleasant man from the pet store asked.

"Yeah, Lenny, I got trouble," Tad said, spitting the words out. "These people are all in with that Claire Hagan broad. She hurt me, she hurt my family."

"Oh, we know all about her, don't we, Billy?"

"Bitch makes it hard for us to do business," Billy snarled.

"This is her niece," Tad said, and pointed to me.

"Oh yeah?" Billy came around the table and put his face in mine. I made the connection, finally remembering where I knew him from. He'd been two years ahead of me in high school. Constantly in trouble, expelled three times. And obviously still a menace.

Jackson got up. "Let it go, Billy. Back off," he said, and pulled Billy away from me.

"You back off." Billy swiveled and smashed his fist into Jackson's face. Jackson hit the ground, hard, and I cried out as Lenny started kicking him in the stomach. Hector lurched over and grabbed Lenny by the collar, pulling him away and tearing his shirt, but Billy immediately jumped on him, pounding him with his fists. Tad turned and ran inside to get some help while Simon gathered his manuscript and took off like a jackrabbit. Allie and I stood helplessly by, watching the madness.

Jackson managed to get to his feet, charged like a bull, and knocked Billy backward across our table. The glasses of wine and cheese platter shattered on the brick patio. Billy landed on the ground with an *ooomph!* while Lenny went after Jackson again, but Hector knocked him down with a good right. The two pet shop boys writhed and groaned on the ground.

Action over, Jackson slumped into a chair, all the adrenaline gone and the pain back, a grimace on his face. Hector grabbed a napkin to clean the blood off his bleeding knuckles as the sound of police sirens filled the air, blotting out everything else. All in all, this sure hadn't ended up being the relaxing, quiet night out I'd envisioned.

# chapter twenty-one

Dear Dr. McQuade,

I just got back from a visit to my doctor and she gave me the results of my bone scan. She told me I have osteoporosis. Can any natural remedies help?

Signed,

Boning Up

Dear Boning Up,

I applaud you for wanting to use natural remedies to help heal your osteoporosis. Even though our bones take a beating as we get older and are also affected by smoking, caffeine, alcohol, and soda, which can leach calcium, our bones are living tissue and can regenerate with the right help. One of the best things to do is to aim for an alkaline diet by eating lots of leafy, green veggies and foods that have a pH higher than 7. You can supplement this with a good powdered green-food drink. Weight-bearing exercise is important, too. Calcium gets a lot of buzz, but strontium is more effective. Research shows it builds better bones and helps reduce the pain of osteoporosis.

Signed,

Dr. Willow McQuade

When they heard the sirens, the pet shop boys pulled themselves together, jumped the picket fence, and beat it across the street and behind the IGA grocery store. A cop car zoomed in and stopped at the curb, a dirty blue Ford sedan right behind it. Two uniformed officers got out of the cop car, while Detectives Koren and Coyle stepped out of the Ford. Coyle, dressed in a cheap-looking blue seersucker suit and wearing shades, and Koren, in a tailored Brooks Brothers suit, took their sweet time as they walked to the entrance to the patio, opened the gate, and came over to us.

When they did, Koren arched an eyebrow and said, "Getting into trouble again, Dr. McQuade?"

"They're getting away," I said, and pointed across the street.

Koren put his hands on his hips and pushed back his jacket so we could all see his gun in its holster. "Don't tell me. Janice. Again."

I shook my head, frustrated. "No, not Janice. Lenny and Billy, the pet shop boys."

"The pet shop boys?" He blew out a breath. "Explain, please."

I told him about the fight. When I finished, he looked at Jackson. "Thought you had a bad back. How did you manage to get into a fight?"

"It's called fight or flight, officer," I said. "He sensed danger, his adrenaline kicked in, and he was able to act. He was trying to help us."

Koren considered this. "Yes, I've heard he's been helping you. The coroner told me he called about the time of death for Sean Nichols. You're a bit off your patch, wouldn't you say, Spade?"

"I'm trying to help a friend, Koren. That's all."

"Dr. McQuade?" He nodded to me.

"Claire Hagan."

"The disability board might be interested in your extracurricular activities when your case comes up for review next month," Coyle said.

"How do you know about that?" Jackson asked.

"We know everything," Koren said, sounding smug. "And I'll be happy to let them know that you're doing quite well. Hell, maybe you don't need that disability after all, Spade."

"That's ridiculous," I said. "He's not doing well; he's in constant pain."

Jackson put his hand on my arm and said, "McQuade, I can handle this myself."

"You can if you get smart and stay out of this case," Koren said. The two detectives headed up the steps and went inside.

"What absolute asses," Allie said. Such a comment was big for Allie, who rarely had an unkind word to say about anyone.

We watched Koren and Coyle as they talked to Tad and a woman I presumed was the manager. Tad waved and gestured. The woman remained calm.

Jackson groaned as he sat down. "I'm going to pay for this big-time."

"He can't touch you," I said, concerned about what Koren might do now. "He's bluffing."

"I meant my back," Jackson said. "It's already in spasm. Those two bozos don't worry me."

Hector sat down next to him. "I can help you. The B-fifty-four acupressure point behind your knees can relieve back pain and pressure. But I'll need to get you on the table. We can go after this."

"I'll follow up with a massage," Allie said.

"Hopefully we can wrap this up quickly," I said. "And get out of here."

A few minutes later, Detectives Koren and Coyle trotted down the steps and came back over to us. "You're very lucky, Dr. McQuade, you and your friends," Koren said. "The manager doesn't want to press charges. She doesn't want any negative publicity. We've also got more important things to do."

"Like find Sean Nichols's and Claire Hagan's killers?" I asked.

Koren pulled me aside and lowered his voice. "Sean Nichols had in his possession an envelope with Claire's name and *Fresh Face* written on it. Know anything about that, Dr. McQuade?"

I played dumb. "He did? Does that mean he stole the formula and killed my aunt?"

Koren's phone buzzed. "That would wrap things up nicely for you, wouldn't it?" He pulled his phone out of his pocket and looked at the message. "No, we don't think it's that simple. You're still on my list of suspects." He eyed Jackson and dropped the phone back into his pocket. "Stay out of this, Dr. McQuade, and you, too, Spade. Let us do our jobs." They slipped through the fence and headed to their car.

The four of us hurried back to Nature's Way and helped Jackson upstairs so he could begin his acupuncture treatment. "Since it's late, I'll do an abbreviated session, but it will still mitigate the tumble you took tonight," Hector said. "We'll follow up tomorrow and Allie can give you a massage then, too."

"I appreciate this," Jackson said.

"Not at all," Hector said. "Now please take off your T-shirt and lie down."

It took some effort, but Jackson managed to pull it over his head. His chest was buff and muscled, with a few distinguishing scars that looked like they could be bullet wounds. Definitely super hot.

He got onto the table and lay on a special body-sized heating pad. Once he was settled, Hector said, "Since you have acute lower back pain, Jackson, we'll want to invigorate your chi and blood to remove the stagnation and unblock the channels, which will stop the pain." He looked at Allie and me. "Do you mind if they watch? Willow is interested in seeing my technique."

"Have at it," he said, turning his head and giving me a deep, penetrating look. "Thanks for the help."

"Quid pro quo, remember? I promised."

"Indeed you did, McQuade." He closed his eyes. "I'll see you on the other side."

We watched silently as Hector inserted various super-thin, pliable needles into Jackson's skin. I glanced at the chart on the wall. For acute lower back pain, the first distal acupuncture point he targeted was Liver 3 on the foot, one of the most important acupuncture points. Jackson winced slightly as he inserted the needle. Next, he inserted LI 4, Du 26, (N-UE 19), and finally BL 40, and then said, "That's enough for now. We'll do more tomorrow."

He adjusted the temperature of the mat and dimmed the lights. "This BioMat is something you might want at home, Jackson. It's a special heating pad that has far infrared healing rays, amethysts, and negative ions. Very therapeutic. A far infrared sauna is also good for detoxification afterward."

"Hmm-hum," Jackson said sleepily.

"We'll leave you now for about twenty minutes. It's okay if you fall asleep."

"Hmm-hum," Jackson repeated.

The three of us went downstairs to get a cup of tea. Hector

and Allie waited at a table next to the window while Qigong followed me as I moved around the kitchen, putting the water on and depositing tea bags into mugs. I'd been in there only a minute when Allie came hustling in with a worried look on her face. "Someone is watching the store," she said, and tugged me on the arm. "Come and see."

Hector stood by the front door, looking through the windowpanes on the top. "They're in the park. I think they have binoculars. Look to the right of your van." I stood next to him and peered out. To the right of our van, I saw two people. I couldn't tell if it was the pet shop boys.

"Aunt Claire has a pair of binoculars, too. I saw them in her bookcase." I ran into the office and grabbed the pair, which sat on a shelf next to new-age DVDs, including those of Catherine Ponder, Louise Hay, and Deepak Chopra. I ran back out and focused on the two shadows, standing to one side of the carousel but just out of range of a large spotlight. Damn it.

"I'm going out," Hector said.

"I'm going with you," I said.

Hector shook his head. "That's not a good idea. Maybe we should call that detective."

I shook my head no. "Not until we have real proof." I turned to Allie and said, "You wait here. If we don't come back right away or you see something bad happen, call the cops and tell Jackson." I checked to make sure I had my cell phone. "I'll call you in a few minutes."

"I don't like this," Allie said, shivering.

"I don't like it, either," I said. "But we're in this now."

Hector and I made our way out the back door, cut behind Nan's Needlework, and crossed Front Street to the other side of the post office. The building blocked our approach. Once across, we headed toward the water and to the path that cut through the back of Mitchell Park and circled behind the carousel.

When we got to the carousel, we could see the two people talking, while one of them, the shorter one, who could be a woman, kept the binoculars trained on Nature's Way. Since the first and third floor lights were on, I figured they were waiting for them to go off before making a move. But as we approached, one of them took off across the street. I still couldn't tell who he or she was. The other person remained in place and I noticed a few strands of long, blond hair snaking out from under the watch cap the person wore. Polly?

We moved closer through the damp grass to the edge of the carousel. A light flickered from the steps of Nature's Way. A signal perhaps? The person with the binoculars ran across the street, and before we could follow, Qigong began barking from inside the store. The flickering light on the steps went out, and moments later we heard a soft whooshing sound. The two people took off at a dead run toward the drugstore and 1st Street while Hector and I ran over to see what had happened. All four tires on the van had been slashed.

# chapter twenty-two

**Dear Dr. McQuade,**
My doctor tells me I've got high blood pressure. I know
I need to manage my stress more effectively, but how
can I change my diet to help? Are there any special
foods that lower blood pressure?
    Signed,
    Too High

**Dear Too High,**
Yes, you are right, handling stress is a top priority when
you have high blood pressure. Qigong breathing exercises can help. Qigong breathing is basically conscious
breathing, with slow, gentle, deep breaths. To learn
how, visit www.SpringForestQigong.com. The right diet
can help as well. You can start by using the DASH diet
(www.dashdiet.org) to reduce both systolic and dia-
stolic blood pressure. This diet, which focuses on fruits,
veggies, whole grains, high fiber, and low-fat foods, can
also help to lower "bad" cholesterol. Fun fact? Chocolate can help, too. The flavonoids in cocoa act as antioxidants and are good for cardiovascular function. Make it
a habit to have an ounce of dark chocolate that is high
in cacao content (at least 70 percent) once a day. Yum!
    Signed,
    Dr. Willow McQuade

"So they slashed the tires and ran?" Jackson asked us. The four of us and Qigong were back upstairs in Hector's treatment room.

"I swear one of them was Polly," I said. "Whoever it was had long, blond hair. Hector chased after them, but they had a good head start."

"Track was not my strong suit." Hector picked Jackson's red-and-white flannel shirt up off the hutch and handed it to him. "Keep warm. We don't want those muscles to tense up."

Jackson sat up, pulled on the shirt, and eased off the table. "Obviously, they haven't given up. Even if they do have the formula. Even if they did kill Claire. Exhibit A." He pointed to my left arm, which was still in a cast. "Like we agreed at the Vine Bar, I think we're going to have to be much more careful going forward."

"Every question we ask seems to stir up a lot of trouble," I said. "I just want justice. I want the truth. I owe it to her."

"Walk me out," Jackson said to me, and took my arm. I felt a zing of electricity pass between us so strong it almost took my breath away. We headed down the stairs in silence, and when we got to the bottom he turned to me. "With everything that's happened, I think we have to consider abandoning the idea that we can solve this thing. Maybe Koren was right, it's better left to professionals."

"You are a professional."

He shook his head. "Willow, I *was* a professional. I'm retired. On disability. I can barely get around. You were right—if it hadn't been for that adrenaline rush, I never would have been able to take on those two boneheads. This is getting complicated. And I'm worried about you."

"You're worried about me?"

He smiled. "Let's just say that you've grown on me, McQuade. You've got guts. I like your style."

"Back atcha, Spade." I punched him on the arm like I was in third grade.

We stood there awkwardly for a few moments, and then Jackson shoved his hands into his pockets. "Guess I should be going."

We walked down the aisle, past the dairy refrigerator, fruit juices, coconut water, and snacks, to the front of the store. I made small talk to dispel any weirdness. "But Hector helped you, didn't he? You feel better?"

"Yes, I feel much looser and my muscles feel energized somehow. I almost feel normal. Thank you, Willow."

"It's part of our personal service."

"Is that right?" He gave me that 100-watt stare and crooked smile.

I felt all gooey inside. "Yes, that's right." It was one of those moments that could go either way. Would we kiss or not?

Jackson leaned in and I closed my eyes. Then the front door flew open and Simon stepped in.

"Willow, you okay?" Simon said as he rushed over to me. He held his manuscript in one hand and a Starbucks cup in the other. Obviously, he'd made it there after all. "I was worried about you." He gulped down some coffee.

Now he was worried? What about during the big fight? And with the cops? Self-centered Simon. But what good would it do to fight? "Simon, I'm fine. Thanks for checking."

"No problem, no problem," he said, clearly hyper from the caffeine. He hooked his thumb in Jackson's direction. "What's he doing here?"

Jackson pushed past him. "I've got to get going. I'm sure you'll be safe with Simon," he said, a bemused expression on his face. "We'll talk in the a.m. I've got an early morning appointment with Hector and Allie. Night."

After Jackson left, Simon processed this development. Willow with another man. "So he's why you don't want to get back together?"

"We're working on the case," I said. "He's helping me figure out who killed Aunt Claire and who stole her formula."

"I'll bet," Simon said, thinking about this. "He's definitely into you. That's just an excuse to hang around."

"Claire was important to him," I said. "That's why he's helping me."

Simon snorted. "Whatever."

I started to turn off the lights in the front of the store. Maybe he would take the hint. "Simon, it's late. I want to go to bed."

He took a sip of his coffee and eyed me over the lid. "Sure you want to sleep alone?"

Actually, I would have liked it if Jackson had slept over, but I kept that idea to myself. For now. "I'm sure."


Okay, so sleeping alone was a lot less fun than sleeping with Jackson would have been. Well, I wasn't exactly alone, since I had Qigong, Ginger, and Ginkgo to keep me company. For some reason, though, I overslept, and the next morning, by the time I'd done a few sun salutations, a seated meditation, showered, dressed, and opened the door to head downstairs, Jackson had stepped onto the third-floor landing and was headed for Allie's treatment room.

"Mornin', McQuade."

"Mornin', Spade. Here for your next session?"

He nodded. "Allie is going to give me a hot stone treatment, and then Hector will give me a tune-up. He's got some exercises I can do at home, too."

Allie stepped out of her room, holding a lavender candle. She lit it with a match and smiled at Jackson. "You are going to love this treatment. It's just heaven. It just melts away stress, tension, and muscle stiffness."

"What exactly are you going to do to me?" Jackson arched an eyebrow.

"I'm going to place smooth, water-heated stones at key points on your back to relax your muscles and tissues, which will release toxins and improve your circulation. After that, I'll give you a full body massage." Her cell phone rang inside her room and she went to answer it. "Come in when you're ready."

"I'll be right there, Allie, thanks." He pulled me aside. "Have you given any thought to what I said about leaving this investigation to the cops?"

"Nothing to think about," I said. "I'm in this thing and I'm hoping you are, too. But you're under no obligation. The sessions are free no matter what. We agreed."

"Uh-huh." He rubbed his chin. "You mean if I don't help you, you're going to do it anyway?"

"You bet."

Jackson blew out a sigh. "I was afraid of that."

Allie came back out and pointed to her watch. "We'd better get started. It's nine and I just booked an appointment at ten. Word must be getting around about our services. Merrily has our cards by the counter."

"And when you Facebook and tweet and get LinkedIn, you'll have even more," I said, glad things were moving in a positive direction despite recent events. People either didn't know or didn't care about what had happened here, which might have a lot to do with an interview that Koren had given to *Newsday*. Not that I was going to thank him.

"I think Claire advertised in the *Suffolk Times*," Jackson said. "Maybe they'll do a story on you. Maybe if you focus on the business rather than you-know, you'd feel better."

"I don't think so," I said pointedly, determined to find Aunt Claire's killer, even at the expense of a promising budding romance.

Merrily ran up the steps, holding an energy drink and wired as usual. "We need to get the bread, and since the van is out, can Stephen borrow your car?"

I fished out the keys and gave them to her. "Can you call the mechanic and have him come over, too?"

"On it." She spun on her heel and ran back down the stairs.

"She's hopped up on caffeine. Just like your friend Simon last night. Kind of late for him to be stopping by, wasn't it?" He folded his arms in front of his chest and appraised me.

"Simon acts on impulse. He doesn't bother with things like checking the time. It's part of the reason we are no longer together."

He arched an eyebrow. "Oh, so you two used to be involved?"

"Yes, but not anymore."

He uncrossed him arms and took a step toward me. "So you're back on the market?"

Before I could answer, Hector came out of the apartment opposite and gave Jackson a once-over. "Feel any better?"

Jackson kneaded his lower back and looked at me. "Yes. And I'm ready for more."

At eleven o'clock, Hector opened his door and invited me in. "We're just about done." Jackson lay on the table.

"How do you feel?" I asked him.

"More opened up. Like the energy is flowing. Does that make sense?"

"Yes, indeed," Hector said. "Okay, now bend your knees to your chest." Jackson did so. "Place your fingertips in the center of the crease behind each of your knees." Jackson managed to do this, too. "Okay, now holding on to the points, gently rock your legs back and forth."

Jackson looked at Hector skeptically. "You're kidding, right?"

"Not at all. Try doing it for just one minute."

Jackson, looking ever more the pretzel, rocked back and forth a few times on the table. "Good," Hector said. "Good. Now let your feet rest flat on the table with your knees bent and relax."

Jackson did as he said. "I do feel like some tension is being released."

"If you do this three times a day, you will notice a difference within a week," he instructed, helped Jackson sit up. Just then we heard a zinging noise, and the glass in the window next to the table shattered. Jackson went down.

# chapter twenty-three

**Dear Dr. McQuade,**
My grandfather has heart disease, and I told him that there were lots of foods and supplements that can help your heart. He doesn't believe me. What can I tell him specifically to convince him to go natural?
   Signed,
   I Heart My Grandpa

**Dear I Heart My Grandpa,**
It's great that you want to help your grandfather feel better and be healthier. First, it's important that he follow the American Heart Association's guidelines for eating healthy. This means eating a varied, balanced diet with lots of fruits and veggies and fiber, 25 to 30 grams a day for heart health. It's also important to achieve and maintain a healthy weight and keep blood pressure and cholesterol at healthy levels. One of the easiest ways to reduce cholesterol is by eating foods that are fortified with plant sterols, which help to block its absorption. You'll find plant sterols in everything from OJ to margarine or in a supplement. Co-enzyme Q10 is another important nutrient that supports heart and blood vessel function. Take 100 to 300 milligrams a day. Whatever you try, though, be sure to check with his doctor first.
   Signed,
   Dr. Willow McQuade

Jackson dropped to the floor, rolled onto his back, and groaned. Blood began to seep through the shoulder of his white T-shirt. His eyes fluttered closed and then opened again, but he had the presence of mind to say to Hector and me, "Get down!"

I did as he said, but then reached up to grab a jade-green hand towel from the table and pressed it into the wound. Hector crawled across to his desk, grabbed his cell, and called 911. Allie and her ten o'clock client, Sammy Braff, the woman who I believed had hypothyroidism, ran in.

"What's going on?" Allie said, clearly in a panic.

"For God's sake, get down and stay down, everyone," Jackson yelled.

The two of them hit the floor and crawled over to us. "Jackson's been shot!" I said. Sammy Braff started to cry. Instead of bawling myself, I kept my focus on Jackson and the situation at hand. Was the shooter still out there? Would the cops get here in time?

Jackson didn't wait to find out. Grabbing the towel from me, he kept it pressed into the wound as he crawled over to the window, inched his way up, and then looked out into the backyard before dropping down again. "Whoever it was is gone."

I crawled over to him. "Where do you think they were?"

"In the parking lot, beyond those trees. It's a straight shot into this window."

"First me, now you. Someone obviously wants us out of the way."

Jackson pressed the towel into the wound and winced, but he managed to give me a smile. "You think?"

Detectives Koren and Coyle arrived ten minutes later and had plenty of questions for us. But my main focus was Jackson. The paramedics who arrived shortly after the detectives looked at the wound and bandaged it to stop the bleeding. They wanted to put him on a gurney, but Jackson nixed that. Instead, Hector and one of the paramedics helped Jackson take the stairs, while uniformed officers secured the scene. On the way down, we told Koren and Coyle about the events of last night and this morning.

"Maybe whoever slashed the tires took a shot at you this morning," Koren said. He flipped through his notebook. "There's definitely a pattern of escalating violence here."

"Definitely," Coyle said. "Look at what happened at the Vine Bar last night. This case is a hornets' nest."

The more we talked, the madder I got. If they'd taken the threats against me seriously to begin with, maybe none of this would have happened. But I tried to keep my cool for Jackson's sake.

One of the paramedics opened the back of the ambulance while his partner helped Jackson in and put him on a gurney; then they slammed the door and took off for the hospital. I headed to my car to follow them there.

Koren and Coyle walked to the edge of the parking lot and looked into the trees. Koren called to the two police officers with him and told them to establish a perimeter and put up crime scene tape to protect the area until the criminalist got there.

When they came over to me, Koren said, "So you and Spade knocking boots or what?" and gave me a smarmy look I didn't like. Coyle laughed into his hand.

"That is none of your business," I said as I reached the car and opened the door.

"Doctor, when it comes to this case, everything is our business," Koren said, slipping his notebook into his inside pocket. "The sooner you accept that, the better off we'll all be."

I gave them a withering look. "You're pretty cocky considering that this is all your fault. If you'd found Aunt Claire's killer, you could have prevented Jackson from being shot. I'm thinking of suing your department for negligence. Tell your chief to be expecting my call."

I really didn't intend to sue, but I did leave a message for the chief of police on my way to the hospital. Koren and Coyle needed to be set straight. Their duty was to protect and serve, but I'd seen little evidence of that so far.

Jackson was in surgery for more than two hours, and it was late afternoon before the doctor came out to the waiting room to talk to me. The bullet had gone right through but he needed to stay in the hospital for a few days before being released. Within a few weeks, he'd be as good as new.

When I walked into his hospital room, Jackson was sleeping. With his long eyelashes and scruffy beard, he looked, well, as Allie had said, yum-*my*. I quietly sat down in the chair by his bed and sent him good vibes while I waited for him to wake up.

He opened his eyes a few minutes later and smiled. "McQuade, you made it."

"You made it," I said, and smiled back. "That's the important part. How do you feel?"

"Like I've been shot." He pushed on a pump connected to an IV bag. "Good pain meds, though. That helps."

"I just can't believe you got shot."

He shaped his fingers like a gun and pretended to shoot himself. "Danger is my business, McQuade."

"Should I contact anyone to tell them about what happened?"

He shook his head. "My ex-wife and I don't talk anymore, and the rest of my family is all at a reunion upstate. I didn't go because of my back. And I didn't want to spoil their good time." He fixed me with a stern look. "I hope this has convinced you to give up the case, Dr. McQuade."

I returned his gaze. "Nope. I owe it to Aunt Claire to get to the bottom of this."

Jackson whistled. "Oh, boy, I was afraid of that."

"Besides, Koren and Coyle are a bunch of asses. I want to prove to them that they're wrong about me." I told them about our conversation in the parking lot.

"I have to agree that there is a high ass factor there."

"So," I said, clapping my hands together. "You're with me when you get out of here. We'll get back on the case when you feel better?"

"I'll need help," he said, not answering my question. Instead he gazed out the window, which had a view of the harbor's twinkling blue water and the pleasure crafts cruising into their berths at the marina next to the hospital. "I'll get a nurse in to take care of me like last time."

"You won't have to do that," I said. "Hector, Allie, and I talked, and we want to take care of you. You can stay with us. With Hector in his room. Aunt Claire has a queen-size bed, so Allie and I will bunk together."

"Willow, you're not thinking clearly. This is getting deadly serious. You'll have to clear out of the store while I'm in here," he said. "Can't you stay with Nick?"

"Not really," I said. "His place is really small."

"Or your mother or sister?"

I made a face like I smelled a can of tuna fish.

"Then stay at my place," he said. "The keys have to be around here somewhere."

"I don't know."

He took my hand. "Just stay there until I'm out. I have a first-class alarm system in place, and I'll request regular foot and car patrols of the store. My neighbor is an ex–NYPD detective. I'll tell him to keep an eye on all of you."

It would be a great relief to feel safe, and I had a responsibility to Allie and Hector and my animals, too. "Okay," I said. "But when you're released, I want to get back to the store. I need to find that formula; otherwise this won't stop. I can take care of you there at the same time."

"I don't want to be any trouble." He attempted to sit up, but abandoned the idea and lay down again. "On the other hand, it would be a good way for me to keep an eye on you," he added, smiling at me, and then he reached back to adjust his pillows. As he did, one of them fell on the floor.

"You'll be my personal bodyguard," I replied as I picked up the pillow and rearranged it so he'd be more comfortable. As I did, I leaned close to him and our eyes met. Zing! I felt the electricity rush between us like a power line and swallowed hard.

He gave me a look loaded with meaning. "Is that all I am to you, McQuade? A bodyguard?"

"That and more," I said, feeling all gooey inside again.

He put his hand gently behind my head and pulled me in for a kiss. Afterward, he smiled and said, "Now that's what I call first aid."


While Jackson was in the hospital, the cats, Qigong, Hector, Allie, and I camped out at his A-frame house in East Marion, a half hour as the gull flies from Greenport. I used the time to have a state-of-the-art alarm system with motion detectors installed in the store and café that I could pay for over time. I also talked to the chief of police, who spoke to Koren and Coyle. He told me that I could expect their cooperation from now on and gave me his cell phone number just in case. The chief also assigned foot and car patrols around Nature's Way, both on Front Street and in back, by the IGA across from the Vine Bar. During the investigation, they'd found one cartridge shell but no gun.

Even though Koren seemed sincere about turning over a new leaf and taking me seriously, I wasn't going to give up on my own quest to discover the identity of Claire's killer. To that end, I'd e-mailed Sue Polumbo three times asking for a meeting. No reply. I'd also gone through every single contact in Aunt Claire's iPhone, but either they were friends and were shocked to hear about her death or they were business contacts for the store. Nothing they said seemed suspicious.

I picked Jackson up at the hospital at ten a.m. on the Saturday following the shooting, and Hector and I helped get him up to Hector's room on the third floor. We took it slow with Jackson, since his back wasn't in great shape and he had a bullet hole in his shoulder, but when we reached the room, he collapsed, exhausted, on the bed.

Jackson ran his fingers through his hair. "Damn, I'm so wiped. This is embarrassing. I'm back to square one. I feel like I did after the accident."

"Just take it easy, Jackson," I said. "It's all about baby steps."

"Yes," Hector said, smiling. "Listen to your doctor."

Jackson nodded. "I know. I'm just frustrated. Before the accident I wasn't used to feeling weak. I thought I'd made some progress but now it's gone."

"I put that warming mat underneath the sheet," Hector

said. "It will help you feel better. In a few days, we'll start treatments again. I'll target your back and your immune system so you heal faster. Allie's massage will stimulate the immune system, too. We'll have you back to yourself in no time flat."

Since the shooting, I was sure we'd have no other clients and that Hector and Allie could give Jackson their full attention. I had no idea how we would build up good will in the community after everything that had happened, but I pushed that thought out of my head for now.

Jackson gave him a thumbs-up. "Thanks, man."

As Hector headed out, Merrily walked in with a strawberry-banana-mango-coconut smoothie I'd ordered for Jackson. It was chock-full of protein, probiotics, and green foods like young barley grasses, chlorella, and spirulina to help build up his immune system and get rid of toxins. Plus it tasted fantastic.

"This will help get you back on the road to recovery." I took the drink from Merrily and thanked her before she left. Putting the smoothie on the night table, I adjusted the pillows on the bed so Jackson could sit up and drink. But first I checked his stitches, which luckily were still intact.

"This looks good," I said, and put the bandage back on the wound. "It's healing nicely."

"It's all that good energy you have, doctor," he said, and kissed me lightly on the lips.

"Hmmm," I said, liking it. "That must be it." I kissed him again and handed him the smoothie.

He took a sip. "This is fantastic." See?

He took another sip and pointed to his bag. We'd made a stop at his house before heading to Nature's Way. "Can you get out my book?"

"Sure," I said, and pulled out the latest Michael Connelly novel he was reading and put it on the nightstand. He'd started the series at the beginning, with *The Black Echo,* and was now on *The Concrete Blonde.* Next, I pulled out a seven-inch portable DVD player along with a stack of Jackson's DVDs, including *The Wire* and *The Shield,* to keep him entertained while he rested. I wanted to get him set up before I went out.

"The prescription for the painkillers is in there, too," he said, pointing at the bag.

In the side pocket was a prescription for an opiate medicine to help manage his pain. Yes, there are herbal options like willow bark, which contains the salicylates that are used in aspirin products, but the effect is mild and takes time to work effectively. An injury as serious as a gunshot wound demands a more intense and targeted approach, one that works quickly. Conventional medicine has its place, and in this case, a prescription painkiller was the way to go.

"I'll get this filled and will be right back," I said. "I don't want you hurting."

"You're the best medicine I could have," Jackson said, giving me a quick kiss. "But the painkillers will help, too. I've only got a few left."

I said good-bye, went downstairs, put Qigong on his leash, and headed outside. The day was perfect, a real ten. Blue sky, sun, no clouds, the smell of salt in the air. The streets were crammed with tourists who were wending in and out of gift shops, antique shops, the bookstore, and new trendy clothing boutiques. I threaded through the crowds and headed for the drugstore, a white clapboard building on the corner of Front and 1st Streets.

I went to the side door, picked up Qigong, and stepped inside to join the drop-off line. When it was my turn, a pert-looking high-school-age girl told me it would be ten minutes, max. She also thought that Qigong was super cute.

I turned and headed down the aisles to check out the products. It's always good to know what the "other" side is doing. There were all the conventional medicines you'd expect. I picked up a bottle of cough syrup and thought about new research I'd read that shows that honey is just as effective as a cough suppressant. A bottle of antinausea medicine could be replaced with a nice cup of ginger tea. As I examined the shelves, I noticed two people—a short redhead about forty pounds overweight and wearing a track suit, and a tall, thin brunette with squinty eyes dressed in a T-shirt and jeans—looking at me and whispering.

Figuring they were gossiping about events at Nature's Way, I ignored them and made my way down the aisle to the magazine rack at the front of the store . There I found the latest issue of *Whole Living* and flipped through it. The magazine had recently been relaunched and redesigned and was packed with useful content. I made a note to order it for Nature's Way.

After ten minutes, I meandered back toward the counter at the back of the store. But I didn't get that far. At the head of the aisle, the redhead I'd noticed earlier planted herself in front of me and said loudly, "So you're the one."

"Excuse me?"

She folded her arms across her chest. "Claire Hagan's niece. The one who's taking over."

"And you are?"

She raised her voice, clearly angry. "The person you've been harassing by e-mail. Sue Polumbo."

People who were waiting in line turned to look at us.

"That's rich," I said. "I saw the e-mails you sent to my aunt Claire. Talk about harassment."

"She deserved it." Her voice rose and she balled her hands into fists and shook them at me. "She almost killed my son Tad!"

This woman clearly had a very short fuse. "Please calm down," I said as I glanced around at the crowd of people waiting for prescriptions to be filled. They were glued to our conversation as if it were an episode of their favorite TV drama. I lowered my voice and said gently, "I understand you're upset, but that was not her fault. You didn't tell my aunt that your son Tad was an asthmatic. She would have told you to see your regular doctor immediately or to go to the emergency room."

"Of course you'd say that." Spittle flew from her mouth.

"Ms. McQuade," the clerk said. "Your prescription is ready."

Sue laughed bitterly. "A prescription? I thought you believed in natural remedies. You're just as much of a fraud as your aunt was."

I moved to the counter, feeling my face turning beet red, paid for the prescription, and turned back to her. "Can we talk about this outside?"

Aunt Claire, Nature's Way, and I did not need anymore negative publicity.

"Here is fine." She put her hands on her hips and narrowed her beady eyes. "What did you want to talk about?"

"I had a few questions," I said. "I'm looking into Claire's murder."

"I didn't kill your aunt," she snapped. "But I wish I had." She put her finger in my face, and Qigong growled.

"Easy, boy," I said.

"Keep that dog away from me," she snarled, practically spitting the words at me.

I picked Qigong up and waited for her to finish her rant.

"Now, I want you to leave us alone. I know you were talking to Dan's neighbor about us. I know that you questioned Tad at the Vine Bar. I heard about the fight." Her voice got louder as she pushed past me and shoved the door open. But before she left, she had one more thing to say: "Your aunt almost killed my son. Nature's Way should be closed down. Stay out of our lives or you'll be sorry."

# chapter twenty-four

**Dear Dr. McQuade,**
**I'm expecting, and the morning sickness has been re-**
**ally tough to deal with. Are there any natural remedies**
**for nausea?**
   **Signed,**
   **Feeling Queasy**

**Dear Feeling Queasy,**
**Nausea is a very icky feeling. The two most common**
**causes are motion sickness and, as you know, morning**
**sickness. One of the best remedies is ginger. You can**
**brew a nice pot of ginger tea or eat candied ginger,**
**which you can find at your local health food store. For**
**motion sickness, homeopathic remedies such as borax**
**(for airplane travel) and cocculus (for a car or a boat)**
**can help. Applying pressure to the P6 acupuncture**
**point, which is a spot two inches below the wrist, be-**
**tween the two tendons, can also ease nausea.**
   **Signed,**
   **Willow McQuade, ND**

I waited a few moments, and then left the drugstore and put Qigong down on the sidewalk. Thankfully, Sue Polumbo was nowhere in sight. Although she'd denied murdering Aunt Claire, she wasn't off my suspect list. She had much too good of a motive. So did her husband and son, for that matter.

Sucking in a deep breath of salty air to calm my jangled nerves, I headed back to Nature's Way. Walking past Mitchell Park, I watched as people walked their dogs and kids played, couples lay in the grass and held hands or gazed at the waterfront. The colorful carousel twirled. Sailboats and yachts dotted the bay. In the distance I could hear a band playing at Claudio's, on the waterfront. At the entrance to the park, near the street, the local shelter had several animals up for adoption. Elizabeth Olberman, Claire's friend who had spoken to me about the pet store opening in town, manned the table where several cats snoozed in a large cage. I crossed the street to talk to her.

"Willow," Elizabeth said as she got up and came around the table to greet me. A large black cat nestled comfortably in her arms. "How are you doing, dear?"

I tried to shake off my encounter with Sue. "I'm fine, all things considered. How are you?"

"I'm well," she said. "Are you looking for a cat to adopt? Midnight is a great feline." She stroked the cat, which began to purr.

"No," I said. "I've got Ginkgo and Ginger and I just adopted Qigong here. I think he was neglected by his former owner."

She scratched Qigong behind the ears and he wagged his tail. Tick-tock. Tick-tock. "What a sweetheart he is. Good for you, Willow," she said. "It's amazing some people are even allowed to have pets. And those new pet shop owners will sell to anybody. No references as with a shelter or a rescue adoption."

"Speaking of the pet shop boys," I said, and told her about the run-in with Lenny and Billy at the Vine Bar.

"Oh my," she said. "I'm not surprised. They've managed to push the hearing back a week, but we're still determined to close them down."

"I'm wondering if they threatened Aunt Claire? Or you?"

She waved that off. "They don't scare me, and they didn't scare Claire. She went toe-to-toe with them. Went right down there and told them what was what."

"So she didn't seem frightened of them?"

A young girl and her mother came up to the table and looked at the cats in the cage. Before she went over to them, Elizabeth added, "She said we had to do what was right. Fear was not an option."

Qigong and I crossed the street and walked past Starbucks. I paused in front of a real estate office to browse the pictures of houses in the window. I couldn't afford it now, but maybe some-day I'd move to a cottage. I was in no hurry, though, as the third floor of Nature's Way with a view of the bay suited me just fine.

In the reflection of the window, I noticed Janice walking toward the post office. I turned from the window to watch her. She wore jeans and a sleeveless blouse and held a very expensive-looking pocketbook, which made me wonder if she had stolen that five hundred dollars from the register or if she was expecting a windfall from the contested will.

But even more suspicious was the fact that she continued past the post office to Nature's Best and met Gavin Milton out-side. She pulled a fat white envelope out of the pocketbook and handed it to him. He opened it, plucked out a big wad of cash, and went inside.

Why would Janice be delivering money to Gavin? Was it from Polly? Did he have a stake in Polly's Peaceful Yoga?

Janice turned and headed back past Mitchell Park. She spotted me across the street but acted like she hadn't and kept going. I decided to confront her.

When Qigong and I got to the middle of the crosswalk, a black Ford truck that looked suspiciously like the truck that had run Allie and me off the road, drove right toward me, going at least fifty-five in a twenty-five-mile-per-hour zone and with, it seemed, no intention of stopping. Realizing this, I scooped up Qigong, ran as fast as I could to the opposite side of the street, and tumbled onto the grass in Mitchell Park. When I got up, Janice was gone.


Janice was not going to get away so easily. After checking to make sure Qigong was okay, I got to my feet and we headed for Polly's Peaceful Yoga. As I crossed Front Street, I spotted Nick sitting in his old Volvo station wagon, fighting with Polly. Polly thrust her index finger in Nick's face repeatedly until he batted it away. Her response was to slap him across the face and jump out of the car. She stalked across the street and into the shop. He yelled after her and began to give chase, but I planted myself in front of him. "Nick, we have to talk."

Looking sheepish, he ran his fingers through his hair. "Now is not a good time," he said, glancing past me to the studio where a yoga class was in session.

I followed his gaze but didn't see Janice or Polly, so I grabbed him by the arm and pulled him toward his car. "Please get inside."

Nick threw Polly's Peaceful Yoga a backward glance, opened the driver's side door, and got in. I got in the passenger side and put Qigong on my lap. "Drive."

I guess he could see by the expression on my face that I

meant business, because he said, "Where?" and turned the key in the ignition.

"Sixty-seven Steps."

He turned the car onto Front Street and drove a mile or so along the tree-canopied road, edged with charming Victorian and Craftsman houses, until he reached the North Road. He took a right, and then a quick left onto the road that led to 67 Steps, a local beach on the Sound. We didn't talk, and the smell of rum was heavy in the car. This, too, would need to be dealt with.

When we reached the end of the road, I got out. The water sparkled like crystals under the sun. Down below, colorful umbrellas spotted the beach. To the right, I could see the tip of Island's End, one of the few eighteen-hole golf courses on the North Fork.

I turned and glanced at Nick, still sitting behind the wheel, motioned him to get out, and then headed down the stairs. Qigong could use a proper walk. And so could I. The view as I descended was breathtaking, the aqua-blue water, the white rocky beach, the large boulders standing in the shallows like sentries. I loved being near the water, and considering how crazy things had been recently, I didn't want to miss this chance to dip my toes in. Besides, I've found that beach walking is good for the soul. And for bearing secrets of the soul.

Nick followed me down without a word. When I reached the bottom, I let Qigong off his leash, walked over the rocky shore to the water's edge, kicked off my Crocs, and put my feet in the water. It felt wonderful. Better than any spa treatment.

He came over and stood next to me. "I know what you're thinking."

"Tell me, then," I said as the water lapped at my feet.

Nick stared at the Connecticut shoreline across the Sound. "You think something is going on between Polly and me."

I turned to him. "Well, is it?" I felt my phone vibrate in my pocket and took it out to see who was calling. Simon. I put it back in my pocket.

Nick sighed. "Years ago, before Claire, yes, we went out a few times. But once Claire and I got involved, it was over. But even though Polly married Gavin, she never quite let go. I think she had the idea that if she got me to come work for her at Peaceful Yoga, it might bring us back together. But I told her I couldn't do that to Claire. After she was killed, Polly came back to me again." Nick turned to me, an apologetic expression on his face. "But I can't do that to you. I've said no to her a dozen times, but she's persistent. She keeps calling. That's why I went there today, to finally have it out. You can see how it went." He pulled a flask out of his pocket and took a drink.

"It's awfully early for a drink. It's not even noon," I admonished as I put my shoes back on and we started to walk on the beach. A seagull landed on a nearby boulder with a conch shell in its beak. Lunch.

"I know," he said, shoving the flask back into his pocket. "A few years ago, I thought I might have a problem with drinking, so I gave it up. After what happened with Claire, I went back to it. Now it's like I never quit." He picked up a purplish-blue stone, examined it, and threw it in the water.

"Alcoholism is a progressive disease, Nick," I said as I stepped among the large rocks at the shoreline. I'd seen many clients who struggled with alcoholism. The best approach was multidimensional and included a support group like Alcoholics Anonymous, counseling, and even acupuncture. Since alcohol keeps the body from absorbing vital nutrients, I also add a combination of supplements, including a vitamin-B complex, vitamin C, selenium, magnesium, and zinc. Amino acids such as carnitine, glutamine, and glutathione can help reduce cravings, as can homeopathic remedies such as Lachesis. And herbs like milk thistle can help improve liver function and support detoxification of the body. I combine such herbs with dandelion to help reduce withdrawal symptoms. I told all this to Nick.

"I know natural remedies can help. But it's hard to admit I have a problem. Especially since I'm a yoga teacher. It sends a great message, you know?" His shoulders slumped.

I touched his arm. "You're human. Aunt Claire's death was devastating for you. People will understand. Especially if you get help."

"The rest of it sounds good. But I've been to AA," Nick said. "And local meetings are out. There are people there I don't want to see. They've threatened me about Polly."

"Who did?" I watched as Qigong darted along the shoreline, sniffing everything. Paradise.

"I'm not supposed to say. It's supposed to be anonymous."

I had an idea of who it was. "Let me guess, Gavin Milton?"

He shook his head. "I really can't say."

"Nick, I'm not going to tell anyone, but I need to know. It might have something to do with the case. About who murdered Aunt Claire and took the formula. You need to tell me."

He stopped and gazed out at the water, as if he might find the answer there. And I guess he did. He turned to me and said, "It's Milton and Dan Polumbo."

"And they've actually threatened you?" I mulled this over as we continued our walk down the beach.

"Yes, the two of them cornered me one night in the parking lot and told me to stay away from Polly. I tried to explain, but Milton wasn't having any of it."

"Polly isn't making it any easier on you."

"That's for sure."

We followed the water's edge around the curve of the beach and came upon Stephen, who lay on a large beach blanket wearing a bright-colored tropical swimsuit and soaking up the rays. I'd forgotten he had the day off. Really, we needed him at the store, but I didn't want to burn out my staff. He was working six days a week as it was. And it was only June. I knew I needed to hire more help, but to do that required money.

I thought he might be sleeping and didn't say anything as we walked past, but Qigong spotted him and scampered onto the blanket, slathering him with a big, sloppy kiss. He opened his eyes. "Hey, buddy! Hey, Dr. McQuade."

"Hi, Stephen. Nick, Stephen is helping out at Nature's Way. Have you two met?"

Nick reached down and shook his hand. "Nice to meet you, Stephen. How do you like working at the store?"

Stephen leaned on his elbows. He had a pretty good tan going. "It's great. I'm really glad to be out of Nature's Best and away from Milton."

"We were just talking about him. Do you think he's, well, dangerous?" I was concerned for Nick's safety and mine.

Stephen sat back up, reached behind him for his sunglasses, and put them on. "Depends on what kind of mood he's in." He waved to someone out in the water. I turned to look and realized it was Tad Polumbo.

"I didn't know you two were friends."

"Oh, yeah, ever since they moved out here."

"But you don't hold a grudge against Aunt Claire, like he and his family do?" If he did, I wondered why he was working for me now.

He shook his head. "No, not at all. It sounded to me like a simple mistake. Sue should have told your aunt everything."

Tad, wearing orange swim trunks, waded out of the water. Droplets streamed from his buff body. He walked over the hard stone beach as easily as if it were sand and came over to us. When he did, Qigong started barking. Did he recognize him? Was he the one who had broken into the store? Or was it the color orange that set him off, the same color T-shirt the intruder had been wearing? Dogs see colors as if at dusk, but it was a really bright orange.

"Knock it off," Tad said, and picked up a big rock.

Nick plucked it out of his hand and threw it on the ground. "Leave the dog alone, son."

"I'm not your son. Back off, old man."

"We don't want any trouble, Tad," I said, picking up Qigong, who stopped barking. "Not after the other night. We were just talking to Stephen here."

"I don't know why you're working for her," Tad said, grabbing a towel that matched his swimsuit and giving me a nasty look. "Her aunt almost killed me, man. You know that. She screwed over your aunt Helen, too."

Stephen was the nephew of Helen from Helen's Organics? He was certainly much nicer to be around than she was.

"I can't deal with Gavin, dude. I told you that. And my aunt Helen is doing fine. Why don't you take another dip and cool off?"

"Maybe I will. But when I get back, you two had better be gone." Tad threw down his towel and headed back in. When he got to the shore, he turned around, gave me one final death stare, and dove into the crisp blue water.

# chapter twenty-five

Dear Dr. McQuade,
I've tried everything I can think of, short of putting a lock on my refrigerator, to lose weight. Are there any natural remedies that can help me battle the bulge?
Signed,
Can't Fit Into My Jeans

Dear Can't Fit Into My Jeans,
You can get your metabolism revved up by drinking green tea. The caffeine it contains helps the body burn fat faster. It's also chock-full of antioxidants. Another good choice is yerba maté, a tea from South America. It will give you energy and appease your appetite.
Signed,
Willow McQuade, ND

On the way back to the store, I got a call from my sister, complaining about my mother, then one from my mother, complaining about my sister. I told my sister, who was worried that my mother was doing too much after her recent hospital stint, to let Mom go at her own pace. And I told my mother to pace herself and not do too much. That seemed to settle things. If only.

I decided to call Janice to see if she'd admit to taking the money from the till, but her voice mail was full. I'd just put my iPhone back into my pocket when it rang again. Randy McCarty from Green Focus.

"Dr. McQuade, I have news."

I held my breath as I climbed the steps and entered Nature's Way. "What is it?" I said as I sat in my desk chair and put Jackson's prescription down on the blotter.

"We've found Dr. Neville," he said. "At his hotel in Chicago."

"And?"

"He did not have the formula."

I felt all the hope whoosh out of me. "So that's that, then."

"Maybe, maybe not. We're going to keep our man on him when he returns to the East End. We'll see what we find. Please keep me posted on any developments there."

I said I would and ended the call, feeling deflated. I really had hoped that Dr. Neville was our man. I needed to update Jackson on everything that had happened and give him his prescription, so I picked up the white package and headed upstairs, Qigong trailing after me.

When I reached the third floor, I heard voices coming from Jackson's room. I thought it was Jackson and Hector talking, but as I stepped into the room, I found someone else. "Simon," I said, feeling my stomach lurch. "What are you doing here?"

He patted Jackson on the shoulder. "Just checking on Jackson here."

Jackson arched an eyebrow suggestively. "He has news, Willow."

More news? I'd had my fill for one day. I handed Jackson the prescription and a glass of water. He opened the bottle and quickly downed two. I noticed a plate with half a garden burger on the night table. Someone had provided lunch.

Simon sat on Hector's bed, making himself at home. He wore tan shorts and a cool Greenport T-shirt with a big flounder on the front. With his sunglasses pushed on top of his head, he looked very L.A. "I've just made an offer on a house. It's a waterfront property. Really sweet."

Wonderful. "Why are you buying a house here?"

He stood and came over to me. "I've been so productive that my agent and I thought it was a good idea. My business manager agrees it's a good investment. So I went for it. Isn't that great?"

"Where is the house, exactly?" I asked, hoping it was at least not in Greenport.

"It's on the Sound, on Moores Lane North, in Greenport, Willow," Jackson said.

Life was just getting better and better. It was not outside the realm of possibility that he had made this move to try and win me back. But I had moved on, with Jackson.

"That's why I called you," he said, and put his arm around me. "Did you get my message?"

"I've been a little busy," I said, pulling away from him and moving closer to Jackson. "Actually, I need to talk to him, if you don't mind."

"You need to talk about the big case? Are you two still working together?"

"Yes, we are," Jackson said, giving him a hard stare.

Simon registered this, and his eyebrows arched like two apostrophes. "Oh, so you two—"

"Are seeing each other, yes," Jackson said, cutting him off. "So if you don't mind."

"Actually, I do," Simon said. "I mean, you may be a nice guy, but who knows you like I do, Willow?" he asked, turning to me. "You know what? I think maybe I should help you with this. You know how smart I am. Besides, it might make a terrific book."

"No, Simon," I said, and went to the door. "Please excuse us now."

He took the not-so-subtle hint and walked over to me. "I'll call you later," he said, and then whispered in my ear, "I don't give up that easily."

"Simon," I said, gritting my teeth. "That's really not necessary."

He kissed me on the cheek. "I want to." He turned to Jackson. "I'm pulling for you, buddy." He pushed past me and left.

"Sorry he bothered you."

"He bothered you more than he bothered me. You okay?" He pulled me down next to him on the bed.

"I guess. I should be used to his shenanigans by now, but he's just so annoying," I said. Not to mention that I didn't need anything else stressing me out right now.

"Agreed," Jackson said.

I blew out a breath. "Let's focus on the investigation." I told him about McCarty's call and the events of the morning, especially Tad.

"He's angry. And so are a lot of other people. With me sidelined, I really think you need to back off the case," Jackson said.

"You know I can't do that," I said, feeling frustrated. "I'm going to try to do some work. I'll check on you in a bit."

"Willow, I want you to seriously think about letting this go," Jackson said. "I'm worried about you."

"I promise you I won't do anything rash. I just need to calm down. Work helps me relax."

He smiled at me. "Why don't you try a nice cup of herbal tea?"

I leaned down, gave him a kiss on the lips, and said, "Who's the doctor here?"

I took Jackson's advice and brewed up a nice cup of ginkgo biloba tea to clear my mind before going into the office. Ginkgo biloba promotes circulation in the brain. This, in turn, improves brain function and also oxygenates the blood, which boosts memory. Plus, the antioxidants it contains reduce the damage from free radicals, causing aging. So all in all, a good tea to drink.

I settled in at my desk and surfed the net for new research about the benefits of herbs, fruits, and vegetables and practices like yoga to blog about and worked on new questions and answers for the website. I also tried to flesh out an idea I had for a piece about natural remedies for dogs and cats. I'd use Qigong as my real-life example. But even with that brain-boosting tea, it was hard to concentrate. I picked Qigong's red ball off the desk and threw it over to him. But it dropped in the recycling bin instead. I retrieved the ball and we had a little game of fetch in the office while I reviewed the case in my mind.

When Qigong tired of the game, I went back to the computer and worked my way through the rest of the Fresh Face e-mails but didn't find anything of importance. I rechecked all of Claire's files again, too, but it was fruitless, so I moved on to bills that needed to be paid, including a new one with the balance due to Helen—which reminded me to call SAVES about her cats—and from other suppliers demanding payment.

There was nothing to be done about the bills at the moment, so I turned my mind to the case again. What should my next step be? I thought about it for a moment, and then did a search for local AA meetings. The meeting Nick had mentioned was tonight. It might be a good idea to stop by and see what Gavin and Dan were up to.

But first I checked in the kitchen for something for Jackson to eat. Luckily, we had plenty of chicken soup with garlic and ginger left. That would make a good start. I toasted up some sprouted-grain muffins and brought it all upstairs on a tray. I found Jackson sitting up in bed. His color had improved and he seemed more robust.

"You look like you're feeling better," I said, handing him the tray.

"I feel better," he said. "It must have been that visit from your ex." He gave me a sly look and tucked into the soup.

"That must be it," I said, sitting on Hector's bed.

Jackson glanced at me over the bowl of soup. "How did you make out?"

I told him about my unsuccessful afternoon's work. "I couldn't find anything. It's so frustrating."

"So what are you planning to do?" He bit into the muffin, slathered with butter.

I sat up a little straighter. "What makes you think I'm planning something?"

He rolled his eyes. "Please, I'm a trained detective. You've got an idea."

"I was thinking of going to the AA meeting tonight. Maybe I can find out more about Gavin and Dan. I still think they're our best suspects."

"An AA meeting? Tonight?"

"Yes."

Jackson took another bite of muffin. "That's my home meeting."

I tried to keep my facial expression neutral.

Jackson, though, looked surprised. "You knew I went to AA?"

"Mike let it slip. But it's no big deal. I know AA works for lots of people."

"Worked for me. After the accident, I kind of went down the tubes. AA helped get me back on track. But I don't know what you're going to find out about Gavin or Dan there. Besides, it could be dangerous. I'll go instead."

"Danger is my middle name. You stay put." I leaned over and kissed him. "But I will be careful."


I pulled into the parking lot of the Methodist church, parked between two VW Beetles, and headed around to the side entrance. The website said that this was an open AA meeting, which meant that anyone could attend, so I felt okay about being here but uneasy about Gavin and Dan. As I entered, I spotted them on the far side of the room in the back row. I didn't see Nick, but I guessed that would have been too much to hope for. I'd have to give him time to realize he needed help.

The room was full of men and women seated in rows of wooden chairs. At the front of the room were banners with the twelve steps and twelve traditions. The leader of the meeting sat at a table below the banners, AA's Big Book in front of him. I slipped into a chair on the far side and slumped down in my seat, not wanting Gavin or Dan to see me, and turned off my cell phone.

The leader started the meeting, and then people shared their experience, strength, and hope. Gavin and Dan stayed mum. An hour later, the meeting almost over, I slipped out and headed back to my car to wait. My plan was to follow them and see what happened.

But as the two men crossed the parking lot, a police cruiser pulled in and stopped in front of my car. Detectives Coyle and Koren got out. I ducked down in my seat and tried to listen.

"Gavin Milton, Dan Polumbo, you are under arrest," Koren said.

Thinking they were arresting them for Aunt Claire's murder, I grabbed the door handle and got out of the car.

"What's this about?" Dan Polumbo said as Coyle clicked the cuffs on.

"You know why we're here," Koren said.

"This is total BS," Gavin said as Coyle cuffed him as well.

I went over to the four men. "What are you arresting them for? Aunt Claire's murder?"

"Dr. McQuade." Detective Koren sighed. "This has nothing to do with you. Please step away."

"Claire?" Dan said, lurching for me, red-faced and angry. "You're related to that woman who almost killed my son?"

"You've got that all wrong," I said. "My aunt did not do anything wrong. Your wife didn't tell her about Tad's asthma."

"Get her out of my face, Koren," Polumbo said. "Or I'll do something I might regret."

"Put them in the car, Coyle," Koren said. He pulled me aside. "Why are you here?"

"I thought maybe I could find something out about those two. Please tell me what's happening! I assume the chief told you my concerns."

"Yes, he told me." He blew out a breath, resigned. "Milton

and Polumbo have been running a betting parlor out of Polly's Peaceful Yoga and that new pet store on Front Street. They've been rotating locations."

I took this in, feeling stunned. So Milton and Polumbo were involved with the pet shop boys? Good news for the animal activists. And that's what Janice's payment to Gavin had been about, too. "Are Polly and Janice involved?"

"No comment."

"But I need to know. Do you have any evidence connecting any of them to Aunt Claire's murder? Did they shoot Jackson?"

"I have no information on that yet," Koren said. "But you need to stay out of this. Go home, Dr. McQuade."

"But . . ." I had so many questions that needed answers.

Koren got into the passenger seat of the cruiser. "Good night, Dr. McQuade," he said pointedly, closing the door. The car drove off, leaving me standing there, feeling frustrated.

When I got home, Jackson's door was partially open and I peeked in. If he was awake, I wanted to give him an update. He was snoring, so it would have to wait. Qigong spotted me, though, and jumped off the bed. He followed me into Aunt Claire's room, where I found a note from Allie saying that she and Hector had decided to run into New York for a new age expo featuring products they might want to sell to clients. Good idea. They'd stay the night with friends in Brooklyn.

I changed into a T-shirt and shorts and snuggled under the sheets with Qigong at my feet and Ginger and Ginkgo at my back. I was more than ready for a good night's sleep, but it would have been more fun to have Jackson with me.

I woke up two hours later, when the door to my room opened. My heart started to beat wildly. Had Gavin and Dan been released and come back to seek revenge? But it was Jackson, who padded across the floor to the bed.

"I thought you were sleeping," I said. "You snore."

He rubbed his shoulder. "Pain woke me up. Since I was awake, I just wanted to check and make sure you were okay. How did it go?"

I told him about the cops arresting Gavin and Dan and their connection to the pet shop boys.

"Maybe they're good for the murder, too," Jackson said as he sat on the edge of the bed. Qigong jumped on my stomach and licked his face.

"Maybe."

"Willow McQuade, what are you thinking?" He peered into my eyes.

"My gut tells me this isn't over. Not by a long shot."

Jackson thought about this. "For tonight it is." He leaned over and kissed me. "We both need to rest," he said, and then sat up and looked around the room. "Hey, where's Allie?"

"She and Hector went into New York for a new age expo."

"So Allie's not here?"

"No," I said, putting my hand on his face. "Did you take something for the pain?"

He climbed into bed with me and pulled me close. "I thought I'd try the natural approach first."

# chapter twenty-six

**Dear Dr. McQuade,**
After I eat anything, especially chocolate or potato chips, I get terrible heartburn. What can I do to feel better?
　　Signed,
　　Burning Gut

**Dear Burning Gut,**
As you've noticed, heartburn is aggravated by certain foods, especially those with a high fat or acid content. So you'll want to avoid them. But herbs like dandelion can ease digestion as well, along with probiotics, which populate the intestinal tract with friendly bacteria. Probiotic "pearls" work best, because they dissolve in the gut, where the friendly bacteria are needed, not the stomach.
　　Signed,
　　Willow McQuade, ND

I woke up a few hours later. Although Jackson lay on his back and slept soundly, a thought niggled at the back of my mind, keeping me from sleeping. I'd forgotten something. Something important. I pulled on my robe, slid out of bed, and headed downstairs, with Qigong trailing after me. In the office I flicked on the light. But as I stepped in, my foot rolled on Qigong's red ball and I hit the floor with an *oomph!* Qigong grabbed the ball and brought it to me. Play catch at 2 a.m.? Why not? But as I picked up the ball, something registered. I thought about our game of catch this afternoon and the fact that the ball had landed in the recycling bin. A light went on in my brain. Could it really be that simple?

I hurried over to the desk and wakened the computer from its slumber; then I clicked on the desktop recycling bin. The computer chose this exact moment to run at the speed of a turtle, so I had time to think. If I was right, and I believed I was, Aunt Claire had left the formula in plain sight for someone who had the intuition to find it. I felt a warm swelling in my chest as I suddenly *knew* she had trusted me to find her treasure. I waited as the seconds ticked by, and finally, the application opened. At first I felt discouraged, because the bin contained more than 250 items. But I knew what would help to show me the way. Before I started, I lit a lavender candle, Claire's favorite scent.

I sat quietly for a moment to center myself, and then I began scrolling through the folder. I found discarded documents and e-mails, all of which I checked but which yielded nothing. Finally, I spotted it at the bottom of the bin, a file named "Fresh Face Formula Final," dated Friday, June 10, the day of her death. I sucked in a breath. Leave it to Aunt Claire to put her back-up copy in the most unlikely of places. But knowing her and how her mind worked, I realized it had been the safest place to put it.

I clicked it open as my heart thudded in my chest and quickly scanned the document. Yes, this was it. There was an introduction by Claire, and then the list of ingredients and how it was to be manufactured.

Wanting to know more about the development process, because I thought it might give me a clue as to who had killed Claire, I saved it to the desktop, activated Track Changes, and set the document in the Original Showing Markup view. This meant I could see all the comments and suggestions from the development executive, Randy McCarty, and there were plenty. The development process had indeed been tortuous and time consuming, covering everything from the consistency of the cream to its scent.

Next, I turned my attention to the ingredients, hoping to find a clue there. These included organic shea butter, sunflower oil, sesame oil, beeswax, willow bark extract, rosemary extract, borage oil, and not surprisingly, lavender oil. I'd seen several of these ingredients recently, and all in one place, but where? Then I remembered.

"This is crazy," I said as I slowly pulled into the parking lot of Helen's Organics. "You've just been shot." I flipped on the wipers as raindrops pelted the windshield.

"What's crazy is you thinking I was going to let you come out here by yourself," Jackson said. Qigong, who sat on Jackson's lap, remained neutral. "Now that we're here, what do you want to do?"

"Go into that greenhouse and see if the formula ingredients match the ingredients she has. I have a hunch it just might."

"I'm not trying to rain on your parade, so to speak, but would that really be so unusual? I mean, this is an herb farm,

Willow. Helen also has admitted that she worked with Claire on the formula."

"That was months ago," I said.

"I know you want answers, Willow, but I think you're grasping at straws."

"There is organic beeswax in the formula," I said. "I noticed new beehives when I came here to pay her, and I saw on the honey labels that it was certified organic."

Jackson shrugged. "Maybe she likes honey."

"No, she told me she just installed them. That was after the formula was stolen. She must have realized that she would need organic beeswax, so she set up the hives."

"So she likes really healthy honey."

I stuck my tongue out at him. "That isn't helping."

"I'm just saying." Jackson shrugged.

"Okay, but there were other unusual ingredients on that list, like lady's mantle leaf extract and plantain leaf extract. People don't just have that stuff lying around. There's no call for it. You have it only if you need it specifically to make something. I just have to check it out." I got out of the car and immediately wished I had brought a jacket. It was raining harder now. Jackson got out with Qigong and followed me.

When I'd visited before, Helen had been in the third greenhouse, and the hives had been directly across from it, so I headed in that direction. The farmhouse on the hill was dark. The moon was hidden behind a cloud, so we used flashlights to pick our way along the path and then entered the greenhouse. As we did, I turned and pointed my flashlight at the hives. Jackson nodded.

Wiping the rain off my face, I went to the spot where Helen had been working and shone the flashlight on the row of bottles on the potting table. The rain thundered on the roof. I pulled out the list and handed it to Jackson. "I'll read them off and you see if they're included on the list of ingredients." I pulled a pen out of my pocket and handed it to him. "If they are, check them off, okay?"

"Got it," Jackson said. "Let's do this."

I picked up the first bottle, which was lavender oil, and read the label.

"So far, so good." Jackson checked it off.

"Plantain oil," I said.

Jackson ran his finger down the list. "Check."

I picked up the next two bottles. "Willow bark extract and borage oil."

"Yes," Jackson said, marking it on the list.

I rattled off the next dozen bottles, everything from sunflower oil to peppermint extract, and they were all there, every one.

"We just need lady's mantle leaf extract," Jackson said.

I picked up the last bottle and smiled. "Lady's mantle leaf extract."

"Spot on," Jackson said, putting the list in his pocket and pulling me into a hug. "Congratulations. I'm proud of you."

It felt good to be right. I beamed at him. "Helen stole Aunt Claire's formula for Fresh Face and was testing it here. We got her."

Suddenly, the overhead lights came on. "Not so fast," Helen said, entering the greenhouse with a shotgun under her arm. "Hands up, you two."

Jackson and I put our hands in the air. "Helen, we don't want any trouble," I said. "Tell me what happened. I just want the truth. We don't have to involve the police." This was a lie but I needed to get her talking.

Helen came over to the worktable and picked up one of the bottles. "I told you what happened. I helped Claire until she decided she no longer needed me. And you know, that made me really mad. So I formulated a plan to take back what was mine. This formula," she said, pulling a piece of paper out of her jeans pocket, "will be worth a fortune to the right company."

"I can't let you do that," I said. "That was Aunt Claire's life's work!"

She motioned the shotgun toward us. "I don't think you have much choice. As you can see, I've got all the ingredients here to make the formula a success. It wasn't easy assembling all of them, but I did. I'm just putting the finishing touches on it now. A prospective buyer is flying in from Japan tomorrow to meet with me. We're talking serious bucks." She motioned around the greenhouse. "With what he's paying me, I'll be able to sell all this and move to Hawaii. I'll be living a life of leisure after over thirty years of tending this farm, first for my old man, then to put my kids through school." She took a few steps toward the door and yelled, "Stephen! They're in here!"

Stephen, my erstwhile assistant and Helen's nephew, ran in. "Hey, boss," he said, giving me a sly and knowing look.

Qigong, recognizing Stephen, started barking. "Shut up," Helen said, and pointed the gun at him.

"No!" I yelled. "Qigong, come here." He came over to me and crawled between my legs.

Helen handed Stephen the gun. "My nephew Stephen is quite a good shot, as you know, Mr. Spade."

"You shot me?" Jackson said to Stephen.

"It was easy," Stephen said, sounding cocky. "I went on the bread run, got the gun from my car, and bang. Done. You went down like a sack of potatoes."

Jackson's face clenched in anger. "You little bastard."

"So you killed Aunt Claire," I said, also simmering with anger.

"Oh, no, Aunt Helen did that." Stephen smiled, keeping the gun trained on us.

Helen moved over to the potting table and pulled out a bottle of flower essences like the one Aunt Claire had taken. "It was easy. I went to visit her, supposedly to make amends. When she stepped out of the office to attend to a customer, I switched the bottles. You know what happened next."

I lunged for her. "You heartless bitch!" The rain pounded on the roof of the greenhouse, and thunder rumbled in the distance.

Stephen pointed the shotgun at my chest. "You don't want to do that. Tell her, Spade."

"Everybody just take it easy," Jackson said, giving me a look I couldn't interpret.

I tried to process what was happening. "So who broke into the shop? You, Stephen?"

"Nichols did that. I hired him, told him to do lawn work to get close to Claire, and then killed him when he was no longer useful. Then you hired me and I had the inside track. Kept us one step ahead."

"And the sabotage? The brick with the note, the AC, and that fish? You stole the money from the cash register and slashed the tires, too? Was it you who tried to run me off the road? Was it all you two?"

"I handled the sabotage," Stephen said, sounding proud. "And both of us slashed the tires on your van."

"But why? Just to make trouble?"

"I'd heard Gavin talking about doing stuff like that to run you out of business, and it just seemed like a good way to keep you on your toes and off the trail of Claire's murderer."

"So who was in the truck?"

He pointed at Helen. "That was my dear, sweet auntie."

"You're not going to get away with this," I said, feeling powerless in spite of my words.

"I believe we will." He swung the gun toward us again and smirked. "We'll go out back and do some digging. No one will ever look for you there."

I hesitated, but Stephen came up behind me and nudged me with the shotgun and we all started walking toward the open door of the greenhouse, Stephen and Helen a few paces behind us. Outside, the rain continued unabated, making the ground a muddy mess. Ahead were the beehives and, beyond that, the fields that stretched all the way to the Sound, where I was sure Stephen planned to dispose of our bodies. I shivered with fear. But Jackson had a look of fierce determination on his face. When we got near the door, he whispered to me, "Get ready."

"Hey, no talking," Stephen said, gesturing with the shotgun. "Move."

We went through the door together, and in the split second before Stephen followed, Jackson pushed me out of the way.

"Go!" he said as I hit the wet ground with a crash. I rolled onto my sprained left arm and groaned in pain. But I was out of the line of fire.

"What the hell?" Stephen stepped through the door and Jackson tackled him to the ground. The gun skittered across the slick ground and lodged underneath a tractor.

Helen lunged for the gun, but I knocked her down and pushed her face into the mud. "How's that for a natural remedy? Mud is great for the skin." She sputtered, but I kept a firm hold on her.

Stephen and Jackson wrestled on the ground for a few moments before Jackson got the upper hand and punched Stephen in the face. He went down only momentarily. Jackson reached for a large yellow flowerpot on the ground and brought it down on Stephen's skull. It split open and blood oozed out of his skull, bright red against his blond hair. Stephen groaned and staggered.

Helen raised her head from the mud and cried, "Stop being such a wuss! Get the gun!"

Blood running down his face, Stephen made a dash for the gun but didn't get very far. Qigong grabbed onto the leg of his jeans and he toppled to the ground. Jackson staggered over toward the tractor and the gun, but after a few steps he fell, hard, onto the ground. I could see that the wound on his shoulder had opened. His T-shirt was now soaked with blood.

I knew I had to get that gun. I rolled off Helen's back at the same time Stephen managed to shake off Qigong, and we both raced toward the tractor. Scampering over the slick ground as fast as I could, I picked my steps carefully, not wanting to go down. But Stephen was right behind me. I had just reached the tractor when I heard a loud groan, and when I looked behind me, Stephen was on the ground with Jackson on top of him. Helen had pulled herself off the ground and was sprinting toward me, her face full of mud, looking like a crazy woman.

"Get the gun, McQuade!" Jackson yelled.

Helen slammed into me, ramming my injured left arm. It hurt, yes, but not enough to distract me. Using all my strength, I elbowed her out of the way, reached next to the wheel base, and plucked out the muddy shotgun, training it on her and Stephen. Rain streamed down my face, but I felt satisfied all the same. "Got it." Jackson gave me a thumbs-up and Qigong barked, both in their own way saying well done.

Once Koren and Coyle arrived at the scene, things moved pretty fast. After taking Helen and Stephen into custody, they confiscated the ingredients for the Fresh Face formula, and yes, they found cyanide in the greenhouse, too. Detective Koren was sure that testing would confirm that it was the same cyanide that he'd found in the vial in my office. All the evidence was there. Add that to my and Jackson's eye-witness report and a conviction would stick.

As soon as I could, I rushed Jackson to the ER. Yes, the doctor said, the wound had opened, but after he stitched it back up and gave Jackson more antibiotics, he said he was good to go. The doctor attending to me x-rayed my arm and told me it was not broken, but he replaced the muddy, ruined cast. When we checked out of the ER, the sun was rising over the bay.

When we got home, I put a note on the door that we were closed, left messages for Merrily, Allie, Nick, my mother, and my sister, and the two of us crawled into Aunt Claire's bed with Qigong, Ginger, and Ginkgo and slept until noon.

When we woke up, feeling battered and bruised, and made our way downstairs, we were greeted by Merrily, Allie, and Hector, who of course wanted to know absolutely everything. During a scrummy breakfast, as Aunt Claire would say, of fresh fruit salad with melon, strawberries, kiwi fruit, and blueberries and whole wheat pancakes that Merrily had made, we told them the entire story.

As we were finishing up, my cell phone rang. It was my sister, telling me that Mother had had her checkup yesterday and everything went well. I didn't even know she was scheduled for one or I would have been there, but I let it go. "Thanks for letting me know."

"Oh, and Willow?"

"Yes, Natasha?"

"We got your message about last night. You were very brave to do what you did. Mother and I have talked, and we've decided that you were right about the whole situation with Aunt Claire's death and your ownership of Nature's Way. I'm sorry we doubted you."

Wow, an apology from my sister. This was a first. I decided to accept it. Who knew when it would happen again? "Thanks, Nat, I appreciate it," I replied as there was a knock on the shop door. "I've got to go now, okay?"

"I'll have you over for dinner next week. Wednesday? Put it on your calendar."

"Will do." I ended the call. Whoever it was knocked again.

Merrily looked at me. "But you put the sign up that says we're closed." She gulped down her energy drink. Her sugar addiction was something we'd have to work on, in baby steps. First, she needed to get off energy drinks and switch to soda or vitamin water made with Truvia, not sugar. To boost energy, I knew she'd benefit from a special sugar called ribose that had zero impact on blood glucose levels. That, along with a good vitamin powder to build up her immunity, ought to provide a good start.

Whoever it was knocked a third time, jolting me out of my prescriptive thoughts. "I'll get it," I said, and went to the door. I looked through the panes and saw Simon. Oh, boy. I opened the door. "Simon? What can I do for you?"

He pulled me into a hug. "I'm so glad you're okay. I heard all about it. It's big news in town."

I stepped away. "I couldn't have done it without Jackson."

"Oh, right. Hey, man," he said, and threw Jackson a wave. "Listen, I also wanted to tell you that I'm headed back to the left coast, but I'll be back in August." He motioned to himself and then to me. "To be continued," he said, and left.

I gave Jackson a look. "He's a slow learner."

"I can teach him real good," Jackson said, smiling. "Don't worry about Simon."

I was about to close the door when Nick came in and also pulled me into a hug. "Thank God you're okay."

I hugged him back. For the first time in over a week there was no smell of liquor on his breath.

He looked at me with kind eyes. "I was sleeping and then at my meeting. My phone was off, but when I heard the news I came right over."

"Your meeting? You mean . . ."

"You are looking at the newest member of AA. I did a meeting last night in Mattituck and one this morning. I've even got a sponsor."

I hugged him again. "That's wonderful news." I looked at Jackson, who nodded. "Come join us for breakfast."

We'd just tucked back into the pancakes when there was another knock on the door. I motioned to Merrily to stay put. "For all we know it's Janice, spoiling our good time." But when I looked out, I saw it was Mr. Matthews, Aunt Claire's lawyer, who stood on the front steps. I let him in and he sat down at the table.

"Would you like something to eat?" I asked. "There's plenty."

"No, I'm fine. I just wanted to stop by to tell you what's happened. I heard about the arrest in Claire's murder, so I called the judge about Janice's action on the will. He said in light of what happened and because of Claire's letter to you, Janice had no grounds to contest it. He's dismissed the case."

A huge load lifted off my shoulders. I would be able to keep Nature's Way open and continue Aunt Claire's mission.

"Thank you so much. We're still in business!" I exclaimed as Jackson hugged me.

"That means I still have a job?" Merrily said. "I was getting worried."

"Yes, Merrily. We all still have jobs to do," I said. "You too, Nick."

"I'm ready," he said. "Let's do it."

"Merrily, turn around the sign. We're open for business!"

"If that's the case," Mr. Matthews said, "could you direct me to the products you mentioned, the tongue scraper and the chlorophyll tablets? I've been to the dentist but I'm still having problems."

I thought of the letter Aunt Claire had left for me: *I want you to carry on my life's work here by helping the community you and I both love.*

"Happy to be of service, Mr. Matthews. This way," I said, throwing a wink at the group still seated at the table while I led him over to the wall of supplements.

I knew that, somewhere, Aunt Claire was smiling.